Volume II

The Haunting of Alexas Mansion

Glenn Slade Clark, Jr.

2014

The Chronicles of Nightfire, Texas, Volume II:
The Haunting of Alexas Mansion

First Collected Edition: June 2014

Published by Clark Ink, LLC. All characters, situations, and other imaginings featured in this publication are purely fictitious and bear no intended likeness to actual persons either living or dead.

This novel was originally serialized from 2005 to 2012 as *The Chronicles of Nightfire, Texas* #4-15.

ISBN-10: 1-61815-094-4
ISBN-13: 978-1-61815-094-3

The Chronicles of Nightfire, Texas

Also by Glenn Slade Clark, Jr.

Cry, Wolf: Shadow of the Werewolf

The Great Debate

Metrognomes: The Shaman's Apprentice

The Chronicles of Nightfire, Texas, Volume I: The Vampire Murders

For a long lost friend.

Contents

Chapter 1
The Ghost of Alexas Mansion

Nightfire, Texas
June 2, 1975
Just after dusk

"Where you goin'?"

Sam turned around in the dimly lit room of his grandmother's house, startled. He had thought he was alone. His mother and grandmother were at his cousin Rose's baby shower. Everyone else, he had thought, had gone out in search of a good time. It was summer after all, and there was no school in the morning. That's why he'd been staying out so late himself.

He squinted his eyes and made out the figure seated in the rocking chair, covered almost completely by an afghan and a shawl. He breathed a sigh of relief. "Oh, you scared me, Mamaw." His great-grandmother had moved in with them only a week before. She was now in her late nineties, and the family had decided that she could no longer take care of herself. She was absent-minded; she was feeble; but she was far from senile, as Sam had come to believe. "Why are you sitting in the dark like that?"

The old woman laughed at this, smiling wide with her nearly toothless mouth. "I wanted to be sneaky's all." A more serious look crossed her face then, or at least it seemed to. The room was very dark. "Now I'ma gonna tell you something, boy. Your Granny and Momma have been tellin' me what you do at night. Your Granny jis' hates it, but I hates it more."

Frustration threatened to steal Sam's temper. He had been through this with every member of his family at least three times. Now he had to go through it with her. He looked at his watch, trying to decide whether or not it was worth getting into it now. "I know what you're gonna say. I shouldn't be workin' for Valen Alexas. His family owned our family on that same property before the Civil War. I was only supposed to be doing it as an after school job, but now school is out and I'm over there all the time. So you don't have to bother. I don't see anything wrong with it. I'm helping him get things ready for his housewarming party. He's fixing the old place up. It was abandoned for more than sixty years before he came to town. He doesn't really have any friends 'cept for me."

The old woman didn't smile, didn't even blink. "They's things you oughta know, Samuel. Things Your Granny don't even know. But I knows it, 'cause my Momma told me. I ain't told nobody else. I'm only telling you. He ain't natural. That man. He's a slave to the Devil."

Sam laughed before he could think to stop himself. "I'm sorry…you're startin' to sound like a friend of mine." He thought about Ray Don, who'd been so convinced several months ago that Valen was a serial killer. Even after the matter had been resolved, Ray still wasn't willing to make peace with the young millionaire. He shook his head, then asked, "Why would you think that? You ain't never met him. Jus' cause his *ancestors* owned *our* ancestors doesn't say a thing about *him*."

"You watch it, boy! His *ancestors*, as you say, didn't own nobody! And if they did…it weren't just any ancestors. They owned my Momma!"

Suddenly slavery had become real for Sam. The institution had been outlawed more than a century before, but here he was, talking to someone who'd heard a first hand account of it; someone who'd been raised on such stories. His tone changed, and he was more respectful. "Mamaw, what are you tryin' to tell me?"

"I set out a book for you, Samuel. I want you to look it through. Come 'ere now."

Sam walked over to her, and she reached with her frail, aged arm to turn on the lamp. The table by the chair held an ancient looking scrap book. "My Momma kept a heap o' these things over the years. She was jis' a little girl when the war ended, but she already had her hobby. She loved scrap-bookin'. I 'spose yer gonna say the Alexases were good people, allowin' a slave to keep a hobby…even teachin' 'em all to read and write. But I tell you…my Momma wouldn't teach me none of that. She knowed it was from the devil. Teachin' us to read the white man's letters, to write the white man's letters. She'd have none of it after they left.

"She could draw too. She could draw anything and anybody. An' this book here she had at the Alexas place. Before they all got run off. And let me tell you about the Alexases…they only ever was *one* Alexas. He never had no wife. He never aged a day. All the slaves were scared of him…but he kept 'em loyal. He kept 'em in his debt by teachin' 'em to read, by teachin' 'em all kind of thing! They didn' wanna leave him. Some even came back after the war and worked in his house. But my Momma learned his secret.

"She would go out in the night. She loved to draw the moon…the frogs on the pond, water black as the sky. She could do it too. Didn' need no light to use her gift. And one night, she saw Alexas and a vagabond out in the wood. They didn't see her. They were arguin', and the vagabond pulled a gun on Alexas, shot him right in the chest. Alexas, she told me, looked down at the wound. He didn' even sway. Then he looked back at the man…and he laughed at him. He laughed. And then…" She looked off, as if regretting that she'd said a word.

"What? What happened?" Sam had been drawn into the story in spite of himself.

His great-grandmother looked at him somberly. "Then he dealt with that vagabond, Samuel." She opened the scrap book and let the drawing stare up at her progeny. "He dealt with him, and my Momma screamed."

Sam's eyes went wide, and a chill ran down his spine, as he stared at the image before him. The paper was yellowed and cracked with age, but the picture was as clear as he imagined was possible. It was Valen. Valen himself. It wasn't just a resemblance. It was a *perfect* likeness. And he looked furious, his mouth covered in blood, his head thrown back, bearing deadly fangs for all the world to see.

"Mamaw…I have to go." Sam backed away and headed for the door.

"Don'ch'you git yourself killed now, boy! He knew! Don't you see? He knew that she saw him! He knows still. He pro'lly knows you from her line now! He'll kill all of us, if he's fearin'."

Sam walked out and slammed the door behind him.

The old woman huffed and shook her head. "I ain't got time for this. I warned him. I did my best. He gonna bring the devil down on this whole house." She rocked for only a moment, then fell asleep, forgetting the episode completely.

Sam rode his bicycle to the Alexas mansion, arriving just after dark. He'd actually enjoyed the time he'd spent helping Valen to fix the old place up. It had fascinated him. There was so much history; so many antiques. It was like a museum. Valen was going to start on the library tonight, and Sam was sure *that* would be very cool.

Sam let himself in with his key and called, "Yo, Valen! You around?"

"In the library!" the man answered.

Valen's pet wolf Raksha came running out to meet Sam. He knelt down and rubbed her neck. She had healed fairly quickly from the wound she'd received from the serial killer eight months before, though she still limped ever so slightly. Valen seemed to think the limp would be gone in no time, though the vet insisted it was a permanent quirk. "Hey, girl. You miss me? It's only been a few hours."

Raksha suddenly turned her head and started whining. She trotted into the living room and whined some more.

Sam followed her and noticed she was staring at the little wooden lamp stand by the couch. There was a picture frame propped up on it, which seemed to be the source of the wolf's agitation. "What is it, girl?"

Valen walked in behind Sam. "Does anything seem different to you?" He beamed, holding out his arms, soaking up the sensation.

Sam shrugged. "No…wait a minute…it's *cool* in here! They finally got the AC working!"

"Yes!" Valen laughed. "Central heat and air is an absolute marvel of the modern age! I thank God for it! Gordon's people finished this evening, just before I got back. I called to invite him and his wife for dinner, but he said he needed to stay home with her and the belly tonight. She wasn't feeling too well."

"When's she due, anyway?" Sam asked.

"Should be September." Valen shrugged, then noticed Raksha and went pale.

Sam turned back to the wolf. "What is it?"

"Nothing," Valen answered absently. He walked over to the lamp stand and picked up the frame with a noticeable tremor. "Just an old picture." He studied it. "The thing is…I don't know how many times I've put it away."

"What do you mean?"

Valen handed the picture to Sam. "I mean…I don't know what I mean. It keeps getting put back on the stand, and I keep putting it away. I'm not sure…maybe someone's playing pranks, but…"

"Not me," Sam assured him. "Maybe one of Gordon's boys, when I'm not around?"

Valen shook his head. "I don't think so. They wouldn't have the key to the old trunk I locked it in the last time."

"Maybe you've been sleep walking?"

"No." Valen laughed shortly. "Not possible. I sleep like the dead."

Sam studied the old photograph. It was brown and gray, it looked really old. "Do you know who these people are? Are these your ancestors?"

"They aren't ancestors, but, they…the picture is from the previous resident, I mean." A thousand memories flooded the vampire's mind. "The one who vacated in 1917. How should I know anything about the people he knew?" But Valen did know. He just wasn't up for telling Sam the rest. He didn't want to deal with it. In the past eight months, however, it had been harder and harder to deny the probability that there was a ghost in the Alexas mansion; a ghost who had knowledge of its surroundings, an ability to move solid objects, and a definite *feeling* about Valen moving back home.

Sam laughed. "Maybe it's the ghost."

Valen looked at Sam, deadly serious. "Let's not talk about it." He smiled, as he took the picture from Sam. "Why don't we go take a look at the library?"

Valen hurried from the room, and Sam made to follow but was stopped by Raksha's renewed whimpering. Sam turned and saw the wolf staring at the old rocking chair. The wicker frame began to creak, and it moved suddenly, turning just a fraction to the left, towards Sam. Raksha growled. "Come on, girl," Sam said. "Let's go." Sam backed out of the room, unable to win the creature's attention. *I'm just gonna pretend I didn't see that*, he thought to himself, though it did little to soothe his nerves.

Sam remained creeped out for the remainder of the time he spent there that night, no matter how hard he tried to convince himself he had imagined the whole thing.

The following afternoon, Ray Don was hurriedly changing his clothes in the men's locker room of the local rec center. He was thinking about how much he hated summer, children, and Old Man Morris. His work time was over for the day, and he meant to make his escape quickly, before any kids could assault him, and before the Old Bastard could think of something menial for him to do.

As Ray finished, he closed the locker quietly and crept towards the exit. He looked carefully around the doorway to his right, but was caught from the other side before he could turn his head.

"Gotcha!"

Ray gasped and turned to his left. "Jenny! Didn't know *you* were still here." He tried his best to smile nonchalantly.

Jenny snickered, tossing back her gorgeous, light brown hair and crossing her arms. "Scared ya, didn't I?"

Ray made a sound somewhere between a cough and a laugh. "No. Losers don't scare me."

"Actually, I was coming to congratulate you on your victory. Your boys slaughtered us on the court today. But next week will be another story. 'Specially now that I know you're such a sore winner."

"Sore winner?" Ray offered a crooked grin. "Something the boys are never gonna give you a chance to be." He heard a noise and turned quickly around...just the air conditioner.

Jenny giggled. "What is it with you? Are you on something?"

Ray frowned. "Maybe I should be. It's just...Old Man Morris."

Jenny laughed. "He really likes you, doesn't he?"

"Likes me? Try *hates* me!"

"Whatever! If he hated you he wouldn't give you more hours than everyone else."

"That's one way of looking at it," Ray agreed sardonically. "The other way is to say if he *liked* me, he wouldn't give me every little degrading task he could invent in his demented old mind." He stole a quick glance at her breasts, wondering if now would be a good time to ask her out for drinks. He studied her posture. *Nah, she's in one of those mean moods.*

Ray hadn't been able to figure Jenny out since she'd started working at the center six weeks before. She paid a lot of attention to him, which would ordinarily imply that she had a thing for him. On the other hand, she was really competitive and wanted to defeat his boys at every game they played, so maybe when she seemed flirtatious she was just trying to find another way to humiliate him.

"What?" she asked self consciously.

Ray smiled. "Nothin'. You're just kinda scary lookin' at the end of the day."

Her eyes narrowed; she opened her mouth to speak…then just hissed and turned away.

Ray laughed, as he made his way to the door. "See ya tomorrow, Jenny!"

"Drop dead!" was all she offered in response.

"Do y'all think it's weird that all my friends are white?" Sam asked.

Bradley looked at him strangely from his position on the cement wall at Hilltop. "No."

Jeffrey Mason laughed. "Yes! It's weird, Spot. Why don't you go make some black friends?"

"Shut up, Jeff," Bradley said.

Jeff lit a cigarette and inhaled deeply. "Ah… mother's milk."

"Why?" Bradley asked. "Do you?"

Sam shrugged. "No; but maybe that's weird in itself. I guess I'm color blind. Is it wrong to be racially color blind?"

"I don't think so." Bradley considered. "I am."

"I'm not!" Jeff said, as he threw a basketball into the air and missed the basket completely. "God damn it! I'm not drunk. That's the problem."

"Well my family seems to have a problem with it." Sam sighed and looked away.

"Well, Sam, you're black," Jeff assured him. The older boy walked over and sat on the bench right in front of Sam. "Your whole damn family is black."

"Thanks for letting me know," Sam said.

"Well, maybe you need to keep that in mind, when you're talking about being color blind. Your family isn't going to want you to forget who you are and where you come from. White people can be racially color blind, and it's a good thing, because it means we aren't bigots. But black people who are racially color blind are damn fools, because it can only mean they don't know how many white people *are* bigots. There *is no* racial equality. It's an idea. It's a *good* idea. But it hasn't been around long enough to overcome history. I'm not saying one race is better than the other. I'm just saying, culturally, we're so different that we can't look each other in the eyes and think that we're the same."

Jeff looked at his watch. "I gotta go, y'all. My brother's s'posed to be in town with his new wife."

"Are they back for good?" Bradley asked.

"I hope not, for their sakes, but Rob did say he was gonna try and find work here." He bounced the ball over to Bradley. "See y'all later!"

"Now what?" Sam asked.

Bradley shrugged. "Dan Parkers?"

"Why not," Sam laughed.

***

Bradley and Sam arrived at Dan Parker's and saw Doris and Helen at a table eating potato chips. They joined them. "Hey, girls," Bradley said. "Where's Mati?"

"At work," Doris answered. "I can't believe that bitch got a job."

Bradley let his mind wander. *Another one bites the dust.* It seemed like only yesterday when there were always twice as many girls at the table. Now Mati was gone too. Of course, it wasn't as if she'd vanished without a trace, like Ann…or been murdered. She'd be back; unlike Bradley's mother; probably unlike Ann too.

"No." Doris said. "No one has heard from Ann. So don't even ask."

Bradley was surprised. "I wasn't going to…"

"Yes," Doris held up a finger, "you were. You always ask about Ann when you get that look on your face."

"So what's new with you two?" Sam asked, eager to change the subject. Bradley had never quite managed to get over Ann since she'd moved to Boston with her family in the fall. Whenever anyone brought her up, his mood changed considerably.

"Clarissa Kran…er…Jordan's back in town. Divorced. So maybe it is Krandall again. I don't know." Doris laughed shortly. "She's apparently keeping her mind on other things by writing a book on Nightfire's local myths. Sure she'll sell a lot of those," she scoffed.

"Clarissa? How is she? Why'd she get a divorce?" Bradley asked.

"I don't know. She didn't get into it. She was too busy asking us about the serial...well...things."

"Oh, come on!" Bradley said, irritated. "I guess my life *is* pretty fucked up! My brother died in the 'war', my dad had a heart attack, my mother was butchered by the serial killer, my girlfriend left me for no apparent reason and moved to another state! But *please* don't walk on egg shells for me! Maybe I'll get a little upset by the topics, but seriously...what the fuck else are we gonna talk about? It's the talk of the town, even months after it happened. So...she was asking about the serial killer? That's no myth."

"You got that right," Sam said. "Just ask Mary. He had that wolf tooth thing to her throat before Raksha took him on." He shuddered.

"Oh, please. Let's talk about something else," Helen pleaded. "I can't sleep when I think about the...that stuff."

"Why not?" Doris asked. "He's dead! They found him dismembered in the woods."

"Yeah, but how do they know it was *him*?" Helen argued.

"The wolf hair on that thing he was wearing," Bradley said, "the weapon in his one remaining hand that was identified as the murder weapon at each scene, the silly picture of Christopher Lee in the guy's wallet that he was obviously planning to plant on his next victim."

Sam laughed. "Some next victim. Guess he picked the wrong guy to try and kill."

"Ack!" Helen clenched her fists. "That's just it though! Who the fuck is it that *did* that to him? How in the hell are we supposed to sleep soundly while *that* guy's still out there? What if he was the real killer and just set the other guy up?"

Bradley shrugged. "Sheriff Cody seemed satisfied."

"But there just isn't enough hard evidence!" Helen protested.

"Hence the tack-on to Nightfire's folk lore," Doris explained. "Some folks seem to think that something from the Mines got him. Something that wasn't happy about his little game."

"The mines?" Sam asked.

"The mines," Bradley laughed. "Just a fairy tale. If there really were any Mines of Sangra Dios, *someone* would have found them by now. It's not like Nightfire's all that big."

"Okay," Sam said, "I don't know anything about these mines of…whatever you call it…but it sounds creepy as hell.

"Sangra Dios." Bradley said.

"Sangra Dios?" Sam translated the phrase in his head. "Isn't *Sangra Dios* Spanish for Blood Gods?"

"Yep." Doris assured him, enjoying the look of panic on Helen's face. "That's exactly what they're supposed to be. Underground vampire sanctuary." She laughed out loud at this. "Can you believe some people take that shit seriously?"

"Can we *please* change the subject?" Helen whined.

"That makes sense though. As far as why Clarissa was asking about the murders," Bradley said. The table went quiet, and Bradley remembered his mother, lying by the car that night…the wound on her throat. "Yeah," he said at last. "Let's change the subject."

"That's what I've been *saying*!" Helen sighed with relief.

Just then the door opened, and a long unseen figure stepped through with a smile. He went to the bar, followed by a stern looking young woman. She seemed almost annoyed at the smile on his face.

"Is that…?" Doris began, as she watched the man order a drink.

"Yeah," Bradley agreed, as he got up out of his chair and went over to the bar.

The man regarded him with surprise. "Bradley?"

"Robert! Long time no see!" He snickered. "Nice mustache."

"Yeah, nice hair." Robert laughed.

Doris and Helen came up behind Bradley. Doris grinned wickedly. "Hi, Robert. Home for good?"

Robert cleared his throat nervously and gestured to the woman beside him. "This is my wife Barbara." He smiled at her. "And, Honey, these are Bradley, Dori and…" he squinted. "Helen? Helen Preston?"

"Jeez! No one ever knows who I am." She laughed.

"No, it's just that you've grown up. The last time I saw you, you were only, what, thirteen?"

Helen shrugged.

"Well, it's very nice to meet you all." Barbara said.

The trio murmured agreement.

"Hey, we…" Bradley looked around. "Where's Sam?"

"He had to powder his nose," Doris answered.

"Oh," Bradley looked to Robert. "Well, we just saw Jeff at Hilltop. He was going home to meet you."

"Yeah, I'm on my way there. I figured it would be better to get a little bit inebriated before going to see the Old Man." The twinkle in Robert's eyes didn't quite fit with the sad smile he offered them. He didn't say it out loud, but his father hadn't approved of his choice in a wife.

"So, you went to school in Boston, right?" Helen asked.

Doris shot her a look of *shut up*.

"Stop it!" Bradley said sharply, recognizing her body language. He looked again to Robert. "So what's it like in good ol' Boston?"

"Well…it's really…*really*…old." He laughed.

Sam approached the group then. He noticed Robert and Barbara. "Hello." He waved.

Barbara just stared, looking offended.

"Hi," Robert said nervously.

"This is Sam," Bradley said. "And Sam, this is Jeff's older brother Robert and his wife Barbara."

"Pleasure," Sam said.

"The same," offered Robert.

Barbara just nodded with a lipless smile.

"Oh, hey! What time is it?" Bradley asked.

Vicky the bar keep answered with a pointing finger, "Clock's right there, cutie."

Bradley studied the clock on the far wall for only a second. "Oh! I gotta go! I'm takin' Sam home, then I promised Ray I'd watch the kids so he can go to dinner at Tom and Abi's." He offered Robert his hand. "It was good to see you, Robert."

"Awe," Doris mocked. "You and Ray make such a cute couple."

"Shut up, Doris," Bradley snapped.

"When are you ever gonna go out with another girl anyway? It's been what…a year?"

"No. It's been seven months…three weeks…and four days." Bradley shrugged helplessly.

"Oh, lord. Alright; you said we could talk about it, so I'm going to," Doris said authoritatively. "You *need* to get over her, Bradley."

"I know. It's not so easy, Dori. We can't all be like *you.*" He smiled tightly, turned, and left.

Sam waved back at the others weakly as he followed. "He's my ride," he offered in apology.

"Yeah, well, I guess we better get going too," Robert said. "It was good seeing you though. We'll probably run into each other again."

"I hope so," Doris said meaningfully.

Robert adjusted his collar nervously and took his wife's hand. "Barbara and I are gonna make a go of it here, I think." He winked at them and waved, as he led his wife back outside and to the car.

Helen sighed. "I don't know why Bradley is having such a hard time moving on."

Doris snorted. "I know. He's such a wiener."

"He's so cute."

Doris regarded the younger girl. "You think so?" She grinned widely.

Remembering how Doris had reacted to learning of her crush on Ray, Helen stammered, "Well…I mean…in a little…cute…sorta baby way."

Doris laughed. "Oh, stop, Helen. You can't fool me. Besides, you're right. He is cute." She shrugged. "I've *always* thought so. You need to go out with him. He is closer to your own age than Ray, after all."

"What? But...he's still hung up on that whore bitch in Boston! I don't think he'll *ever* get over her."

"At least you know he's loyal. Besides," a grand scheme instantly formed in Dori's mind, "all he needs is for someone to remind him he's a man. Then he'll be back in the game." She pointed at Helen. "And you can make your move."

"You're awfully pensive tonight," Tom said as he joined Ray and Abi at the table.

Ray looked up. "Hm?"

Abi laughed. "He said you're pensive, Ray. Quiet. You seem deep in thought."

"In fact," Tom added, "you've seemed sort of spaced out since you got back from Europe last year. Is there any particular reason, or are you just...reflecting?"

Ray smiled. "Reflecting, I guess."

"Well, fill us in? Share you're insights on life."

Ray considered. There was just too much to tell. He had always trusted Old Tom, but how far could that trust be taken? And would his confession even be met with belief? These were staunch Roman Catholics he was dining with after all. Did he really want to tell them what he'd seen and learned across the sea? Could he ever, realistically, tell them what terrible secret knowledge had robbed him of his faith? Ray frowned as he thought about Alexas Mansion. The renovation. *Why did that screwy millionaire have to pick this moment in time to take up residence in Nightfire?*

"Oh, my," Abi shook her head. "I think that lost him."

Ray looked over to his hostess. "I'm sorry. I just have a lot to think about. Regrets, maybe?" He shrugged. "I don't know. But, there's a definite shadow over my heart that wasn't there before I left. Before Vietnam changed everything." He laughed bitterly. "And I wasn't even there." He waved a finger at his journalist friend. "Now that's irony."

"Ray, what are you talking about?" Tom asked with genuine concern.

"It's just…I guess I saw a lot of things in the years I was gone; enough to change my perspective on everything. It's sort of a lot to take in. I guess I'm trying to reconcile.

"Then, coming home to a town where my best friend is dead, just in time to move in and play house with his younger siblings after their mother is murdered by that *animal.* And I *still* haven't heard from Lee. It's been the better part of a year."

"Is he in trouble, Ray?" Tom asked.

"I don't know. It's just that I haven't heard from him. It bothers me." Ray didn't want to tell them why; or, rather, he didn't want to burden them with it.

"So what's this change in perspective you brought back with you all about?"

"Sorry. No press." Ray smirked.

"Ray, we're worried about you, son. I'm asking as a friend."

Ray shook his head. "I can't. Not yet." He forced a smile. "Just…give me some time to process it all. It's not that I don't want to tell you, Tom. It's just that I don't know how." *And I don't want to see you get hurt.*

Tom nodded his head. "Fair enough."

"So what's new with you?" Ray asked.

Tom sighed. "Oh, Rita quit today. She's going back to Louisiana to spend more time with her grandchildren and such."

"Your secretary?" Abi asked. "But she's been there twenty years!"

"I know. Figure she deserves a rest. I'm running an ad. It's gonna be hell without her though. I hate answering the phone."

"Oh, well. It'll be okay. Enough brooding for tonight." Abi smiled and held out her hands to each of them. "Now let's say grace before the food gets cold."

Ray took their hands dutifully, all the while thinking them fools for wasting any time at all on a prayer. And as he thought them fools, he suffered all the more, because he envied them their foolish bliss.

Sam studied the drawing that his great-great grandmother had made, alone in his room just after dark. He'd always had a talent for drawing as well, and now he knew where he got it from. The knowledge failed to comfort him.

He'd done all within his power not to even think about the picture, but every time he was alone, it came back to him. He finally had to sneak the ancient scrap book into his room and make a lingering study of it. It was uncanny. It was Valen…but it couldn't be. The picture was over a hundred years old. Valen couldn't have been more than twenty-one? Twenty-two? Actually,

Sam realized, he had no idea how old Valen was. Could someone's genes actually ignore so many different lines of marriage that they produced a spitting image of a long dead ancestor? It seemed more than a little bit unlikely. At the same time, to think that this Valentinus of the Old South was the same as the Valen he knew today was even more preposterous. People didn't live that long; and even if they could, they wouldn't look so young.

He studied the fangs on the drawing and shivered, as he remembered something Doris Gardner had said. *Sangra Dios.* The Blood Gods. Could there be some truth in that? Was it possible? Mamaw had called Valentinus *unnatural.* What had her mother really seen? He wondered.

Sam gave the image on the yellowed paper one last protracted stare before closing it back in the book and sliding it under his bed. "No." He shook his head as he stood to leave. "That's ridiculous," Sam assured himself, as he headed off, once again, to work with the man himself.

"You seem pensive," Valen said to Sam, as they continued their work in the library.

"Hm?"

Valen laughed. "You're awfully quiet tonight. Is something wrong?"

"Oh no. Just thinkin'." He changed the subject. "You have got a *lot* of books! Good thing this room's so enormous."

Valen looked around with wonder himself. "Yes, I..." he stopped himself. He had almost made a reference to having planned the building of the library. "I think my ancestor anticipated that the library would grow; hence the shelves from floor to ceiling."

"I guess you and he had a lot in common. Good thing he anticipated that his descendants would also be bibliophiles." Actually, Sam found the whole thing disturbing. They'd been going through the boxes that Valen's friend Julius had sent marked "Books." There were so many of them, and some of them were *so* old. Sam hated himself for thinking that it added some credence to the Eternal Valentinus theory, so he kept shaking the thought off; but every time that Valen spoke, Sam tried to get a good glimpse of his teeth. So far no fangs.

Raksha ran to the door, whimpering instead of growling. The hair on the back of Sam's neck stood up, then there was a quiet knock.

"I'll be right back," Valen said as he rose and went to answer the door.

Ghosts don't knock on the door, Sam thought to himself. *And Vampires don't…EXIST!*

Sam opened another of the seemingly endless boxes of books and reached in to pick one up. It was a very worn tome, without anything written on it at all. The faded ones drove Sam nuts. He hated having to open them, hoping they didn't crumble in his hand, just to figure out the title, author, and category.

He opened the book very gently and noticed on the first page, hand written, was "1917." At the bottom of the page was a signature:

Getting excited, Sam put the book down and picked up the one beneath it. It was the same, from 1916. He flipped through to see all the handwritten pages. This was a journal! If anything could possibly put Sam's questions to rest, it would be this discovery. Unless, he realized, Valen decided to hide them.

Sam quietly put the books back into the box and closed it. He then moved the box behind all the others, so that he'd have an opportunity to get to it later, before Valen came upon them himself.

Valen opened the door and gasped. "Clarenda?"

The girl laughed. "Clarissa," she corrected him with a smile. "I guess you've heard about me, then, even though you got the name wrong. So you probably figured I'd be coming by, considering the stories about this place."

Valen had absolutely no idea what this Clarissa was talking about. He was still too shocked by her appearance to stop himself from gaping. "How…" he managed to stammer. Not wanting to reveal his ignorance, he started over. "How can I help?" He smiled at her.

"Well, I'd like to see the house sometime. I'd love to talk to *you* about the legends of the hauntings. I know it's a strange topic for a book, but you don't find many towns around like Nightfire. The macabre mythology is very unique."

"I agree." Valen looked to see Raksha by his side, simply panting. He smiled and gestured apologetically. "Come in!"

"Thank you." She stepped through the doorway and knelt down to scratch Raksha on the head. "Hi, doggie! What's your name?"

"Her name's Raksha," Valen answered. "She's a wolf."

She regarded Valen skeptically. "You read Rudyard Kipling much?"

He laughed. "No one's ever caught that before. Yes."

She smiled. "Me too. Dad brought me up on it. So how did you hear about me? My parents?"

"Actually, I…don't have any idea who…your parents are." He offered a sheepish grin.

"Really? Well, they're Ted and Elizabeth Krandall. Mom's written some stuff on Nightfire's history. I guess I'm following in her footsteps, except that I'm tackling it from another angle." She stood, and she was very close to Valen when she smiled, and the twinkle in her eyes was so familiar. "It's funny you called me Clarenda."

Valen nervously ran a finger through his hair at the temples. "Really? Why's that?"

"Well I had an aunt. Well, a great-great aunt I guess. I don't know how it all figures. My great-grandma's sister. I'm actually named after my great-grandma. They were twins. Am I rambling?"

"It's all right."

"You're cute." She giggled.

"I…"

Raksha perked up and looked at Valen, laughter in her eyes.

"I'm sorry." Clarissa covered her face. "I get nervous, then I get unreasonably honest. I didn't mean to make you uncomfortable." She looked him in the eyes again. "I just really want to do this book, and it wouldn't be complete without a chapter on the old Alexas mansion."

Valen laughed and met her gaze. "I like honesty. Don't think anything of it."

"So, where's Mrs. Alexas?"

"Um…there's no Mrs. Alexas. It's just me and the dog…er…wolf. Um, so, it's strange I've never seen you before."

"I was married and living in Denton. But, now I'm divorced." She offered a coy smile. "I guess I'm looking for something to occupy me."

"I…um…" Valen pointed behind him. "You should come meet my friend Sam. He's helping me with the library."

"Oh, sure. I didn't realize you had someone over. I mean…I didn't mean to keep you from anything."

"That's all right. It's this way."

Valen led her to the library and made introductions. Sam had heard about Clarissa and her project earlier at Dan Parker's. He offered to tell her about his encounter with the Vampire Killer, and she seemed interested.

Looking around, Clarissa finally said, "Wow! This library is *incredible*! I've never seen such a collection!"

Valen beamed. I've been collecting books for years." He laughed. "And reading them."

Clarissa giggled a lot at his comment; more than most would. Sam took note of it and smiled to himself. She nodded her head. "It's good to be well read." Her eyes narrowed as she regarded Valen. "Knowledge is power."

He lit up at this. "Exactly."

Her smile stole his breath. "Well, I guess I'll go. I don't want to keep you from all this. But maybe I can come back," she considered, "when the place is all fixed up?"

"Or sooner," Valen offered a little too eagerly.

"Hey, that works for me. The sooner the better. Let me give you my number." She fumbled through her purse until she'd found a pencil and a scrap of paper. "It's actually my parents' number. I'm staying with them, until I can figure out what I'm gonna do with my life." She jotted the number down and handed the paper to Valen. "I guess I'll just…" She pointed to the library doorway.

"Oh, no, I'll see you to the door," Valen exclaimed.

Sam and Raksha exchanged a look after the slightly older pair had left the room. Sam laughed. "Yeah. I think he's hooked."

The wolf exhaled dramatically and looked to the doorway.

Sam marveled again at how human the wolf's expressions could be.

Ray put off getting the kids in bed another minute and answered the unexpected knock at the door. "Doris?"

"Hey, Ray, is the wife around?" She smirked.

Oh, great. She's hitting on me again. He looked her over. *The funny thing is, I probably would, if not for the fact I lived on the couch here.* "He's upstairs…"

She pushed past Ray and into the house. "Hi, kids. Y'all are up late. Is Ray corrupting you?"

"Yes!" Kate answered. "He's letting us watch Johnny Carson."

"It's summer." Brendan shrugged. "We got no responsibilities." He winked at her.

Doris laughed.

"Dori," Ray said, as he closed the door. "You okay?"

"I just came to see Bradley."

"Well, he's in his room getting ready for bed, or already sleeping."

"Perfect!" Doris went to the stairs and made her way to Bradley's room.

"Doris!" Ray gave up. "This is weird." He looked over and noticed Brendan and Kate watching him. "Watch TV! Don't wanna miss Carnac." He pointed sternly, and they turned their heads.

Bradley sat on his bed, shirtless, holding a picture of Ann, wondering for the millionth time why she'd left him. The door swung open, and he started. "Dori? You scared the shit out of me! What's wrong?"

She closed the door behind her and smiled. "Nothing."

He stood, uncomfortable. "Well I was just getting ready to…"

"Go to bed?" She looked down at his hand. "Or jerk off to that picture of Ann?"

"Picture of Ann?" He pretended not to know what she was talking about.

Doris reached over and snatched it out of his hand before he could do anything about it. "Aha! I knew it!"

"Well I..." He looked down. "I wasn't going to jerk off. I was just...thinking about her."

"Well, stop, Bradley. This is the problem. You *have* to stop obsessing over Ann! Don't you realize that there are other girls who are interested in you?"

"But they just aren't Ann."

"Good! Bradley, It's time to get over it. Have fun. Live life. Go out with other girls!"

He shook his head. "I couldn't. I couldn't ever be with anyone other than Ann. She was just so..."

Doris cut him off, putting her lips to his, grabbing his butt, and pulling him close to her. The kiss took on a life of its own when Bradley responded. He pulled back, utterly confused. "Okay, so...*maybe* I could..."

"Shut up, Bradley." Doris grabbed him by the belt buckle, grinned, and pushed him down onto the bed. She unzipped her dress and let it fall to the floor.

"Doris! You're...crazy." He laughed out loud.

"Just your luck, Stevens." She straddled him and reached again for his belt buckle, unfastening it with expertise.

"What are they doing?" Kate asked Ray, who'd gone pale.

"They're just, eh, cleaning." Ray answered.

"Well they sure are cleaning *loud*." Brendan complained.

"What are they cleaning?" Kate asked.

"Erm...the...rugs?" Ray laughed into his fist, not knowing what to make of the whole thing. "They're cleaning the rugs, okay? It takes a lot of work."

"It sounds like they're jumping on the bed." Kate observed.

"Well," Ray offered helplessly, silently cursing the thinness of the walls, "they're cleaning them on the bed."

"How come she keeps yellin'?" Brendan asked.

"Bradley's yellin' too! Didn't you hear him, he just said 'Oh, yeah!' " Kate said.

"Gosh," Ray said. "I am craving ice cream like mad! Anyone interested?"

"Yeah!" the kids shouted in unison.

"Thank God!" Ray opened the front door.

"We have ice cream in the refrigerator," Kate pointed out.

"It's not my favorite. We need another kind."

Kate and Brendan joined him in the doorway, and he quickly ushered them out.

"Where are they gonna sell ice cream this *late*?" Brendan asked skeptically.

"We'll *find* someplace," Ray said, as he took out the keys to Bradley's car.

After Sam had gone, Valen grabbed a book from the shelf and walked upstairs, leaving Raksha asleep in the library. He went to one of the guest rooms; the one that he remembered most fondly. Seeing young Clarissa Krandall had jarred him. She looked *so* like Clarenda had, all those years ago.

He closed the bedroom door behind him and raised his eyebrows, calculating. "Fifty-eight years ago." He studied the bed where Augustin had slept. He caressed the antique wooden post, as if it could bring the young man back. "Is it you, Augustin? Are you the one...haunting this place? Or is it her?" He smiled, staring at the bed, as though watching someone sleep. "How she loved you. How I loved you both. We were quite a threesome. The very best of friends." A tear crept from his eye, as he remembered. "I'm so *very* sorry. I've always been so very sorry."

He lay down on the bed with the book, pretending that his old friend was there beside him. "I remember reading to you, and this was your favorite." He opened the volume and began to read aloud. " 'It was the best of times, it was the worst of times, it was the age of wisdom, it was the age of foolishness...' " He put the book down beside him, still holding it. "I don't know why it was your favorite. It was such a sad story to me. Now those first lines remind me of you and your sister in more ways than I can count." He sighed heavily, as tears began to flow freely. "I miss you both so much. I miss all that we had in those few, brief years. God forgive me for all of it...God forgive me."

After lying there a while, Valen began to doze, knowing in the back of his mind that he had to get up before the sunrise, but also knowing he had hours yet to lie in bed and remember.

He opened his eyes a crack as a chill disturbed him. A silhouette seemed to float in the air at the foot of his bed. He closed his eyes, dismissing it.

"Murderer..." a voice whispered.

A dream.

"I hate you." The voice was louder.

Valen opened his eyes now, coming fully awake at the site before him and pushing himself back on the bed in terror, as the spirit of Clarenda Richardson pointed straight to him and accused him with a soul-rending screech, "*MURDERER!!!*"

Chapter 2
The Trouble with Doris Gardner

Ray was startled the following evening by the sound of the phone slamming against the wall and back onto the receiver. He jumped up from the couch, where he'd been reading, and went to see what was wrong. "What the *hell* is the matter?"

Bradley sighed loudly and dramatically. "Doris isn't coming to the phone when I call."

Ray shrugged. "So maybe she's not home."

"Yeah." Bradley laughed bitterly. "That's what her mom keeps telling me."

"How many times have you called?"

"I dunno. Twelve?"

"What? Are you serious?" Ray shook his head. "*Maybe*...she isn't home!"

A knowing gleam came into Bradley's eyes as he argued, "No. She's there. I called Helen and Mati just after noon, and they said they'd *just* dropped her off half an hour before. But I had called her twenty *minutes* before, and her mom said she wasn't there. I called Helen again a few minutes ago, to see if she'd heard from Dori, and she said she'd *just* gotten off the phone with her, but when *I* called, her mom said, 'Sorry, Bradley, she's still not back.' She's hiding from me, Ray. I *know* it!"

Ray looked at Bradley as if the younger man had gone completely insane. "So when exactly did you turn into a chick?"

"What?"

"Bradley, what's gotten into you? *Twelve* times? Guy's don't do that shit! If she wants to blow you off, then go out with someone else! Show her she's not worth it."

Bradley shook his head slowly. "But it's...I just...what's wrong with me, Ray? Why do girls do this shit to me?" An idea struck him then. "*You* could call her! Then you'll see. If she answers for you, then we'll have proof!"

"Proof? You're fucking insane! I'm not playing your weird *Days of Our Lives* man-woman of the week psycho game of phone tag!"

Bradley looked away. "It's just like Ann all over again."

Ray sighed, and he reached for the phone. "Move."

Bradley got out of the way, as Ray dialed the number. "I knew you'd do it."

Ray rolled his eyes, noting how the crazed gleam in Bradley's eyes got worse with every spin of the rotary dial. After a few rings, Dori's mom answered, sounding well past irritated. "Mrs. Gardner, hi. This is Ray Don."

Relief washed over Rebecca Gardner then. "Oh, hello, Ray! How can I help you?"

"I was just wondering if I could speak with your daughter for a moment."

"Of course! Hold on." She spoke away from the phone as she called Doris, telling her who was on the phone.

Ray heard a muffled, brief argument, then, after a notable silence, Doris was on the phone. "Hey, Ray, what's up?"

"Thanks, Mrs. Gardner. Please tell her I called." Ray hung up the phone before Dori could respond. He looked at Bradley and shrugged. "She wasn't home."

Bradley growled, "It's because you're living with us. She knew you'd tell me!"

Ray grabbed Bradley by the shoulders. "Bradley! Snap out of it. Reclaim your balls! Why do you let chicks do this to you? Seriously! You're acting like a mad man." He mussed the younger man's hair and held up a finger, speaking sternly, "No more phone calls! At least not today. Okay? If she wants to call you back, she will. This is *obviously* not getting you anywhere."

Reluctantly, Bradley nodded his head. "Yeah. You're right." After a pause, he added, "I guess."

Ray sighed, relieved and pissed off all at once. "Women," he snarled. He made up his mind to hunt Doris down and find out what was going on. If he could keep Bradley from getting his heart stomped on again, he would do whatever it took.

***

The previous night's apparition had shaken Valen Alexas to the bone. From the moment she'd vanished before his eyes, he hadn't been able to escape the accusation. *MURDERER*. The word turned over in his mind without relent. Was he? Was it true? Of course it was; but never a friend. He hadn't been the one…or had he? And *never*…that wasn't exactly true either. There had been an incident just after he'd turned… He stopped himself, just as he had the night Bradley Stevens had confronted him on the porch. It was too painful a memory. It had nothing to do with the ghost of Clarenda Richardson *or* her young brother. Or did it? *Was* it his fault? Ultimately?

"Hey, Valen. What's up?" Sam's voice rang out, though not as cheerfully as usual. Maybe it was Valen's own mood making the young man sound somber. In his ominous state, the vampire hadn't even noticed Raksha going to the door, or Sam walking into the house.

"Sam! I didn't hear you come in."

The teenager regarded his friend. "Really, Valen. You look like you've seen a ghost or somethin'."

Valen wanted to tell him right then. He had to turn to someone with this. "Well…I…It's actually…nothing at all." Valen forced a smile. He couldn't bring himself to do it. How would Sam react? The boy had become his only real friend in the past several months, and he wasn't prepared to lose him. He noticed the purple folder in Sam's hand. "What's that?"

"Uh..." Sam thought about it. He had taken the picture that his great-great-grandmother had drawn with the intention of asking Valen about it in person. Now that he was standing right before him, however, he just couldn't imagine accusing his friend. That's how it would come off, after all. And then Valen would think Sam was crazy for buying into the weird folklore of Nightfire's long-time residents. "It's nothin'. Just some stuff I meant to drop off at home." But he *had* to know. "Hey, Valen..."

"What, Sam? You look frightened." Valen giggled at his friend's unusual state.

Sam's eyes widened, and he forced an enormous smile. "Oh, no! I've just had a long day's all. Bradley finally got over Ann and hooked up with Dori, but now she's ignoring him too. Poor guy's really losin' it."

"That's horrible." Valen shook his head. "I just want *something* to go right for that boy." He smiled. "Were you going to ask me something?"

"Yeah." *Just do it, Sam. It's not like he bites. Well...Oh, just ask him!* "I was just wondering if you knew *any*thing about the history of this place. I mean, like, the slaves."

Carefully, Valen asked, "Like what?"

"Are you familiar with the name Daisy Jacobs?"

Valen's heart skipped a beat. Did Sam know? He *couldn't*! "I...can't say that I am. Really, how should I know anything about *any* of the previous residents, other than the fact that this place was willed to me by one of them?" He softened. "But don't worry, Sam. We still haven't finished in the library. I expect that is going to be the biggest part of this renovation. Surely something will turn up in there. Valentinus was quite a meticulous record keeper from what I've seen. Why do you want to know, anyway? Was this Daisy Jacobs a relative of yours?"

"Someone I know was just wondering if you knew is all. Said Daisy was a slave here, just before the war. I said I would ask." Sam thought about the drawing in his folder again. How would Valen react if he pulled it out and noted how similar, scratch that, *identical* he and Valentinus looked? Ultimately, he decided against it. For the time being.

He thought about the box of journals he had found, wondering how far back they went, remembering what his Mamaw had said days before. *...they only ever was* one *Alexas.* He decided to change the subject. "So what were you doin' before I got here? Thinkin' about Clarissa Krandall?" He laughed.

"Indirectly," Valen muttered. "I think she's very friendly. I wonder what else she's going to include in her book."

Sam shrugged. "The Vampire Murders, The Mines of Sangra Dios, the Witch's Tree, the Devils of the Wood, that two-hundred-year-old homeless guy, the telekinetic twins who killed all those Yankees right after the Civil War, the Indian ghost lake massacre of 1957, where they found all those arrowheads. I don't know. I'm new here, remember? I'm just learnin' it all myself." He laughed. "Maybe she'll even interview Mary the Witch."

"Mary the Witch? Who is that?"

Sam giggled. "She's supposedly this psychic lady who lives in a trailer at the edge of town. She reads palms and crap like that for money. I think her real name's..." He searched his brain for a moment. "Donavan! Mary Jean Donavan. Mati and Dori went to get their palms read for a laugh not too long ago. I think Dori took it seriously, which is strange for her. I didn't think she took anything seriously."

Donavan! Valentinus knew the name. He wondered if it were the same Mary Jean Donavan whose mother he'd met in the late twenties; the psychic woman his old friend Tex McCoy had always been so grumpy about. "That's very interesting. You know, I bet if you dug deeper, you'd find even *stranger* tales from the history of this town."

"Like what? I mean, for real, what could be stranger than that Indian ghost shit at Lake Nightfire?"

Valen shrugged. "It's a hunch. That's all. I only wonder what Clarissa will dig up."

Doris Gardner went to her window, after the third sharp tap had startled her. Her stomach lurched when she saw Ray Don in the yard, getting ready to throw something. She hoped he was alone, as she opened the window, stuck her head out, and whisper-shouted, "Ray, what are you doing down there?"

Ray shouted up, "I just wanted to talk to you, Dori!"

Doris cringed. "Shush! My parent's are in their room watching TV. I'll come down." She closed the window then and made her way downstairs and to the front porch.

Ray walked up to the giant porch and sat on the old wooden swing, smiling smugly. "Guess you finally made it home. So…"

Dori sat beside Ray on the swing, looking guilty. "Look, Ray…I know, okay? It's not as bad as it looks."

"It's not?" Ray shook his head. "Listen, Doris, you can't do this to Bradley. He says it's like Ann all over again." He found satisfaction in her disgusted wince. "You're not planning to move suddenly out of state are you?"

Angrily, Doris snapped, "It's not like that. I'm *not* her. I just needed a day to think is all. I like Bradley. He's a good kid. I was just trying to help him get over *her*. I thought he needed a jump start." She sighed. "But then he got all mushy on me, and I tried to blow it off, but it's like he just replaced Ann in his head with me. But I'm not…I didn't mean for anything like that to happen. I thought he'd just wake up and realize that there are girls besides Ann, and he wouldn't want me again." A sadness entered her voice. "That's the way it usually goes. It's all I ever expect. No one actually wants to *date* me." She laughed bitterly. "What man would ever be proud to say 'I'm Doris Gardner's boyfriend.?' None that I know."

"This is a new side of you." Ray chuckled. "I didn't think you were the type to *want* a boyfriend! And if you are, then what the hell's wrong with Bradley?"

"Well…why want something that you can't have, Ray? Everyone just treats me like a slut."

"You *are* a slut!"

"Shit, Ray!" Dori's jaw dropped, "You are *such* an ass hole!"

"What? Doris, let's revisit reality for just a second. You meet a hot guy, you throw yourself at him and do everything you can to get him into bed. Then, you move on to the next guy. You talk trash. You dress like you've got something to sell. I mean, if you want to be treated like a nice girl, maybe you should try playing the part. *Date* someone. Don't just jump right into bed. Show him that there's more to you." He shrugged. "Maybe show Bradley."

Doris shook her head, flabbergasted. "You're unbelievable. If you weren't telling the absolute truth, I'd probably get Daddy's gun and shoot you right here." She nodded. "Maybe I do need to try a different approach, Ray. But that doesn't change the fact that I wasn't interested in Bradley. I mean, he's *hot*, but he's so needy right now. I just don't think we'd work out. I'm too much of a bitch to help him through all his mental shit. Face it. He needs someone who can be more understanding. I'm just a fuckin' bulldozer." She met his eyes. "Kinda like you." She punched him playfully on the shoulder.

"Are you gonna talk to him then?"

"I've been thinking all day what I'm gonna say. Of *course* I'm gonna talk to him. But it's like I told you, I wasn't prepared for the need to. I honestly expected him to treat me like yesterday's newspaper afterwards. I just needed some time. I care about him. I don't want to lose him as a friend, or for things to get all…weird."

Ray was glad he'd gone to see Doris. It was good to learn she had a conscience. Even a misguided one was better than none. He stood up. "Well, I better go. I told him I was taking the car to get gas for in the morning. I guess I'd better do that too." He rolled his eyes and moaned. "*Jesus* money's getting tight."

As Ray walked across the yard, towards his car, Doris called, "Hey, Ray!"

He turned.

"Bradley's lucky to have you, you know? You're all right."

Ray laughed. "Thanks." He thought for moment, before he said, "I guess you're all right too."

***

Late that night, Valen Alexas stood outside the rusty, vine-covered trailer home of Mary Jean Donavan, wondering what to do. How much could he actually tell her? Would she recognize him? Would she know his secret before he even spoke? How much of her mother's gift had she inherited? He felt silly, standing there, unable to bring himself to even knock on the door and say hello. He turned to leave, preparing to signal Raksha to his side.

The door opened audibly. "Don't be shy, now that you've waited out there for so long."

Valen turned back around to see the very image conjured by the words *Mary the Witch*. The woman grinned like a panther out of the jungle, her face framed by ivy that grew along the doorway.

"I'm sorry," he said. "I didn't mean to bother you so late."

"No bother, Mr. Alexas. Come in." She vanished into the shadows, leaving the door open behind her.

Valen noticed the lights coming on through the dark orange curtains in the windows. He looked behind him, finding Raksha's eyes in the distant shrubbery. He doubted she'd need to rescue him, but it was a precaution he knew better than to neglect; especially considering his enemies' attempt on his life several months before. Valen entered the trailer.

The dwelling was small and lonesome to behold. He wondered at her ability to live in it, so removed from the rest of the town. Then he thought of his own seclusion. He had more space, but no neighbors to speak of; not within sight of his mansion. But at least he had Raksha.

"Do you keep pets?" he heard himself asking.

She was seated at her little round table, waiting. "I've never *kept* a pet, but there are some who choose to stay. There's a cat who seems to like me. I raised it from infancy. Of course, we all know about *your* pet, Mr. Alexas. I hear you raised *her* from a pup. I take it she's your greatest comfort. Why else would that be your first thought upon noting the loneliness of my home?"

He smiled. "She is. I have no more loyal friends."

Mary nodded. "Would you like me to read your palm? The Tarot? The crystal? How can I help?" Her eyes narrowed. "Your heart is very heavy, Mr. Alexas. You've come here with a purpose."

"I seek your…advice. And please, I am Valen."

"Call me Mary Jean."

He smiled. "Mary Jean, I have a ghost in my mansion. I have heard you are the expert on such things." He decided to take a chance. "I knew of your mother, in Rolling Rock. A friend of mine was something of a rival of hers. He witnessed her abilities on many occasions."

"Yes," Mary Jean acknowledged. "She spoke of you. Tex's vampire. I knew you were the one who'd taken up residence here, but I didn't know you were *Tex's* vampire. I remember him. He was a beautiful man. Is he well?"

Valen was relieved at how comfortably the revelation seemed to pass between them. She knew who he was and what he was, and she wasn't horrified in the least, and neither was he. "He is. I saw him last in Amarillo. Very healthy, so he said. He also claims to be retired, but he's a man, even at this age, who doesn't stay quiet very well. He actually reminds me of…" He paused. "I don't know if you know Ray Don."

She nodded. "I haven't seen him in years, but his personality is well known."

"Well, they have a lot in common. Too bad Ray doesn't seem to like me…at all. But I suppose Tex and I had our rocky episode…"

"When he found out? Mother told me about it. You employed her to track down your secretary, to prove your innocence."

"Ah, you know more than I'd expected about me. And you have your mother's eyes. Is she…"

"No. She passed about seven years ago. Very peacefully, in her sleep."

"If only we could all go like that." Valen came back to the present then. "I apologize for so digressing. It's not often I can speak openly about anything at all. But now, I need help with this ghost. She thinks I'm a murderer."

"Is it someone you killed?" Mary Jean asked, almost amused that such a creature could see himself as anything less than a murderer, especially after what he'd obviously done to the serial killer the previous year.

"No!" Valen stopped. "Not intentionally. Not directly." He looked at her pleadingly. "I don't know. If I were her, perhaps I'd think so. I don't know. But I loved her. I loved her so much." He thought some more, as tears danced on the surface of his eyes. "I wanted to protect them, but I may still be the *reason* that they died, though I was not the one. I only kill strays, vagabonds, people who no one would miss, people who would cause more harm than good by going on another day. It's the Rule of Nightfire. We set it down when the town was founded. It prevents suspicion…even then, I wouldn't have touched them."

"But you wanted to," Mary said.

The tears at last escaped the vampire's tortured eyes, and he blurted a barely controlled, "Yes!"

Mary Jean tried to be sympathetic. She'd pondered the existence of creatures such as Valen since she was a child. She had thought about what it would be like to have to exist on the blood of other humans in order to survive. For a creature with conscience, it would be an utter hell, she had decided. A vampire would have to separate itself from humanity, in order to stay sane. It couldn't enter into society, as this one had done so many times. She found herself wondering if the creature before her were indeed sane. She put a hand on his arm, across the table. "Valen, I will do what I can to help you."

"Thank you," he said, as he wiped his cheeks on his sleeve.

"We need to understand this ghost, if we are to send her to the light," Mary Jean continued. "Or even if we are to reconcile the relationship, so that the both of you may exist in peace. But it's preferable to send her to the light. It's where she should be, but she has something she can't let go of. Apparently, that something is you. I suspect she wants you brought to justice."

Valen considered that. "I think she means to destroy me."

"How so?"

"I don't know. But there was a violence in her eyes…murder. She's strong too. She's able to move things, to unlock and open heavy chests. If she believes I killed them, she may mean to take revenge herself."

"So, *can* we prove to her that you are innocent?" Mary Jean asked, skeptically.

"The test of that would be proving it first to myself." Valen looked away, through the darkness outside the window, as he remembered all the horrid things about his past.

"We can do it." Mary assured him, seeing the goodness in him through his tears. "Would you like me to come by?"

"Yes, but not tonight. I haven't…fed." A guilty shadow passed over him as he said it.

"We are what we are," Mary Jean said. "And we must obey our natures. I will come when it is convenient for you." She handed him a card with her number on it. "Call at any hour." She studied the shaken creature. "Where do you sleep?"

The question seemed to startle him. "I can't…we don't reveal such things. To anyone. Forgive me. But I assure you it is a safe place, for now. I don't think she can hurt me there. But I don't think she's active during the day, which is strange."

Mary Jean nodded. "My mother always said that ghosts were more potent at night, because that's when more people tend to believe in them. It gives them strength."

"It makes sense." Valen stood to leave. "Thank you. I already feel much better, knowing there's someone on my side. We're getting the mansion all fixed up, and I'm going to have a housewarming. I'm inviting everyone. I'd be honored if you'd come."

Mary Jean cackled. "We'll see, my little butterfly. I'm not much at parties, unless I'm working."

"All the same, I hope you'll come as a guest. Leave your cards at home. It doesn't seem you really need them anyway."

Mary winked, and Valen departed with a boyish grin on his tear-streaked face.

Bradley walked through the doors of Dan Parker's the following afternoon not knowing what to expect. Doris had finally called him back and asked him to meet her, so that they could talk. He found her sitting at a table with Helen and Mati. He waved, and the two Preston sisters got up suddenly and went over to the game room, apparently to play pin-ball. Bradley's stomach twisted, as he approached.

"Hi, Bradley," Doris said nervously. She forced a smile and gestured with her hand. "Sit."

He did. "So, what's the deal?"

Doris exhaled slowly, then said, "I think we've had a mis-communication."

"How could we have miscommunicated? You wanted me, I wanted you…so we did the right thing, right? Now we're together. I mean…we should be. Right?"

Doris looked miserably into Bradley's eyes. "No. I'm sorry, Bradley…I didn't mean to give you the wrong idea. It was just a thing we did for fun. I was just trying to help you get past Ann. As a friend."

"As a friend?" He shook his head in bewilderment. "Dori, friends don't fuck!" He snarled and turned away. Then he turned back, staring her down. "That's the trouble with you, Doris! You just…you don't have any respect for anybody else. You don't take *anything* seriously. Anything! I mean…did you really think getting my heart *crushed* by someone else was going to help me?"

Tears were welling up in her eyes. "Bradley, I didn't mean to…how could you be crushed? It was just one night."

Angrily, he answered, "Well, for some of us, one night's all it takes to change everything."

"Bradley, I'm so sorry. I honestly didn't know. I thought you'd *want* to move on. That's how it usually works out for me."

"Like I said. That's just the trouble with you. You couldn't even *fathom* the possibility that you could actually *mean* something to someone."

"You mean so much to me, Bradley, as a friend. All I wanted to do was be there for you, but I went about it all wrong. I'm just not the right girl for you. You need someone better."

"Well I want *you.*"

"That's not possible. Can't we still be friends?"

He looked away and said sharply, "I don't know." He shrugged.

Doris wiped her eyes. "All I can say is that I hope you'll forgive me. I promise, I'm still your friend. I'll always be. I'm not going to run away like Ann did."

"Whatever." He sighed. "Just, leave me alone." He didn't meet her eyes. "I'm still your friend, Doris. I just need some time to adjust. I guess I have a lot to learn." His tone went bitter. "Thanks for teaching me."

Doris stood, sniffling. "I'll go."

"See ya." Bradley still didn't look at her, as she put a hand on his shoulder, took it away quickly, and walked out the door.

Helen came over to the table then. "What the hell is going on?"

Bradley glanced over and saw Helen's older sister standing at the entrance to the game room, shaking her head. She went back in, and Bradley looked at Helen. "Nothing. Just…Doris."

"Is there something going on between you two?"

"Apparently not. But that didn't stop her the other night." A tear rolled down his cheek.

Realization dawned on Helen's face. "That *bitch*! Every time I say I think a guy is cute she…" Helen stopped suddenly, realizing what she'd just said.

In spite of his tears, a smile curled Bradley's lips. "You told her you thought I was cute?"

Helen's face turned beat red. "Well…well…"

"Well?" He was laughing at her discomfort, already beginning to heal.

"Well I'm gonna go play pin-ball. I almost beat Vicky's score." She stood and backed away shakily. "And, you know, she's going on that cruise and all, so if I beat it now, I'll actually be able to enjoy the victory for a while." She turned and walked back towards the game room, then turned back around and added, "But, you know…if you need to talk…or something. I can…well, you know. I'm willing to listen." She turned back around and bolted into the game room, covering her face.

Mati's laughter trumpeted out from the game room only a moment later. Bradley shook his head, even more perplexed by women than he'd been when he'd arrived.

Robert Mason was the next to fill the empty seat at Bradley's table. "Girl troubles?"

"How did you guess," Bradley asked sarcastically.

Robert laughed. "I know Dori. She's always been a…" he searched for a nice way of putting it, "…free spirit." He put a bottle of Budweiser down in front of Bradley and popped off the cap. "Here, take two of these and call me in the morning. Call it a pain reliever."

Bradley studied the bottle, feeling like a virgin all over again. "Serious?"

"Don't tell me you never had a beer before?" Robert's eyes went wide. "What do you do to cope?"

Bradley shrugged. "I just…suffer."

"Well, here, take it slow." He put another bottle on the table. "Then follow it with this. Jeff's been busy doing who the hell knows what, and I've been needing a new drinkin' buddy."

Bradley took a sip and made a terrible face, sticking out his tongue as if the action would remove the taste.

Robert laughed. "It's an acquired taste, but I promise it dulls the pain. Sort of like a good friend. It's even there to celebrate with you when you're happy. I can't believe you're this old and you've never had a drink."

Taking Robert at his word, Bradley tilted the bottle back and chugged the first half of it.

"Woah woah woah! Slowly!" Robert laughed, then he dismissed it. "Well, you're gonna get drunk anyway. Guess it doesn't matter." He put a hand on the younger man's shoulder. "There are other girls, Bradley."

Bradley noticed a fraction of Helen that was visible from his vantage point, and he silently agreed.

By the time Sam and Mary arrived, it was evening, Helen still hadn't left the game room, and Bradley and Robert had gotten completely drunk.

Sam noticed Bradley's disposition right away, then he saw Mati and Helen in the game room and decided to go find out what was going on. He and Mary walked into the game room, and he asked, "So what's the deal?"

Mati answered irritably, "She *won't* leave!"

"I can't!" Helen pleaded. "Just wait a little bit longer!"

"What's wrong," Mary asked.

"She doesn't want Bradley to see her. Says he has to leave first."

"Why?" Sam asked.

"Because she accidentally told him she thinks he's cute. Then she made an idiot out of herself and ran in here to hide. We ran out of change like an hour and a half ago."

Sam laughed and looked at Mary, who was also giggling. He turned to Helen. "You think Bradley's cute?"

Helen groaned and put her hands up to her face. "Crap! Now the *world* knows!!" She glared at her sister. "Thanks, *Matilda*!"

"Well, what're my options, Sis? Either I tell the world or I *move in* to the game room with *you*!"

"Why don't you just go for it?" Sam asked.

"Maybe 'cause Bradley has baggage?" Mary pointed out.

"Exactly!" Helen said, pointing at Mary.

"Exagly!" came Bradley's drunken voice from behind them. "Exagly what?" he slurred. He looked at Sam. "I zaw you, Zam. I waned to zay hi." He held out his hand and shook Sam's. "Hi."

Sam started laughing hysterically. "Bradley, you are hammered!"

"I'm pervegly all righd, Zam. I juz wanna tell Helen zomething." He turned to her, not quite comprehending that everyone was laughing at him. "Helen, you don' have to veel embrazed. I am cute to you too." He managed to register the blur that was Helen looking perplexed. "I zaid I think you're cute too. I would like to go out on a date with you, maybe. Zometime." He stopped and put a hand to his face. "Oh." Bradley collapsed onto his knees then and threw up all over the floor.

Helen had no idea how to react. So she just stared.

"Shit, Bradley!" Mati exclaimed. "How many beers did Robert give you?"

Sam turned and saw that Robert Mason was passed out on the table. "Looks like they lost count."

Bradley crumpled onto the floor and passed out in his own vomit.

Mary asked Helen, "You gonna take him up on his offer?"

Helen shrugged, trying not to see the mess on the floor that had just asked her out. "He's having a really bad day."

Ray was watching meaningless tripe on TV with Brendan and Kate, when there was a knock at the front door. He answered it to find Doris Gardner on the other side. "Hey."

"Ray, can we talk?" she asked.

Ray turned to the kids. "I'll be on the porch. Stay put." He joined her outside. "What's up?"

"Well, I've been thinking. I've been thinking and thinking and *thinking*."

"Yeah, I know that must be hard for you." He smirked.

"Shut up, jackass. I'm trying to get this out. I've been thinking…"

"So you've said."

She ignored him. "…about what you said. I already talked to Bradley. I don't know how it went, but I was honest, and he got the message. Don't know if he'll ever wanna speak to me again…but I did what I could."

"I still don't know why you couldn't jus keep seeing him."

"Well maybe I'm interested in someone else."

"No shit. Try *everyone* else."

"No, I mean what you were saying last night. I mean seriously. Maybe I do want something serious. Something real."

Ray laughed out loud. "Yeah right. The trouble with you is…"

"That I don't have any respect for anybody else. That I don't take anything seriously. That I couldn't even *fathom* the possibility that I could mean something to someone."

Ray nodded his head. "Not bad. You really *have* been thinking."

"Well, that's not all there is to me, Ray. I already told you why I'm not the right girl for Bradley. I need someone more like me."

"Like who?"

"You?"

Ray was stumped. "I'm not like you."

"You're enough like me. I'm a bitch. You're a jackass. We'd make such an obnoxious pair."

"Ooh. That's tempting." Ray rolled his eyes.

"Please, Ray. I've had a rough couple of days. Can you take me seriously for just a few minutes? I want to show you that I'm more than just the slutty girl who's always chasing after you."

"And everybody else," he quipped.

"Shit! Never mind. I should have known better than to think you'd be capable of an adult conversation. Last night, I guess, was just a fluke."

Ray thought about that. "Sorry. It's just too easy. Maybe I'm just uncomfortable."

"Why?"

He looked at her as if she'd just escaped from the funny farm. "Because, I could maybe consider it. I'm actually sort of curious whether you can pull it off. But Bradley is my best friend. He still *thinks* he's in love with you. I can't just say, 'Oh, sure, Doris, I'll go out with you. Bradley won't mind.' I have to at least talk to him about it. And it could be a while before I really can. Maybe when he finds a new target for his mindless infatuation, we can talk."

Just then, Bradley's car pulled up. "Oh, shit." Doris muttered.

Sam and Mary got out of the car and lifted Bradley out, each holding an arm over their shoulders, dragging him, though he was almost trying to walk.

Ray was freaked. "What happened to him?" He couldn't hide the panic in his voice.

Sam smiled up at him. "How do you make Bud *weiser*?"

Recognizing his own joke, Ray understood. "You send him to school." He smacked Bradley softly on the head.

Bradley vomited on Ray's feet.

"He's having a bad day," Mary said.

Ray looked over to Doris.

"We'll continue this conversation another day," she said. She giggled, slapping Bradley on the butt as she walked past him.

Ray watched her walk away, then he turned his attention to Bradley's rescuers. "Thanks for bringing him home. Let's get 'im inside and cleaned up. Then I'll drive y'all back to your car."

When Bradley seemed to have recovered from his hangover, late in the afternoon on the following day, Ray decided to feel out the Doris situation; not really sure where he meant to take it. Bradley was finally dressed and eating in the living room. Brendan and Kate were playing outside with some of the neighborhood kids. "Feeling better, I see."

Bradley put down his sandwich. "I'm really sorry, Ray. I should've taken it slow, like Robert said. But *he's* the one who passed out on the table. I think." He shook his head. "Actually, I'm not quite sure. It's kind of a blur."

Ray sat down in the chair beside the couch. "Well, you asked Helen Preston out, then you threw up on her. Sam and Mary dragged you home, then you threw up on *me*."

"Oh, shit. I guess I've managed to run off *everyone*."

Ray laughed. "I doubt it. But I wouldn't expect to live it down anytime soon."

"Yeah."

"So how did things go with Dori?"

Bradley sighed. "Wish I could forget *that* part. I told her to fuck off. Well, pretty much. We're still friends, I guess, but I don't know."

Ray laughed. "She actually…"

The phone rang.

Bradley hopped up and answered it. "Hello?"

"Hey, Bradley, it's Helen."

"Oh, shit."

"Well, it's nice to talk to you too!"

"No! I mean, I'm sorry about last night. Ray says I…" he decided not to remind her that he had asked her out. He'd had enough rejection to last him awhile. "…threw up on you. I figured you were calling to cuss me out."

Helen laughed. "Well, you didn't throw up *on* me. Just in front of me. But Ray's a Texan. That gives him a license to exaggerate."

Bradley laughed. "I like that. I'm gonna steal it from you."

Helen giggled. "Well…do you remember what happened *before* you threw up all over my face and in my mouth?"

Nervously, Bradley ventured, "I…asked you out?"

"Oh, good. You do remember. Well, now that you're sober…um…"

"Are you asking if I still want to?"

"I guess. Yeah."

"Yeah!" Bradley couldn't suppress the relief in his voice. Suddenly things were looking up. "I mean…if you want to."

"Sure! That's why I called. That, and to see if you had survived."

Bradley giggled. "I'm all right. 'Specially since you called me."

The conversation went on for several minutes, before they actually made plans for that night. When Bradley got off the phone, he was beaming.

"Unless you threw up on someone else too, I gather that was Helen?" Ray smiled. "You're giggling like a school girl."

"I have a date!" Bradley declared.

Ray decided this wasn't the best time to bring up Doris. "That's great. Romeo returns. Didn't take long."

"Maybe Doris was right. I guess I just needed a jump start."

Ray said nothing, as he watched Bradley bounce up the stairs to get ready.

Helen flat out refused to go to the Witch's Tree, so Bradley found himself parking by a dock at the man-made Lake Nightfire. "Why did you wanna go someplace and sit in the dark anyway?" Helen asked.

Bradley shrugged with a grin. "Just wanted to get to know you better."

"You've known me since…forever." She laughed. "But alright. I guess if we're on a date, we should get to know each other better. Different? Whatever. So what's it like living with Ray?"

"It's…weird. Sort of like all I could ever ask for, but not exactly what I think I need? I don't know. He's replaced half my family. He's like my parents and my brother all rolled up into one. And then, he's just Ray. It was weird having him there for Christmas. He's got no family of his own. Not really. We've sort of adopted each other, but I guess it's hard to identify which part of the family he is."

Helen giggled. "Doris says he's your husband."

"Doris…she's a piece of work. Why are you friends with her anyway? I mean, don't get me wrong. I like her. As a person."

"She's crazy. I guess she's like a habit, you know? I can't stop being her friend now. Plus she's best friends with my big sister. I think she's after Ray." She smiled. "He cracks me up! He's just so witty. So charming. Such an arrogant ass! But, you know, he really cares about people. He *really* loves you. You should have seen him tell Ann off in church that day. It was *great*! He told her exactly what he thought of her running out on you. You're so lucky to have him."

Bradley nodded. "I know. I think Doris is more than she appears to be too. She acts like a slut. She *is* a slut." He smiled. "But she means well. She knows what she's doing too."

"You nailed her didn't you?" Helen asked.

"It was just a thing. She just wanted me to stop moping over Ann." He looked at her with a mischievous grin. "It worked."

"So what was it like?"

"It was…*great.* I mean, I only ever did it with Ann before. It's not like I have much to compare it to. But yeah, she knew how to do things. She has great tits."

"They seem small to me," Helen said, noting the strangeness of her lack of jealousy.

"Well, they aren't gigantic or anything. But they just worked for me. Just so soft and…pointy." He laughed. "I guess it was her nipples."

"I've never done it before," Helen announced. She giggled. "When I was little, I used to want to lose my virginity to Ray. Isn't that funny?"

Bradley laughed. "When you were *little*?"

"Yeah, I know. It's crazy. I was like eleven."

"What did you think it would be like at eleven?"

"I used to just think about his lips touching mine. His hands feeling me, you know. Just being together in an intimate way. I didn't picture a porno or anything."

Bradley moved closer to Helen and put his arm around her. "Porno. That's what Doris is like." He chuckled, as he allowed his hand to travel to Helen's breasts.

"What are you doing?" Helen asked with a tremor in her voice.

"Getting to know you better." He leaned in, his face nearly touching hers. "Your tits are bigger that Dori's." He kissed her, and she kissed him back. He let his other hand travel up her leg, until he'd crossed the line.

Helen pushed him back. "Wait! Stop it."

"But I...what's wrong?"

"I'm not your rebound girl, Bradley."

"What? I'm over Ann."

"What about Doris?"

"Her too! Come on...it's just for fun."

"Take me home." Helen crossed her arms and looked straight ahead.

"Are you *serious*?"

She said nothing.

Confused, Bradley straightened in his seat and started the car. "Alright."

Ray had agreed to watch the kids while Bradley was out with Helen. He hadn't anticipated anything strange happening at all. His life had become so domesticated in the past few months that he sometimes even forgot to brood over his deadly secrets. But when the phone rang that night, though Ray didn't know it when he went to answer, everything he'd hoped to escape was waiting on the other end. "Hello?"

"Howdy, Ray. It's Todd at Dan Parker's."

Ray was unprepared for that. He and Todd weren't really close. In fact, Todd was one of the last people Ray would have expected to call him at home. "Hey, Todd. What's up?"

"Somebody keeps calling for you here. He won't leave his name. This last time, he said he'd call back in half an hour. I tried to give him your number, but he didn't want to call you at home. I'm sorta sick of him calling, so I thought I'd see if you wanted to come down here and see what the hell he wants. Get 'im to leave me alone."

Ray's heart filled with hope and dread. "Sure, Todd. I'll be right there." What else could he say? He had no way of knowing if more of their enemies had tracked him down or if Lee was finally making contact. He also had no choice other than to take Brendan and Kate along with him. "Hey, boy and girl," he said as he hung up the phone. "I need to go down to Dan Parker's to talk to somebody. Y'all are gonna have to come along."

"Will you buy us hamburgers?" Brendan asked.

"No," Ray said.

"Then we aren't going," Kate said.

"Have fun. We promise not to get kidnapped," Brendan said.

"Damn it! I don't have time to negotiate! Get the hell in the car. I'll buy you hamburgers, but you owe me chores."

"And Dr. Peppers?" Kate asked.

"Anything your evil little hearts desire. Just get in the car."

The children obeyed with greedy laughter, and Ray remembered that Bradley had the car. "Shit!"

"Don't say shit," Kate scolded. "That's a nasty thing to say."

"I'll try to remember that," Ray muttered.

He went to the phone and looked up Mary's number on the notepad beside it. He called her.

"Howdy-do!" Rang the happy voice on the other end of the line.

"Howdy, Mr. Rhodes. Is Mary in?"

"She just…oh, hang on a minute."

"Hello?" Mary asked.

"Mary! What are you doing?"

"Ray? I was just leaving to pick up Sam."

"Can I possibly get you to pick me up first and drop me at Dan Parker's? It's urgent. Someone's going to call me there in less than thirty minutes, and I don't have a car."

"Sure, Ray. Le'me call Sam and let him know. Then I'll be right over."

"Thank you! I really owe you one." Ray hung up the phone and stared at the clock, counting the seconds as he waited.

***

Bradley drove the short distance from the lake to Helen's house slowly, not wanting their date to end like this. When he finally had to stop in front of her house, he waited until she'd opened the door, then he broke the silence. "I'm sorry, Helen. I'm really sorry."

Helen paused, then turned to him. "No, I'm sorry. I guess I should have said no to parking at the lake in the first place. I should have known the message I was sending."

"No, I shouldn't have even *suggested* it. I mean, it was our first date. I'm just in a confused place right now. I hope you don't hate me."

Helen smiled brightly. "I don't hate you, Bradley. I think you're sweet. Girls have just fucked you up."

"But not you," Bradley insisted. "You're different. You're…nice." He smiled. "Can we try again? You could be the girl who gets my shit together. Give me a second chance. I promise I'll slow down."

She shook her head, smiling, and leaned over to kiss Bradley on the cheek. Then she pulled back, and she looked into his eyes. "I smeared lipstick on your face."

He simply stared into her eyes, and before he knew what had hit him, their lips met. She crawled back into the car, and they both started losing control, tasting each other's kisses, groping in the dark.

A tap on the window stopped them abruptly.

"Hi, Dad," Helen said. "I was just saying goodnight."

"Get yer ass in the house," Helen's father growled. "And you," he said to Bradley as Helen made her way from the car. "Get the hell out of here before I rip your nuts off." He slammed the car door shut and turned away, following his daughter, shaking his head as she straightened her skirt.

"Sorry, Mr. Preston," Bradley shouted after them. "I'll call you, Helen!" Bradley drove off laughing hysterically.

Mary agreed to watch over Brendan and Kate while Ray was on the phone, once they'd arrived at Dan Parker's with just a few minutes to spare. Ray raced ahead of them and went right up to the bar. "Hey, Todd. Sorry, I had to track down a ride. Has he called back?"

"Not yet, but I'm sure he will."

"Whew! Good. Two hamburgers and two Dr. Peppers." He looked at Mary. "Make it three Dr. Peppers. And an order of fries."

Beth Green approached Ray then. "It's too late to feed those children so much food. They'll have nightmares."

Ray turned around and faced her. He rolled his eyes. "Oh, fuck."

"They should be in bed. And you shouldn't swear in front of them."

Ray leaned over and whispered in Beth's ear, "Well, I would say call their mother, but she's dead." He backed up and resumed his normal volume. "I guess that means it's up to *me* what they do. Why don't you call *my* mother? Oh, but that's right, she isn't speaking to me. I guess you're just gonna have to go home and worry yourself to *death*."

"Raymond Don! You are a menace! I should have them removed from your care and put into a foster home."

"I'm pure poison. Please swallow me!"

Beth gasped dramatically and stormed away in a red-faced rage.

The phone rang.

Todd answered and quickly held the receiver up to Ray. "Your secret admirer."

Ray took the phone and dragged it to the other end of the bar. "Who is this?"

"Who do you think? Glad to hear your voice. I've been worried sick for months."

"Lee!" Ray actually jumped up off the floor with joy. "You're all right! I've been worried sick too! It's been *eight* fucking months! Where have you been?"

"It's a long story, man. I'm safe though, for now. I think I've got it figured out."

"What do you mean?"

"I mean who to trust and who not to trust with our…discovery. Is it…?"

"It's safe. What are you talking about?"

Lee seemed to hesitate. "I'm with the Nephilim in London right now. They're the ones to trust. They've promised to protect us from the Prieuré de…"

"No, no, no! Lee, get out of there! They aren't trying to help! They ransacked my hotel and wrote creepy weird Bible verses all over the bathroom mirror! Get away!"

"That doesn't make sense. It has to be a mistake. These guys are as benign as it gets. They think that they're…well, I guess I shouldn't get into it all over the phone. I need to cut it short. But they've sent a representative to make contact with you in Nightfire. We need to trust them. Things have gotten bad. I'll explain when I talk to you again."

"Lee! Get away from there! These people are *not* benign!"

"Well, that's no way to talk about an old friend, is it?" a man with an Irish accent said from behind Ray.

Ray turned and paled at the sight of the man before him. It was too late. The Nephilim had Lee, and now they had him too.

Chapter 3
Secrets of the Nephilim

"Christian Rivers," Ray said to the Irishman. He turned his attention back to the phone. "Lee! This is not a good thing."

The voice on the phone still thought otherwise. "I'll call again, Ray. Christian will explain everything."

"I'll bet. Talk to ya soon, Lee."

As Ray hung up the phone, Christian smiled. "Come on, Ray. Let's get a table."

Ray looked over to Mary and the kids.

"Don't worry. I won't bring them into this," Christian assured him. "I assume you haven't told anybody. I figured you'd go to the press first."

Ray regarded the man. "Maybe I just wanna sit on it awhile."

"A good notion. At least till you can figure out who to trust." He looked over himself at Mary and the kids. "Lovely children. Not yours though?"

Ray sighed. "Fuck you. Let's get a table. *They* stay out of this."

"So, how do you *feel* about the stories that have grown around this place in all the years it's been abandoned?" Clarissa Jordan asked. "How many years was it again?"

"Fifty-eight," Valen answered with a smile, as he looked around the cozy den of his mansion. "And as to how I *feel*...I suppose you need to be more specific. I'm sort of like the new guy in town."

Clarissa jotted down his answers on her note pad. Then she looked up, beaming. "I know what you mean. I've been gone awhile, myself, and I feel almost like a new kid too. Okay...that's not true." She giggled. "I just desperately want something in common with you." She laughed out loud.

Valen regarded her as though she were the strangest person, then he laughed himself. "You are so...unique, Clarenda."

"*Clarissa!*" She shook her head, still smiling. "Gosh, it's so *strange* that you keep calling me that. It's not like it's a very common name. Aside from my own great-grand aunt, I've never heard of anyone else having that name. And it's not like you knew *her*." She laughed. "She's been gone since..." a realization hit her. "I guess she's been gone since the same year this mansion was vacated." Another thought struck her, and she laughed.

"That's it! *She's* the ghost of Alexas Mansion. She croaked, saw it was vacant, and moved right in."

Valen paled.

"What's wrong? It was a joke. I didn't mean it. Are you mad…about the ghost rumors, I mean?"

"No." Valen snapped out of his daze. "I'm sorry. My mind went somewhere else. I'm not mad. In fact, I think it's part of what's kept the place from being overly vandalized. People fear the supernatural."

She nodded, making a note. "Especially in Nightfire." She looked up from her notepad. "But kids have been breaking in for decades. For some reason it's always been thought of as a great spot for a date. I never thought so. No offense, but who wants to go to a haunted house to make out?"

Valen laughed in spite of himself. He perked up, and he noticed Raksha staring past him. He heard violin music. "Do you hear that?"

"Hear what?" Clarissa asked.

"Sounds like a violin." Valen cocked his head, listening. Absently, he added, "It's probably nothing. Just the…air conditioner."

Clarissa went on, oblivious, "So, when it comes to the history of this mansion, do you know enough to speculate on, say if there really *were* a ghost, who it might be?"

Valen shrugged. "Your great-grand aunt probably *is* the one." He forced a laugh.

Clarissa giggled. "No, really."

"Oh, I don't know. This place is *so* old. It's been here since the town was born. My family had been in this house, along with slaves and…friends, for seventy years before they left it. That's a lifetime, if you think about it."

"So the Alexases were slave owners!"

"It was the way of things back then. Slaves were common."

Clarissa nodded with a bright smile. "I guess I just think cowboys and Indians when I think about Texas in the 1800s."

"In fact," Valen went on, "the slave quarters are still standing on the property. Come to think on it, I'd be surprised if there were only *one* ghost haunting this old mansion."

The music suddenly grew much louder. Valen jumped up, looking all around, for surely it was in the very room with them.

Clarissa jumped up, and Raksha howled.

"What's wrong," Valen's guest asked, concerned. "Why's she howling?"

Valen regarded the young woman, realizing she didn't hear the music. "I just…must have startled her. I have a terrible headache." He motioned with his hand for Raksha to be quiet. The wolf obeyed, though she continued to stare into the air, as if something were hanging suspended right in the center of the room. Valen put a hand to his head. "I'm very sorry about this. I think it might be a migraine. I have to tend to it, before it knocks me out. Can we continue this some other time, Clar…*issa*?"

Looking perplexed, the young woman agreed. "Sure, Valen. I'm sorry you've got a headache. Hope you feel better."

She gathered her things, and Valen walked her to the door, seeing that she made it to her car. When she'd gone, he closed the door. The music had stopped. He looked down at Raksha. "Am I going mad?"

The wolf simply watched him.

"They can't...*both* be haunting me." Valen felt himself cold with sweat, as he wondered if all of his immortal sins had finally come to find him.

Back at Dan Parker's Bar and Grill, Ray sat at the table across from the Nephilim. "So, what? Are you gonna kill me?"

"Come 'ere to me now, Ray. Have we ever tried to kill you before?"

"No, but you never trashed my hotel room before either."

Christian sighed. "And we haven't yet, either. Weren't we the ones who helped you all along in Europe? Didn't we get you and Lee out of jail in Paris?"

Ray remained hostile. "Maybe you thought we'd just hand it over if you made friendly. Now that it hasn't worked, you started playin' nasty. And that won't work either. I'm *not* handing it over to you, just because you say I should. I mean, seriously, Sion's given us the same load of shit. 'Oh, we have your best interests at heart, boys. Give it to us. Don't give it to those spooky tall people!' "

Christian seemed amused. "We aren't *all* tall, lad. Not anymore."

"What the *fuck* is that supposed to mean?"

"Let me put your mind at ease, Ray. I won't try to talk you into handing it over tonight." He held up a hand. "I promise! We can just sit here passin' the crack. In fact, I just want to tell you who we are. Maybe let you sit on it awhile, like you said. Think it over. And, in all fairness, the least you can do is hear me out, seein' as I've come all this way to have a visit."

Ray scoffed. "Yeah...*visit.*"

"Just let me tell you the story."

"Fine." Ray shrugged. "Go ahead. But make it a good one."

"I guess I'll just take it from the top, then. It starts in ancient Egypt, when the..."

"Wait a minute," Ray looked at his watch. "*Ancient Egypt?* I don't have all god damned night!"

"Fuck's sake, Ray! Will you let me tell the story?"

Ray just gestured for the man to continue.

Christian nodded his appreciation. "Ancient Egypt...when the pharaohs still had the divine secrets. The Nephilim existed as we are now. Organized as we are, I mean. Sion existed too, though they didn't call themselves that. That's just a recent thing. The Sions were simply...sycophants, I s'pose you'd call 'em. They followed the powers around, always hoping to find a shred of the secrets. They wanted to learn the divine rights. A good number of 'em were priests, as you might have guessed."

"Oh, yeah," Ray said sarcastically. "I guessed that."

Christian ignored the interruption. "Well, the Nephilim weren't privy to the secrets of the pharaoh, per se. We were guardians, more like. Just as we are now, but back then we were acknowledged. We were advisors to world leaders, protectors of those who needed us, keepers of many ancient secrets. People feared us. They knew of our origins, as the descendants of the union between angels and humans. The Nephilim were known both as warriors and as spiritualists. Our god was known as Aten. This was a god not known to the Egyptians at the time. They would hear of him later on, when a Nephilim actually became

Pharaoh, but the real story begins much earlier, during the reign of Sequenenre Tao II."

Ray held up a hand. "Okay, Lucky, not only am I completely lost at this point, but you're boring the *shit* out of me! You're just rambling on like I have any *idea* what your talking about. I don't know anything about Sequen-whoeverthefuck, or his secrets."

Christian looked sheepish, as he considered who he was talking to. "I apologize," he said at last. "It's all common knowledge, once you've been in the order a few years. I'll back up and assume you know nothing.

"Point one: who the Nephilim were and *are*. In the *oldest* days imaginable, when human beings first began to spread across the African continent, the celestial guides that Aten had put in place to look after them became jealous of their bonds with each other. Celestials, or angels, gods, whatever word works for you, they were directly created by Aten. Sometimes by each other. Sex was something they envied in mortals. Especially when the humans began carrying on about it so. The celestials could generate bodies for themselves, if they so chose, and some of them disobeyed the wishes of Aten, and they sought physical unions with humans. This practice went on for centuries, even after the Reprimand. These unions are what created us.

"We were born half man and half celestial. Men of extraordinary height and strength. We were a terror, in the early days. We had an insatiable need for meat. Some even turned to cannibalism. But we eventually managed to organize ourselves. That's when we began honing our abilities.

"The *natural* humans, while they still feared us, began to seek us out when there were tribal disputes, because we were renowned for our wisdom as well as our ability to crush our enemies. They sought us out when they were having trouble with ghosts, or when someone had angered a god, because we were also known for our psychic attributes."

"Wait…you're talking like you were *there*," Ray said.

Christian laughed. "No, no, no. Not as far as I *remember*. I'm only thirty-two. This is just the history." He went on, "So, as the generations passed, the Nephilim married and had children of their own. Surprisingly, many of their own offspring were merely human, inheriting none of the divine strengths of the Nephilim. Down the line, the Nephilim gene, as we call it now, would manifest itself at random. The later generation Nephilim, like myself, didn't have the great height of the first generation. They appeared much more human, but beneath their skin lay something more. Nephilim are often mind readers, seers, prophets.

"As the Order of the Nephilim took shape, we made it our priority to watch *all* of the Nephilim bloodlines, as they spread, waiting for the dormant genes to add to our ranks. Nowadays, the lines have grown so large that we can't make contact with every one born. We've even lost track of some of the lines altogether. But most we still watch, which is why the people began referring to us as the Watchers. And there is *one* line in particular, as you'll have *surely* already gleaned, that we watch closer than any other.

"Now, taking us forward to the reign of Seqenenre Tao II and who the Sions were. There had been a Nephilim bloodline that we had been watching for some time, which had come to our attention in a certain desert prince named Abram. This line eventually became entangled with the Hyksos kings, who were in competition with the *legitimate* pharaohs of Egypt. A Nephilim prophet, who had been arrested for attempted rape, proved himself to Apophis, the Hyksos ruler, and became quite powerful as a result. This Nephilim prophet is someone you may have heard of in Sunday school as a child. So to make it less confusing, we'll just call him Joseph."

Ray interrupted, "Okay, how is *that* supposed to make things less confusing? How many Josephs were there in the Bible? Are we talking about Joseph with the obnoxious coat, Joseph from the manger scene, Joseph of Arimathea…?"

"Oh, I guess you're right," Christian conceded. "This was the one with the 'obnoxious coat.' As you might know, Apophis made Joseph a governor, second in power only to himself.

"Now this was all happening, remember, in the *Hyksos* kingdom. The predecessors to the Sions were still apparently loyal to Sequenenre, the *legitimate* Pharaoh of Egypt. Now, the legitimate Pharaohs had a history much older than any modern-day scholars would dare to believe. Like the Nephilim, they had once enjoyed direct access to the minds of the "gods." In fact, they had a secret magic of sorts which allowed them, upon their death, to join the gods themselves; to actually *become* gods, as they understood it. This was what had always drawn the interest of the Nephilim. Some of our number even became priests in the Pharaoh's court in order to assure the secrets were never lost. We protected the pharaohs, as they were nearing their deaths, in order to assure they had the opportunity to pass these secrets on to their successors. We had no interest in attaining these secrets for ourselves. Only in preserving the tradition.

"This is where it gets complicated, so I'll simplify it as well as I can. The predecessors of today's Sions were after the secrets of the pharaohs. Being masters of infiltration then, as well as they are today, the Sions became priests in his court just as some of the Nephilim had done. They witnessed several key points of the mystical ceremony; though, of course, the true secrets they sought were only passed from pharaoh to pharaoh. After several generations, this began to frustrate them. No matter how close they got to each pharaoh, the secrets never came to them. Ultimately, they decided to take the secrets by force.

"Now the Sions were, and still remain, experts at infiltration, as I've said. They were also masters at hiding their tracks, which is why they didn't confront the pharaoh himself. Instead, they managed to infiltrate the highest levels of King Apophis' *Hyksos* court, knowing that he had a Nephilim prophet at his right hand. They convinced the king that, in order to fully legitimize his reign, *he* should have the secrets of the ancient pharaohs, and that he should stop at nothing to acquire them. Somehow or another, the Nephilim governor Joseph wound up entangled in this plot, as did a couple of his sons, and it's not quite clear whether the Nephilim or the Sions are more to blame for what happened…"

"How convenient," Ray grumbled.

"In all fairness, Ray, this part's important. This is the origin of Sion."

"So what happened?" Ray asked.

"The legitimate pharaoh, Sequenenre Tao II was murdered, betrayed by a 'Sion' priest in his court to Joseph's sons. The group attempted to force the secrets of the ancients from Sequenenre through threats and torture, but the mighty pharaoh would not submit. They lost their temper with him, and they lost control. They killed Sequenenre before the secrets ever left his lips. The secrets were lost. They had died with Seqenenre. And the Sions became obsessed with somehow restoring them.

"They formed a brotherhood that was tasked with passing along the rituals, as far as they had known them, that were used in the raising of the pharaohs to godhood. Over time, of course, the meaning of these rituals has been lost to the groups who still use them, groups such as modern-day Freemasons, but the point has always been simply to keep the rituals intact.

"Some time after the murder of Sequenenre, Joseph's daughter Tiye married a descendant of Sequenenre Tao II, named Amenhotep III. Their son Aminadab was born Nephilim, a prophet like his ancestor. What made this Nephilim so special, however, was that he was destined for the Egyptian throne.

"Before Aminadab ascended to the throne as Pharaoh Amenhotep IV, the Nephilim had made themselves known to him. We had initiated him into our order. Still, it was a surprise to us when he named our god, Aten, the god of all Egypt, in place of their traditional deities. He was eventually deposed, and he fled with his mother's people, who still regarded him as their pharaoh. They referred to him as the "Mosis," a title meant to acknowledge his position in their hearts. For he was still *their* pharaoh. This title was later thought to have been his actual name, *Moses.*

"This is the point in history, when the Sions first latched on to a particular Nephilim bloodline. They had seen the power of long-lived Joseph, over the years, and now his grandson *Moses* struck them as a pharaoh who knew something the others did not. He had a power that they hoped would grant them their prize. Indeed, *Moses* became the greatest of the prophets in his day. To some, he seemed a celestial being himself.

"Sion followed Moses' bloodline through the centuries, just as we did. Unfortunately, they managed to manipulate it, where we sought only to protect it.

"After his death, Sion convinced the followers of Moses that we were the enemy. We found ourselves slaughtered by them wherever they found us. It was one of many points in history when the Nephilim appeared to the outside world to have been exterminated. But we survived, and we kept on watching.

"The line produced many powerful prophets, as well as a line of kings, and then, one day, it produced something more. It produced a Nephilim so powerful that nothing could be hidden from him. He could change the molecular makeup of things, he could defy the laws of physics. He was a healer, a great teacher. He was the *messiah* that the prophets had foretold.

"The Sions had plotted to use this Supreme Nephilim to conquer the Romans. If they could not become gods themselves, they would at least *control* one and thus dominate the world. They had burned visions of conquest into the people's minds for so many generations, that many of them were disappointed when this messiah could not be made to fight. So impossible to control was this Nephilim that, even when they killed him for his failure to comply, he wouldn't stay dead. In fact, he didn't give up the ghost, so to speak, until, as a very old man living in…"

"Jesus," Ray interrupted.

"Precicely."

"No, I mean Jesus *Christ* you are fucking *insane*!"

Christian offered Ray a tolerant, blank expression. "Ray, I think you know now the *significance* of what you have. The *reason* both Sion and the Nephilim are trying to get it. We don't want the wrong sorts of people getting their hands on those…"

"Ray!" Interrupted the voice of Kate. "Mary has to go, man!"

Christian smiled. "It's all right. I have no more reason to hold you here. Just think about it, Ray. Think about what you've gotten yourself into." He shook his head. "You have the same propensity for trouble that your father had. You remind me of him."

Ray turned on the man angrily. "My *father*…is an asshole!"

"He…*is*?"

"I don't know how the hell you think you know that old son of a bitch, but I'm sure it has something to do with the war, and I'm sure I don't *give* a fuck, because you just said it to get a rise out of me. Mission accomplished!" He pointed right at Christian. "*Don't* bring up my family. Ever!" He grabbed Kate's hand. "This is my family now."

Kate looked up at him. "Don't say 'fuck,' Ray. You'll burn for it."

Christian giggled at that. "God go with you, Ray Don." He watched Ray leave with Mary, Brendan, and Kate, then he turned to a dark-skinned man seated across the room and nodded his head with satisfaction.

The other man came over to him. "Well?"

Christian replied, "A place called Alexas Mansion. Every time I brought *it* up, he thought about the mansion. I almost didn't get a name, but I'm sure that's it."

The other man smiled broadly. "I knew you were the right man for the job. I know exactly where it is. In fact, you'd be surprised who lives there."

Christian thought about it. "Not... *Valentinus* Alexas?"

The other man nodded.

"Fuck's sake," Christian mused. "By the way, why was he speaking about his father as if...?"

The other man patted him on the shoulder. "*Long* story. And, frankly, after listening to you ramble on about Nephilim history forever, I'm all done with long stories for the night. So, let's go check in to the hotel and get some rest. You've had a much longer trip than I have, *Lucky*."

Christian stood and grumbled, "What is it about you Americans? You equate anything Irish with that *fuckin'* leprechaun."

The other man shrugged, as they walked away from the table. "He pushes some damn good cereal. You know...marshmallows. Good stuff."

"It's crap," Christian said, and the pair left the bar and grill, seeking shelter for the night.

After dropping off Ray and the children, Mary picked Sam up at his house. She'd been quietly dreading it all night. Normally, she let Sam drive her car when they were together. Tonight, however, she needed to remain in control. She needed to be strong. She had to get everything out in the open, so that they could deal with it. She drove to a park near Sam's house and led Sam to a rickety wooden Bench by a little playground.

Sam laughed as he sat beside her. "Funny place for a date." He smiled.

She struggled not to be charmed by him, and she said humorlessly, "I don't see anything funny about it."

Sam decided to ask, "What'samatter, Mary? You been real quiet. Now you're actin' mad."

She looked him in the eyes. "Sam, tell me what's wrong with this place? Where would you rather be spending time with me?"

Sam decided to be honest. If she was having a PMS moment, there wouldn't be anything he could do to please her anyway. He shrugged. "I guess, with all the park areas in Nightfire, it just seems this one's not exactly…the pick of the litter. I mean, this bench is *rotting*, Mary. The slide over there is warped. I don't know how kids don't all get stuck and jumbled up in the middle." He laughed, but she did not join him. "We could have gone to Hilltop, if you wanted to be outside."

Mary shook her head. "You just don't understand, do you?"

"What am I supposed to be understanding? I don't think I'm following."

"Sam…are you ashamed of who you are?"

"What?"

"Don't you see? This is *our* park, in *our* part of town. Of course Hilltop is in better shape, because the town puts out the money to keep it up just as sure as they let this park go all to rot. That's because Hilltop is where all the *white* people go, Sam. The *white* people hang out at Dan Parker's. You always want to be with the whites, Sam. You *never* want to do anything with your own kind."

"My own kind?" Sam was shocked and a little bit mad. He hadn't seen this coming, but thinking on it, he saw the truth in it. At least the truth as far as his closest friends all being white. "It's not like that, Mary. I'm not ashamed. I'm proud of where I come from. I'm proud of who I am. But Ray saved me from getting my ass whooped when I first came to town. Bradley took me under his wing and showed me around, making sure I wasn't made into a target for being the new kid in town. Valen gave me a really good job…"

"But see? That's the thing, Sam. Do you think these people really *respect* you? Ray gets in fights for the sake of getting into fights, Bradley probably wanted to be the cool white guy with a *black* side-kick. Just for novelty! And Valen! Valen *Alexas*! I have *never* been able to see why you took that damn job! His family *owned* your family, Sam! Taking that job makes you the epitome of an Uncle Tom!"

"I am *not* an Uncle Tom, Mary! That's just not right. And you like my friends yourself. Unless you've just been two-faced all this time and never let it show."

"Yes, I like them, Sam. I really do. They're good people, in spite of it all. They *have* been good to you, even if it does serve their own agendas. But the problem is you *only* spend time with them! You're even starting to *talk* like them! I just don't understand it. You go around with them, hanging out at their white parks and white restaurants, like their little pet. All the while your family and mine have this run down park and neighborhoods that aren't nearly as nice, because *your* friends don't bother to do anything about it. If there's a pot hole on Bradley's street, how long does it take the town council to have it patched up? And have you noticed the street *you* live on, Sam? It's nothing *but* pot holes! Carmilla Franklin has been going to the town council for *years* to get the roads fixed over here, and *nothing* has been done."

"But my friends aren't *on* the town council," Sam protested.

"You're missing the point, Sam! You're missing it completely! I hear people talking all the time. Your cousins make fun of you. Your neighbors shake their heads. They feel sorry for your granny that her grandson wants to be some rich white man's little slave, happy as Uncle Remus!"

"I'm not a *slave*! He pays me *and* he's my friend! Get over slavery already, Mary! It was over a hundred years ago, and neither one of us was even there!"

Mary stood up, livid. "Get *over* slavery? That's what our people have been *trying* to do! *Fighting* to do for all this time. Yes, over a *hundred* years! And it isn't long enough. Maybe in a *thousand* years, Sam. Maybe, if we're blessed by some miracle. Maybe then all the races can look each other in the eyes without harboring some resentment, however slight it may be. But today, Sam, in 1975, we can't even get our *streets* paved just for the fact our skin's so dark!"

She shook her head before going on, tears rolling down her cheeks. "The church is having a Juneteenth festival, you know. Or maybe you don't. There's gonna be a big dance that night. I'd hoped you'd ask me. But Juneteenth is probably too *black* for you, Sam. I've had to accept that. If you even know or care what it's all about, I don't know." She shook her head and choked out, "And I don't care."

"Mary..." Sam stood and went to her, but she held up a hand.

"I'm sorry, Sam. You don't know how much I love you. But I can't do this, okay? I'm too involved with what the rest of us are fighting for. It just kills me the way you shrug it all off. 'Get *over* slavery'?" She shrugged, wiping the tears from her eyes. "Get over *me*, Sam."

Mary got in her car and drove away, leaving Sam dumbfounded in the park, staring at that rotting old bench and wondering who he was.

Ray walked into the offices of *The Nightfire Chronicle* the next afternoon and was surprised by a new face. "Hello. Is Tom in?" He pointed to the old man's office behind her desk.

"Yes," the young woman said with a contagious grin. "He's in a meeting though, can I take a message?"

"Uh, sure. I'm Ray, by the way."

She giggled. "I'm Trish. I'm Tom's new secretary."

Ray smiled. "Right. Well, I was just seeing if Tom was free for lunch. I felt sorry for him having to work on a Saturday and all."

Trish made a face, brushing a strand of curly red hair away from her cheek. "So did I. I told him I'd come in and help. We already grabbed lunch too."

"Really?" Ray considered that. "Tom never told me he'd hired anyone to replace Rita."

"I just started yesterday."

"And already devoted enough to come in on a weekend."

"I guess Tom has that effect on people." She winked.

"I guess he does." Ray looked again to Tom's office door. "Well, tell Old Tom I dropped by."

"I will. Good meeting you, Ray."

"You too." Ray turned and left, wishing he knew what it was that was bothering him.

That evening, Bradley came bounding down the stairs. "Hey, Ray!"

"Yeah?" Ray didn't look up from the book that he was reading as he lounged on the couch.

"You don't have any plans for tonight, right?"

Ray put the book down and sat up with an amused grin. "I don't know. Why?"

"Well, 'cause I just worked it out to where I can see Helen again."

"Convinced her ol' man what an upstanding citizen you were, eh?"

"Not exactly." He laughed. "No, I don't think there's a chance in hell…but I did get them to agree to letting Mati chaperone."

Ray laughed out loud. "Ooh! Fun times!" He shook his head, still giggling. "Yeah, I guess I can look after the kids tonight. But then, who's gonna watch over me?"

"I think you're old enough now to look out for yourself," Bradley answered. "Well, they're already on their way over, so I guess I'll go wait outside."

Ray tensed suddenly, as he dared to broach a touchy subject. "Hey, Bradley…"

"Yeah?"

"Uh...so you're pretty much into Helen now, right?" He cleared his throat.

Puzzled, the younger man answered, "Sure."

"So then, you don't have any feelings for Doris?"

Bradley scoffed, "Hell no. She's a dirty slut."

Ray nodded his head. "Well, good. I think. So how 'bout if *I* asked her out?"

Bradley felt as if the wind had been knocked out of him, but he managed to answer, in spite of his suddenly dry throat, "Well...I mean..." He thought about it. He *shouldn't* have a problem with it. There was no sensible reason to deny to Ray the girl he'd let go. "Why?"

Ray shrugged, fearing he'd flipped a switch. "Iduno. She's...there?"

Bradley nodded, considering, then said earnestly, "But she's a dirty slut."

"I can cope with that."

"Well then, sure. I mean...if you really *want* to. It's not gonna bother me. Now that I've got Helen."

A car pulled up in front of the house and started to honk. "That's them!" Bradley said. "Gotta run."

Ray called after him, "So I can call Doris? You're sure?"

"Yeah, Ray," Bradley assured him as he walked out the door. "Go for it, you crazy bastard." He closed the door and bounced right over to Mati's car.

Ray leaned back on the couch, wondering when the last time he'd asked someone's permission for anything had been. "That went better than I thought it would." He breathed a great sigh of relief.

Valen Alexas hadn't been awake for very long when he heard the violin music coming from the music room. Raksha's ears perked up. Valen walked up to the door and considered opening it. It was a difficult decision, considering how hungry he was after a long day's sleep. The music grew louder, more energetic. He raised his hand to the doorknob. *It's just a ghost*, he thought. *What can a ghost do to such a creature as* me*?* He began to move his hand away, the hunger winning the argument. *It can wait.* The image of Clarenda's apparition assaulted his thoughts then. He recalled every horrific detail of it. *I don't think I want to see her again just yet anyway.* Of course, he had to acknowledge, Clarenda hadn't been the one whose violin music had always made his knees tremble.

A voice came from the room then, as the music stopped. "Something else, then. He always loved this one." The music began anew, playing one of Valen's favorite old melodies.

His hand clasped the doorknob, leaving his hunger behind, and he threw open the door. "Augustin!"

But there was no one. There was only emptiness. Silence. Raksha whined at his side. Stunned, eyes still searching the room desperately, Valen said to the wolf, "I think it's time to go hunt. And when we get back, I'm going to call Mary Jean."

The lights in the movie theater went down, and Bradley and Helen were already making out in the seat beside Mati. She groaned and turned to Sam, who they'd picked up along the way. "So what's wrong with you, anyway? You look like Bradley always did before," she gestured with a thumb to the couple on her other side, "*this.*"

Sam sighed, not meeting her gaze. "Mary dumped me."

"What? Why?"

A deep voice from the speakers began to speak, as the screen showed an underwater image, *"There is a creature alive today, who has survived millions of years of evolution. Without change, without passion, and without logic."*

Sam answered, "This movie's probably about *her.*"

"It lives to kill."

"That's not Mary! What happened?"

"A mindless eating machine."

"Well, I guess she *does* have passion. I don't know…"

"It will attack and devour…anything."

"You don't know what?" Mati asked distractedly, as she listened to the trailer.

"You don't think of me as a pet, do you?"

People from the row behind began shooshing them.

Mati laughed. "No! Why? Did Mary?" She watched the image of a woman swimming on the screen and grabbed Sam's arm intensely, gasping. "Oh!"

"It is as if God created the devil and gave him…"

"What is it?" Sam asked.

Mati shouted out along with the voice from the speakers, "Jaws! I can't *wait* to see that movie!"

The shooshing became much angrier. A voice from off to the side even shouted, "Shut up!"

Mati whispered to Sam, "Keep it down, Sam. We can talk *after* the movie. Your voice really carries."

Sam just shook his head and tried to get enthused about the movie, pretending not to even remember what Bradley and Helen were doing a couple of seats down the row. Pretending that he didn't desperately wish *his* girlfriend were with him, doing the same. But as he continued to watch the chilling preview for *Jaws*, all he seemed to want to do was go swimming.

A knock at the door took Ray away from the TV.

"*The Saturday Tonight Show*'s about to start!" Brendan called after him, as Ray went to answer the door.

"I know. I'll be right back." He opened the door to find a smiling, blonde Irishman standing on the porch. "Get away from here!"

"Come'ere to me now." He handed Ray a card. "I just wanted to give you the number of my hotel, in case there's any trouble. You can reach me any time."

"The only *trouble* I anticipate is standing on my porch right now."

The Nephilim whispered, "No, Ray. I'm not your only worry. Sion's here as well. We are watching them. We're watching them watch you."

Ray slammed the door in the man's face.

From the other side, Christian shouted, "Well, if you change your mind, I'm still in town." He whistled a tune Ray had never heard as he walked away, back to the hotel.

"Who was that?" Brendan asked, as he sprinkled pretzel crumbs on the face of his sleeping sister.

"No one. Just watch TV."

Ray peeked around the curtain, wondering how much faith to put in the Nephilim's latest warning.

At the Alexas mansion, Mary Jean Donavan finally opened her eyes. She turned to Valen. "He doesn't want to talk. I think he's embarrassed."

Excitedly, Valen asked, "So it's definitely a male presence in here?"

"The one who came forward when I called, yes. But I sense *three* presences aside from ourselves, watching us."

"Three?" Valen tried to decide who the third presence might be.

"Yes. The boy seems friendly, but apprehensive. The woman is hostile, but we already knew that. And the third one…" She concentrated. "Male. He comes off as simply curious, amused. Doesn't actually feel like a ghost at all…" She shook her head. "That's funny. I don't feel him anymore." She smiled at Valen. "Ah, well. Old houses are funny like that. So many entities. I would like to come back tomorrow, early, and stay here alone while you're out hunting. I think, if you're not here, I can get Augustin to speak to me. I might be able to find out what his sister is up to."

A tear escaped Valen's eye as he nodded. "Yes. Of course."

Mary Jean put a hand on his shoulder. "I know it's hard, learning that people you loved are not at peace. We will help them, Valen. I promise you. We'll clear this whole thing up."

"Thank you. I'll call you tomorrow night, as soon as I wake."

Mary Jean nodded and showed herself to the door.

Once he and Raksha were alone with the spirits, a voice sent a chill down the vampire's spine. "Valentinus Alexas."

Valen spun around with a gasp, then slowed his breathing, as he acknowledged the third presence. "Dominic Babylon." He laughed shortly. "Not a ghost at all."

The dark skinned man stepped out of the shadows. "I am here to know your answer to a question, old man. We need to know where your loyalties lie. Are you with your friend Julius, loyal to the Nephilim? Or are you still loyal to your mortal family, devoted to the Prieuré de Sion?"

CHAPTER 4
THE VAMPIRE'S DREAM

"Raksha," Valen said.

The wolf simply whined, and Valen looked at her, completely perplexed.

Babylon smiled bitterly. "She knows better than to attack a Nephilim, old man."

Valen smiled back bravely. "Who said I wanted her to attack you? Perhaps I was just showing you that we're not alone."

The Nephilim shook his head slowly. "This isn't personal, Valentinus. I know my relations with your kind have been less than civil ever since my brother went vampire. I've been working on coming to terms with it. It's the Nephilim way. We must accept what is, remember what was, and prepare for what is yet to be."

"That's good to hear. So, if it isn't personal, what?" the vampire asked.

Dominic's eyes narrowed. "You don't already know?" He studied the vampire's eyes. "No." He shrugged. "We thought you did."

"What is it?"

"You are familiar with a young man named Raymond Don?"

"Yes."

"Well, then you should know that he's hidden something on your property that is of interest to both the Nephilim and Sion. He's put himself in a deadly position. And you with him. So where do your loyalties lie?"

"What are you talking about? What has he hidden?"

Dominic shrugged again. "If you don't know, I really shouldn't tell you. Especially since I don't know where your..."

"Stop it," Valen said harshly. "You *know* where my loyalties *must* remain. You know the sort of man I am."

Ray picked up the phone and dialed Dori's number. She answered on the first ring, "Hello?"

"Hey, Dori."

"Ray? Do you have any idea what time it is? My parents could have answered."

"Yeah, but they didn't. Lucky me."

Dori snickered. "Oh. Feelin' lucky, are we?"

"I'm always feelin' lucky. So, anyway, I've got the kids tonight, but I talked to Bradley about, you know, what we had discussed."

Doris started laughing, "And how did *that* go?"

"Better than I'd expected. He's into Helen now."

"Shit. Guess *I* was easy to get over."

"I thought that was the idea."

"Yeah," Dori conceded. "I guess."

"So, now you've got your chance."

"Are you saying you wanna…"

"I'm asking you out. You know, if you haven't got anything better to do."

"I think my schedule's pretty clear. When did you have in mind?"

"I don't know. Tomorrow?"

"Sunday? What will Jesus think?"

Ray laughed. "So, what'll it be? Are we gonna do this thing? Or should I give the honor to someone else?"

"Arrogant bastard. How could I refuse?"

Ray laughed, and Dori joined him.

Mati pulled up to the Stevens house, as Bradley and Helen continued to make out in the back seat. She had already dropped Sam off at home, without having had the chance to ask him what had happened between him and Mary Rhodes. "We're here!" After getting no response, "Hey, Bradley! Detach! My sister needs to breathe!"

Bradley slowly pulled away from Helen and smiled at Mati. "Where did you say we were?"

"Your *house*? You need to get back to your husband and the children."

He looked out the window. "Oh, we're here already?" He opened the door, then leaned over to kiss Helen goodbye. The kiss lingered.

Mati honked the horn, and Bradley jumped. "Come on, Stevens! I don't have all night!"

"Sorry." He laughed. "I'll call you tomorrow, Helen."

"Bye!" Helen blew him a kiss, and he caught it. Mati rolled her eyes.

When Bradley closed the door and started walking to the house, Helen crawled into the front seat with her sister.

Mati drove off silently.

"So what's up your ass?" Helen asked.

"Nothing. It's just irritating when you have to sit next to two people sucking each others faces through the whole movie."

"You're just jealous."

Mati hissed through her teeth. She waited a moment before responding. "You know what? I really am, a little, on some level. Since Scott broke up with me, I haven't had much opportunity to meet anyone. I miss him. But that's not what's really bothering me, Helen. This whole thing with you and Bradley just isn't *right*."

"How do you mean?"

"Well, for starters, there's the way you just reacted to my statement. You didn't get angry or offended. You just don't seem bothered by the possibility that you and Bradley aren't right for each other. And, if you think about it, what do you and Bradley even have in *common*?"

"Well, we like..." Helen thought about it.

"Making out?" Mati asked. "There's more to a relationship, Helen. Bradley may not even know it, but he's using you. How can you believe him if he says he really cares? I mean, look at his history! He's like Romeo! One second he's completely head over heals for Rosalind, who he can't have so he wants to kill himself, obvious solution! Then, he meets Juliet like the next *day* and forgets Rosalind even existed, goes totally gaga over the new girl, loses her too, then kills himself. Hello! He's so *manic*! That's who you're going out with. I just don't wanna see you get hurt. I think what Bradley really needs is to be single for a while. He needs to focus on *Bradley*, not Bradley *and*. He has a lot to work out in his own head, and he's using girlfriends to hide from it. That's why he gets so clingy."

"Jesus shit." Helen said matter-of-factly. "You are *so* jealous."

Mati groaned and rolled her eyes, trading the subject in for silence for the remainder of the trip.

By sunrise, the vampire was dreaming. It was rare that Valen had dreamt since his conversion nearly half a millennium before, and now dreams were not for him what they had been when he'd been mortal. Dreams were not escapes. Dreams were not symbolic manifestations of the sub-conscious. Dreams were old thoughts, buried memories, coming to the surface with more clarity than when they'd actually been happening.

It was the summer of 1914, and it was raining. Valentinus waited in the shadows of Nightfire's hotel, watching for prey. The pair he was eyeing now was abnormally attractive, like something from a painting. Valentinus mused to himself how moments like this made him *wish* he could paint. He studied them. They seemed lost and frightened, watching the rain from beneath the awning.

He approached them cautiously. They were young, surely not old enough to have become the sort the world would never miss. At least not old enough to have earned it. Still, if they were here alone, with no one to wait for them, the Rule of Nightfire would not protect them from the others. Valentinus decided he had to leave. He couldn't rescue *every* wayward soul who didn't deserve to die.

Just then, the boy turned his head and made eye contact with him. He then tugged the sleeve of the young woman and whispered conspiratorially, "Look."

She turned and saw Valentinus, who was puzzled by them both. She looked to the boy, confused. "What?" she whispered. "You make it seem as if something were out of place."

"But look at him," the youth insisted. "He's *weird*."

The girl sighed and turned to the vampire. "I'm sorry, sir. He's a very strange young man at times. He hasn't any manners."

Valentinus surrendered to the fact he was now involved with this pair, and he laughed quietly. "Not a problem. After all, manners can be so boring."

She and the boy both laughed. They turned to face the vampire completely, as they backed away from the edge of the porch, farther under the shelter of the overhanging roof. "My uncle is sending a car for us. But maybe he's waiting for the rain to die down."

Valentinus laughed with relief. The pair were not unaccounted for. The others would not try to feed on them. "It is a dreadful night for driving." He extended his hand to the boy. "I'm Valentinus Alexas."

The boy took his hand and smiled. "Augustin Richardson. This is my sister Clarenda." He jerked his head in her direction.

Clarenda offered her hand, and Valentinus took it. "A pleasure to meet the both of you. Who is your uncle? Perhaps I know him."

Augustin answered energetically, "Jacob Richardson. We're going to live with him now, since our parents died from fever last month. My dad grew up here. We'd been traveling for over a year when they got sick, and we had to come home. They didn't last long once we did."

Clarenda nudged him. "I'm sure we don't want to bother everyone we meet with all the details, Augie."

"He didn't *stop* me," the young man argued

Valentinus laughed at the boy's spirit. He liked him. Liked them both. And he did know their uncle. He even remembered their father Thomas, now that he knew who their uncle was. He remembered them as boys. He remembered *their* parents, and the dates of their births. The town was Valentinus' flock, and he did what he could to watch over them all. He noticed the case Augustin held at his side. "Do you play?"

"No, I'm just holding it to look good," Augustin answered flatly.

Clarenda slapped his arm. "Augustin! Be polite! You're too old to be…"

"Okay. I play. In fact, I play better than anyone," he boasted. He looked keenly into the vampire's eyes, "I'm enchanting when I play. You'll fall in love with me, if ever you witness it."

Valen didn't know quite how to respond.

Clarenda shook her head and rolled her eyes. "So cocky! If you're so good, then why is it that you're seventeen years old and you've never had a girl take interest."

He laughed. "Plenty have taken interest."

"Really? Then why haven't I heard anything about them?"

He shrugged and looked at the vampire. "None of them ever seem to interest *me*."

Clarenda smiled at Valentinus. "One day he'll grow up. I'm certain of it."

"I hope not," Valentinus said. "The world is never as kind to men as it is to boys."

Augustin replied, "Some see it the other way around, Mr. Alexas."

A car pulled up in the rain, and a man shouted for the young pair. They said their farewells to Valentinus, and he offered to come by, assuring them that he *did* know their uncle, and see that they had everything they needed the following night. He watched them drive away in the rain.

An ageing wolf materialized from the shadows behind him. The vampire regarded the creature. "I like them, Tonkawa. I hope their uncle doesn't cause them more trouble than they've already seen."

The wolf looked at the vampire tiredly.

Valentinus laughed. "If you're thinking I'm being too optimistic…" He sighed. "You're right. We'll have to keep an eye on them."

Ray pushed his way through the crowd that was leaving the Methodist church. He was the only one trying to get *in*, and he was swimming against the tide. He found Reverend Michaels in the crowd and headed straight for him.

"Ray!"

He stopped and turned, surprised by the voice that had called his name. "Jenny? I didn't know you went to this church."

She smiled. "Well, I don't. Not usually. But Mr. Morris said this is where *you* go to church."

Ray scoffed. "I don't go to church."

Jenny looked perplexed. "Then…what are you doing here?"

"Oh, I…" He looked over to the pastor, "…needed to talk to the preacher." He studied her. He'd never seen her in her Sunday best before. She was gorgeous. "So, you just came here because you thought I did?"

"Well, you know, I thought maybe I should get to know you better. Outside of work. I mean, if you're not seeing anybody." She turned bright red. "Jeez that was stupid."

Taken completely aback, Ray fumbled, "N…no, no. I'm not…" He considered his impending date with Doris Gardner. "I'm not seeing anybody, really."

She lit up. "Oh, well then do you wanna get some lunch?"

Jeez, she really is forward. "I can't today. I have to talk to the preacher. But, maybe…"

"Some other time?"

"Absolutely." He flashed his most charming smile.

When he made his way through the crowd to Reverend Michaels, he blurted out, "Can we talk?"

"What's wrong, Ray?"

Ray thought about the Nephilim. He thought about his treasure. He thought about the Prieuré de Sion. "I've got some theological questions."

The pastor studied him. "They must be pressing on you greatly. I've never seen anyone look so disturbed by simple 'theological questions.' Come to my office. We'll see what I can do to help."

The vampire's dream continued, as he relived those early days of friendship with the Richardson siblings. He'd loved them both, but he'd bonded with Clarenda first.

He went to the door, and there was Clarenda with a basket of fruit and a smile. "I hope it's not too late. I know you said your work kept you away during the day, and I just wanted to thank you for coming to my rescue last night."

Valentinus remembered the previous night, when he'd come upon a strange man assaulting the young lady. It had cost Valentinus no effort at all to pull the man off of her and break both of his arms. He'd seen Clarenda on her errand and back home safely after that, then he'd gone back to the man's hotel room and waited. "It was nothing, Clarenda. It was my pleasure to play the hero."

A strange look came over her then, a wrathful look. "Did you hear what happened to him?"

Valentinus didn't answer.

"They found him this morning, dead in his hotel room. No one knows who he is or where he was from. And it didn't look like he died from what you did to him, but what could have caused it? He just went back to his hotel from the doctor, and he died. Do you think it was God?"

Valentinus shook his head. "No."

"Well, I hope he's burning in Hell. I hope he never stops screaming."

Valentinus was shocked by the heartlessness of the young beauty. "Miss Richardson, you astound me."

She smiled, and his heart warmed. "I thought we'd taken care of this already. Call me *Clarenda*."

Later that night, Valen saw to it that the man's body vanished from the coroner's, before it could be examined. It was a great risk, and a breach of the Law that he'd left a body, but he'd done it for Clarenda's peace of mind. He didn't want her ever to wonder if that man were still lurking in the shadows. He wanted her to sleep well, knowing that he was dead…and in Hell, if that's what she needed to believe.

Clarenda came over more and more frequently over the next few months, at risk of the townspeople talking. Half in love with her, Valentinus ignored the threat of gossip. He was drawn to her intelligence, her silken white skin, her dark golden hair, the grace with which she moved, the depth of her amber-colored eyes. They talked for hours. She read every book she could get her hands on, just as he did, so their conversation never lacked for a topic. They spoke of art and politics, history and romance. She kissed him one night, as they sat together beneath a tree, staring out over a pond in the woods, just outside of downtown. It was the most alive Valentinus had felt in decades. "I love you, Valentinus. I want to marry you."

"That's very noble of you." He laughed. "Your uncle needs you."

"He's insane, Valentinus! Surely you know…"

"Yes," the vampire admitted. "I have known a while now."

Desperately, Clarenda explained, "He beats Augustin! He *hates* him! That's why he's never come with me, though he wants to, terribly. He was very taken with you the night we all met. But Uncle Jacob gets drunk and hurts him so frequently, the bruises never go away."

"I didn't realize…"

"You know everyone in this town, so tell me, how did Uncle Jacob get like this?"

Relieved that the conversation had taken a new direction, Valentinus explained how three years before, Jacob Richardson had left his wife for another woman. It hadn't worked out. His wife had remarried and found happiness, started a family. Jacob realized what he'd lost and just went mad. He'd been getting progressively worse ever since. He hadn't left his house now in a year and a half.

"You see then, don't you?" Clarenda pleaded. "If we were married, I could leave that house and take Augustin with me! You do think I'm pretty, don't you?"

Tortured by the reality of it, Valentinus answered, "Yes, Clarenda, you're beautiful. The most beautiful woman I've ever known."

"And you love me, don't you?"

Tears threatened the vampire now. "I do. It is true. I will not deny it. But…"

Clarenda's countenance fell. "But? What is it?"

"I can't marry you. I have…other commitments. It wouldn't be right for me to lead you on. I have to remain honorable, don't you see?"

"I think I understand." She began to cry, quietly. "It's some-one else?"

"It's complicated." He shook his head. "There is no finer woman than you. I am a lonely creature, it's true. I desperately need you to be my friend. To *remain* my friend."

"So…she lives afar." Clarenda nodded her head. "And you insist on being loyal to her. I should have expected no less from Valentinus Alexas." She looked him in the eyes. "My heart is broken, my friend, but I think I love you all the more for it. There's no more noble man than you."

"Then…?"

She smiled through her tears. "We'll remain friends." She put a hand on his, then turned from his gaze and quickly changed the subject. "Augustin wants to come with me, as I said. He finds you strange, which is complementary coming from him. But he's so embarrassed of his bruises. He feels like less of a man for them."

"Bring him," Valentinus said urgently. "I will teach him how to fight. I too have seen the world, and I have learned the art of hand to hand fighting from ancient sources. Few in America know such skills as these. I'll teach them to Augustin." He smiled at her, and he kissed her on the cheek, savoring the aroma of the blood beneath her blushing skin. "Bring him tomorrow."

Ray followed Reverend Michaels through the little building to his office and sat at the chair in front of his desk.

"So, what sort of *theological* questions bring a church-hating young man like yourself racing into the church as if it mattered to you?" The twisted little man sat down across from Ray, as he cackled.

Ray considered the question, not wanting to sound like he actually cared. He shrugged. "I'm just curious."

"About?" the preacher prodded.

"About...things like...the Nephilim." Ray looked expectantly at Reverend Michaels.

"Ah!" The older man cackled some more. "It never fails to amaze me how the ones who actually *read* the Bible are the very ones who never seem to believe in it. Not many people would even know what in the hell you were talking about, son. Fortunately for you, I happen to have read the old book. So what's your question, specifically?"

"How do you reconcile that, for one? And what are they? What's their agenda?"

Reverend Michaels laughed hysterically.

Ray straightened up and looked irritated. "What's so damn funny?"

The preacher wiped a tear from his eye. "You're serious, eh? All right." He composed himself. "The Nephilim were said to be the offspring of human women and the 'sons of God.'"

"But I thought Jesus was the only *alleged...*"

Reverend Michaels held up a hand. "Precisely. That's why no one ever likes to acknowledge that particular story from Genesis. And so it's led those who do to speculate. Some say the sons of God were angels, others extra-terrestrials. Still others use it to support polytheism. It's always sounded a little like Greek mythology to me. The Nephilim were the heroes of days gone by. Men of renown. They show up later in Numbers and Joshua as well as in several extra-Biblical scriptures. They were thought to be very powerful. It's speculated Goliath was a Nephilim. In fact, some translators have replaced the mysterious word 'Nephilim' in Genesis and the others with 'giant.'

"As for their *agenda*...the Bible doesn't say. To be heroes perhaps?" He shrugged. "I don't know. No one really knows anything about it. Many scholars feel safe in dismissing these creatures as folk lore, along with *most* of the book of Genesis."

"What about Moses? Does anything in the Bible support the idea that he was in actuality a deposed Pharaoh?"

Reverend Michaels seemed to like the idea, as he pondered it. "Now that *would* be something, wouldn't it? That would ruffle a lot of feathers." He shook his head. "But, no. The Bible, well, actually...I think I should reread Exodus with the idea in mind and see if it fits. He *was* raised in the *house* of Pharaoh, after all. That's an intriguing notion. But I've never heard it before. And the Bible pretty much paints the picture that he wasn't." He leaned forward. "What else have you got for me?"

Ray laughed. "Okay, amazingly you haven't thrown me out yet, but this one'll probably do the trick. What if you found out that Jesus didn't die on the cross or ascend into Heaven? What if you found evidence that all that was just a lie, and he actually went on to live a normal, not-so-virginal life? What would that do to your faith?"

Surprisingly, the preacher's only reaction was a raised eyebrow and a shrug. Then, "Between the two of us, I already think that. My faith's intact."

"You *what*?" Ray couldn't believe it.

"Ray, why don't you tell me what you saw in your travels? Was it the tomb in India?"

Ray's jaw dropped. "I'm not *seriously* hearing this shit come out of your mouth! You're a Methodist minister! You're supposed to be brainwashed!"

Reverend Michaels grinned. "The Bible's a book of illustrations, Ray. Examples of how to live our lives. Metaphors. I'm not supposed to be saying any of this, now, so let's keep it between the two of us. I'll tell you a secret, too. Not a preacher comes to this little church in Nightfire without having gotten into trouble where they were before. So, if you ever run into anything weird, even after I'm gone, you can come here and talk to the preacher about it almost sure he'll take it seriously. That said, what is it you need from me, Ray? Is this discovery what's taken you away from God?"

Ray stammered, "It just…Lee's the same. I don't get it. There can't be a God. All the miracles were lies. Don't you see? Everything the Church stands for is a lie."

"I disagree. It's just not the *absolute* truth is all."

Ray shook his head in frustration. "But…what if you found the *evidence*? And I mean *more* than just a tomb? What would you do?"

The preacher became instantly serious, and he put a hand down harshly on the desk. "I would keep it real quiet." He fell into thought for a moment. "Have you ever heard of an organization called the Prieuré de Sion?"

Ray slumped in his chair. "You're shitting me."

"I take it that means yes. Ray, people have *died* over this. I'll tell you the sin that landed me in Nightfire. I was *looking* for the evidence. It just made so much sense. I thought it would *enrich* my relationship with Christ to know he'd lived a fully human life. The bishops didn't see it that way. The thing is, the trails all run cold. People *have* found the evidence in the past, Ray. But all those people are dead. The Prieuré de Sion saw to that."

Ray was pale. "So…if there were, say, *another* group who said they were the *opposite* of Sion, would you put your life in their hands, if they offered?"

"I've never heard of an opposing order to Sion."

"Try the Nephilim."

"What? Are you saying they still exist?"

Ray shrugged. "The Bible *says* they do, doesn't it?"

"Yes, but that verse was written untold *thousands* of years ago. Even if you believe it applied then, that doesn't mean it still applies today."

"Well, it does."

Reverend Michaels considered that silently, then made up his mind. "Ray, don't trust any of them. Don't trust anyone you meet. *Anyone* could be a Sion assassin. They're clever. They have a penchant for untraceable poisons. Be careful who you drink with." He paused, then added, "And don't involve me any further, if it can be helped. I'm alive today, because I never found the answers. I'm in Nightfire today, because of how openly I pursued them. Whatever evidence there is, at this point, I don't want to see it." He looked sadly into Ray's blue eyes. "I'll be praying for you, son."

"Whatever helps you sleep at night, Bob." He laughed as he stood to leave. "This is not the way I envisioned this conversation going."

The preacher shook his head with a weary smile. "That makes two of us."

After Ray had left him, Reverend Michaels opened his Bible, wondering at the many surprises his tenure at Nightfire had offered him, eager to read over the Book of Exodus with Ray's new perspective.

The vampire's dream continued. At first, Clarenda began to bring Augustin with her, then the boy started showing up on his own. Some nights even before Valentinus had risen. The vampire would go into the den just after he woke, and there would be Augustin, sitting on the couch with his feet propped up on the table. "Do you like how I broke into your house?"

"No," Valentinus would answer, always with a loving smile. He taught the young man how to fight, and Augustin proved an excellent pupil. Valentinus taught him all of the ancient techniques he'd learned from Julius. In little time, they'd become playmates, and Valentinus was like a boy himself again. It was a second youth, and much better than the first. This, Valentinus thought, was what being seventeen *should* have been. But he'd been an aristocrat. He'd been spoiled. He'd let vice take a hold of his destiny. And then there had been D'artagnan. But Valentinus did not like to think on him.

Augustin was a free spirit such as Valentinus had never encountered. If he was half in love with the sister, he was *completely* in love with the brother. The boy had a way of bringing him out that he became quickly addicted to.

One night, Valentinus went into Dan Parker's Saloon, and there was Augustin, engaged in an arm wrestling match with one of the more dangerous looking patrons. Of course he won, against all odds, and didn't seem at all exerted afterwards. He seemed to have an endless store of energy. In a way, Valentinus fed on him, without ever taking the boy to his lips.

Augustin approached Valentinus and slapped him on the arm. "Let's go for a swim!"

"It's late."

The boy shrugged, "It's always late when we're together. Besides, we'll have the pond to ourselves. Come on, Valentinus!"

Unable to resist his enthusiasm, Valentinus consented and found himself following Augustin into the woods behind Dan Parker's Saloon. Soon they were at the hidden pond, surrounded by trees and darkness, bathed in moonlight. The water wasn't still, though there wasn't any wind. It was rippling with unseen intrusions to the surface, gently splashing against the shore, like a living, breathing thing.

The vampire was always bombarded by memories in this wood. This was the place where he had once tried to stop the werewolf Sebastian Barnes from murdering a young girl named Anabell Richards. He'd failed. He wasn't an Ancient and didn't have the strength to overpower a werewolf. His failure had led the town to near ruin. This was also the place where, only days before, Clarenda had kissed him, and he'd been forced to disappoint her. This pond represented failure to him. Surely nothing good could come from it.

Then he saw Augustin, without hesitation, shed his garments and test the water with his toes, giggling like a child. Valentinus was dumbstruck by the sight. He'd never seen a body so perfectly sculpted. Not even D'artagnan, who he'd thought to be the most beautiful man when he'd still been human. Even after, for a time. Augustin turned to him with the brightest smile. "It's just right. Get in with me, or I'll throw you in."

The feeling of sheer euphoria at the vision before him continued to grow, as Valentinus allowed himself to be pulled in by the affectionate gaze of the amber-eyed beauty. His face so perfectly crowned with unruly curls. Valentinus imagined running his fingers through them, as he…fed. He removed his clothing, then stepped up to the pond's edge and put a toe in, pretending. "That's far too cold. I won't get in."

"I swear I'll throw you, Valentinus." Augustin giggled.

"You couldn't."

"I could, just like you taught me." He grabbed Valentinus then and knocked his legs out from beneath him with a well placed kick, then threw him in. Valentinus surfaced to the young man's laughter, then Augustin jumped in after him, splashing loudly, as he pounced on him, pretending as if he were going to drown him. They threw each other all over the pond, and they laughed until their sides hurt. This was the mortal frivolity Valentinus had so yearned for. The camaraderie with another being he'd so lacked for all these centuries.

Suddenly, Augustin grabbed both sides of Valentinus' face and said, "If it were not so *wrong*, I would love you, Valentinus." He kissed him on the forehead. "You're a wonderful friend." Then he surprised the vampire further by hugging him tightly and resting his head on his shoulder, his heart pounding urgently against the vampire's chest.

The beating heart and the scent of the living blood within was almost enough to break Valentinus' reserve. He returned the embrace and closed his eyes, letting his mouth drift ever closer to his new friend's exposed skin. His lips parted automatically at Augustin's throat. *I mustn't*, he thought. *He must remain as he is.* He pulled away, stroked the young man's cheek, and kissed him on the forehead, fighting against his darkest desires. "Your friendship means the world to me. We should get back." They smiled at each other, lingering, both unsure what to do next. At last Valentinus moved to the shore and got out of the water. He could feel Augustin's eyes on him as he dressed, as well as Tonkowa's. Though Tonkowa had been dosing, the vampire could tell.

Ray and Dori walked into Dan Parker's, hand in hand, and quickly found a table. On the other side of the building, they could see Rubin Santana and Dirk Arnold arm wrestling. Rubin won, of course, because he was huge.

I hope he doesn't come over here, Ray thought. "So, where the hell else is there to go for a date in this town?"

Doris laughed. "Lots of places, if you're a kid. Or if you just wanna get down to business." She narrowed her eyes at him.

He shook his head and laughed. "I wouldn't mind a little privacy. I'm pretty hungry though. I skipped lunch."

"Why?"

Ray shrugged. "Just forgot. Had a lot on my mind."

"Such as?"

"Nothin."

"You're useless." She waved over at Rubin. "Hey, Rubin! Over here!"

"What the hell did you do that for?" Ray whispered, upset.

Dori looked surprised. "He's my friend."

"*Him*?"

"Yeah, since we were kids."

Rubin walked over to them, running a hand through his hair at the side and tucking it behind his ear. "Dori, you so desperate for love you got a table with *him*?"

Dori laughed. "Relax, Santana, you had your moment to shine."

Ray's eyes went wide as he regarded Dori.

She went on, fondling Rubin's shirt where he stood. "You cut your hair! It used to be so long!"

He ran his hand through it again. "It's still too long for some folks' taste. I'm tryin' to get a better job and do something with my life."

"So become a dancer. You'd make an *awesome* stripper."

"Not my thing, but I'll give *you* a show…"

Ray stood up. "Hey, go push your burrito someplace else!"

"Touchy, Ray. It's not like y'all are on a date or…"

"Yeah, we are. So bug off you son of a…"

"How's your jaw, Ray?" Rubin asked.

"Why you…"

"Hey!" Dori stood up and got between the two men. "No fighting. I'd don't particularly want to get kicked out of here tonight."

"Whatever, Dori." Rubin stomped off angrily. "Have fun."

Dori laughed as she sat back down.

"What's so damn funny?" Ray asked, exasperated.

"You are."

"Me? What about *you*? You mean to tell me that you and *him*…"

"It was a long time ago, Ray. What? Like you don't have a history?"

Ray sighed. "Everybody has a history. But does *everybody's* history have to include *you*?"

"So charming."

"Maybe this wasn't such a good idea."

"Right. We knew that. We're just seeing how long we can pull it off for, remember?"

"We must be out of our minds."

"Precisely. That's why we have to see what happens. It's just for kicks. It doesn't have to work any longer than we want it to. We don't even need anything in common, except for…certain things."

She put a hand on his arm, and he laughed in spite of himself. "What happened to looking for something more *real*?"

Just then, Bradley and Sam walked in and joined Robert and Jeffrey Mason at the bar. Ray stood up. "Come on, let's go talk to Bradley."

"Ooh! Now I feel like the *other woman*."

"Shut up." Ray led Dori over to the bar. "Where are Brendan and Kate?"

"They're at a sleepover." Bradley met Dori's eyes for only a moment, then looked away and asked the ground, "So what are y'all up to?"

"Just a date," Ray answered.

"That was fast," Bradley muttered.

"Well, you said it was…"

Sam interrupted, "You two are going out? Since when?"

"Since right now." Doris grinned.

Jeffrey snickered at this, but surprised everyone by making no comment. Ray glared at him incredulously.

Todd the bartender put a Dr. Pepper down in front of Ray. "I know your poison, and ya look like ya need it."

Robert noticed Bradley's discomfort, and he put a beer down in front of him. "Ya look like ya need it."

Bradley chugged it instantly.

"Whoa! Slow down, tiger," Dori laughed.

"Really, Bradley. I don't wanna clean up your puke tonight," Ray added.

"How 'bout you, Sam?" Robert asked.

"I don't wanna clean it up either!"

"No." He gestured to Todd, who passed him a bottle. "Beer?"

"No thanks. I'll stick to Dr. Pepper."

Todd put one on the counter in front of him.

"I'll compromise," Ray said, as he grabbed a glass from behind the counter and poured his Dr. Pepper into it. He then poured some of the beer into it as well and stirred it with a straw.

"Nasty," Todd said.

"So who's filling in while your cousin's on her cruise?" Ray asked.

Todd groaned. "Our other cousin. James." He looked to Sam. "He's a piece of work. Frankly, I can't wait for Victoria to get back. Being around James is kind of like…eating raw coffee grounds."

Sam contemplated that quietly, not at all sure what to say. Everyone else laughed.

"What's wrong, Sam?" Ray asked.

"Nothing. Everything. Mary broke up with me."

"What? Why?"

"Mati told me," Dori said. "She said she didn't get a chance to ask you what happened."

"Well, it's sort of a long story," Sam told her. "Complicated anyway. I don't know. I'm pretty sad. It's like she wanted me to choose between her and my friends. I couldn't do it. So she chose for me."

The group did their best to try and comfort Sam, as he filled them in on all the details. After not much time, however, Ray and Doris decided to leave.

When they got outside, Doris wrapped her arms around his neck. "Finally! I thought we'd never be alone." She kissed him on the lips, then smiled up at him. "I want you, Ray."

Instead of answering her out loud, or even making a sarcastic remark, Ray kissed her back.

She laughed. "I knew we had something in common. How long has it been for you?"

Ray exhaled dramatically. "Too long."

"So take me home with you."

Ray studied the ominous storm clouds that covered the stars from view, as the wind blew his hair in all directions. "I don't have a room. Just a couch."

"That'll do."

"Maybe for you. I need more room."

"The hotel then."

Ray thought about Christian Rivers. "No. There's someone staying there I don't want to run into."

She pushed him up against the wall. "Think of a place! Or I'll take you right here." She looked at the sky. "And we'll probably get rained on." She lit up. "We could use Bradley's room."

"No we couldn't."

"That house is full of rooms! Why don't you have one?"

"The two empty rooms…depress me. They remind me who's not in them. I can't even go in there. Neither can the others. I'd rather just sleep on the couch."

A light drizzle began to chill them. "Bradley's room then," Doris said. "It has to be. He's not dead. And I've done it in there before."

Ray rolled his eyes. "Don't remind me."

"Come on, Ray. He just got here. He's hanging out with Sam and the Mason boys. He won't be home for hours. We only need…twenty minutes?"

"Oh ye of little faith." He sighed. "All right. Let's hurry. Looks like we're in for a hell of a storm."

The vampire's dream spanned years. His house was never empty now. Clarenda and Augustin came over every night. They had become a family. Augustin had taken over the music room, and he played his violin like the devil, seducing Valentinus all the more with every stroke of his bow.

Eventually, Augustin became confident enough, and angry enough, to strike back at his uncle when the beating was eminent. Jacob never touched him again. Instead he began taking it out on the townspeople, who would have preferred if he he'd remained a hermit.

By the spring of 1915, Jacob Richardson had been killed in a gunfight just outside of Dan Parker's Saloon. Clarenda and Augustin, now partial owners of his estate, let it fall into disrepair, choosing to spend all their time at Valentinus' mansion instead. Their other sister never came to lay any claim on Jacob's estate either, as she was happy where she was, with her husband and their daughter, and had no need of the old man's property.

By 1917, Valentinus, Clarenda, and Augustin were the perfect threesome. Old Tonkawa would have made it four, if he'd not spent so much time asleep. Valentinus worried that the wolf was near its end, and knew he needed to raise another. He dared not divulge to the mortals how old Tonkowa actually was, considering he'd acquired him as a pup in the winter of 1887. Such a lifespan was unheard of, even for a wolf of Tonkowa's sort.

It was interesting to Valentinus to note how differently the mortals he'd become so intimately entangled with would treat poor, old Tonkowa when he was awake. Clarenda regarded the creature as merely decorative. So long as he remained "adorable and fuzzy" there wasn't a problem. When the creature would get sick, however, which seemed to be happening more and more frequently, she would scream and unleash such a fury, as if he'd done it deliberately to spite her. Such moments made Valentinus very uncomfortable. Yet he always managed to forget the cruelty that should have been undeniable within Clarenda's spirit.

Augustin, on the other hand, saw Tonkowa as a wrestling partner, plain and simple. He seemed not to realize the growing frailty of the beast. And Tonkowa visibly appreciated that about Augustin. He would allow himself to be spun around on all fours, or on his side. Augustin would laugh when Tonkowa tried to walk afterwards and fell over from dizziness. This is how they would play. Augustin's reaction to the old wolf's bouts of sickness was no different than his normal treatment. "Tonkowa! Did you throw up? Don't be sick!" And then he would attack the poor creature with playful fur-ruffling and slaps on the side.

Valentinus loved them all. He loved sitting on the couch beside Clarenda and listening to Augustin play his music. Clarenda was not as taken with it as he was, but she would sit with them anyway, smiling that not-so-genuine smile of hers. Valentinus took advantage of every opportunity he had to simply gaze into her eyes.

The bond between Valentinus and Clarenda continued to grow. It was clear she was in love with him, and she had made no efforts to land a husband. He feared she'd become a spinster for life, and what a crime it would be for such a beauty as she. He tried to encourage her to meet other young men. She simply had no desire. He was all she wanted.

Valentinus yearned to tell her the truth. That he was not human, that he was, in fact, something evil, something demonic. But what would that solve? She'd never have believed him. Not unless he showed her. And that was not possible for him. It would have violated her sacred innocence. So she went on loving him, and he went on pretending to be something he was not.

His bond with Augustin also continued to grow. The young man was so open, so unafraid of taboo. "I'm tired. Let's go to bed."

Not understanding, the vampire simply smiled, as if to wish him sweet dreams.

"Come on," Augustin said, as he began to climb the stairs. "My bed's big enough for two."

Not knowing at all where this would take him, Valentinus followed. They got into Augustin's bed together, and they held each other like lovers. "See? This is nice." Augustin whispered in his ear. "No sin in two friends *sleeping* together." It was seemingly such an innocent thing.

And that's exactly what they did. They slept. It was the safest Valentinus had ever felt, laying in that bed with Augustin. It seemed he should never have been anywhere else.

It was that very year, just when everything seemed so perfect, that everything suddenly began to crumble. It started with the letter from D'artagnan. Then Augustin had innocently stumbled upon the Mines…

***

Valentinus awoke with a start from his dream. Someone was screaming. He left his resting place and rushed upstairs. He looked around, dizzy from the intensity of his dreams and the suddenness of his waking. Instinctively, he opened the door to the room that had been Augustin's. He went in, leaving the lights out, half expecting to see the young man lying their, waiting for him to crawl beneath the covers beside him. Instead he saw the darkness, interrupted by an occasional burst of lightning. The tempest outside was perhaps the source of the sound he'd heard, the scream, though it had sounded like *her.* The way she'd screamed on that last night…

"Valentinus."

He turned and gasped, for there she was, in her nightgown, holding a candle. She looked completely tangible, not like a spirit at all. "Clarenda…"

"Yes, dear one. It is I." She smiled, and she stepped closer with every beat of the vampire's heart. "Did you hear my scream? Murderer. Were you dreaming of the old days? Before you condemned us to *this*?"

Valen said nothing, as she came right up next to him, so close he could feel the warmth of the candle.

"Well, I'm a strong ghost, my love. I have both the will and the strength to see that you *join us*!" She lunged forward with the candle suddenly, and the flames quickly took to Valen's shirt. He batted at them to no avail, as Clarenda's ghost watched with laughter. "I know how to destroy you, creature from Hell! You can't survive fire! You'll burn up just the same as any mortal!" The flames began to burn his skin, his face, his hands. Somewhere within his own, wordless screaming, he heard the anguished cry of Augustin, shouting helplessly, "No!" But then his own screams drowned all other sounds out, as the candle's fire sought to carry out Clarenda's revenge.

CHAPTER 5
THE PHANTOM'S FURY

Raksha bounded into the room, alert and horrified. She saw the ghost of Clarenda Richardson laughing like a villainess from a fairy tale, and she saw her master burning.

Valen batted at the flames with his burning hands, screaming, accomplishing nothing. He saw the wolf, as lightning from the storm outside once again lit the room. "Raksha!!! I'm dying!!!"

Ignoring the phantom, who she knew was more than a match for a mere wolf, Raksha abandoned all caution and leapt at Valen with all her strength, feeling the flames take to her coat as she accomplished her aim. She knocked Valen over into the great window with such force that he broke right through the glass and flailed out into the air, far enough from the ground that, had he been mortal, he would have joined Clarenda just as she'd planned. And she would have enjoyed the irony.

It wasn't until several moments after he'd hit the ground and been soaked to the core that he realized the incredibly heavy rainfall had saved his life and extinguished the flames that sought to consume him. It was just then that he had another realization, moving his arms and legs experimentally, that the nauseating crunch he'd heard when he'd hit the ground hadn't been any of *his* bones. He looked around frantically in the rain, but the torrent made it difficult to see. "Raksha!"

He found her very near to him, not moving. He went to her and saw the bone of one of her legs sticking through the skin. "No!" He put a hand to her shoulder, and she opened her eyes, unfocusing, and whined. Valen scooped her up in his arms and carried her to his car. "Hang on, girl." He laid her gently in the back seat, and she yelped in pain whenever he moved her legs. Valen could hardly breathe. If he was injured himself, it was the furthest thought from his mind. He placed a loving kiss on her snout. "Don't leave me, Raksha."

Valen looked to the broken second story window, and he watched Clarenda fade from sight.

Bradley didn't feel like staying out as late as he usually did. Sam was bringing him down, though he knew he probably owed him. He hated himself for it, but he had to admit he was letting Ray's "date" with Dori get to him way more than it should. *So Mary Rhodes dumped you*, he thought abut Sam. *At least she didn't start dating your best friend like five minutes later.*

After dropping Sam off at home, Bradley drove back to his own house, and a wave of irrational panic shot through his gut, when he saw Doris Gardner's car parked in his driveway. All the lights were out. He started trembling and felt the sudden urge to urinate. "Fuck," he said. "Why do I care?"

He sat in his car awhile, telling himself he was waiting for the rain to die down. Finally, he got out, not caring that he was getting soaked, refusing to run. It wasn't raining as hard as it had been, but it was still coming down pretty good.

Bradley opened the door quietly and crept into the living room. The couch was empty. That feeling of sheer panic began to take hold again. Trembling, Bradley walked up the stairs and opened the door to his room.

There they were, sleeping soundly in his bed, their nakedness barely covered by his sheets. A wordless snarl twisted Bradley's face, and he knew he wasn't going to let them off easy. Gnashing his teeth until the side of his jaw hurt, Bradley slammed the door with all the power in his arm, and he stormed off to Brendan's room, slamming that door even harder.

Ray and Doris were instantly awake, their hearts beating fast. "What the fuck!" Dori exclaimed.

After getting his bearings, Ray let out a long, anguished breath. "Oh, shit. Bradley's home."

Dori snickered. "Oops."

Ray gave her a look that told her he was anything but amused.

"Samuel, what's the matter, son?"

Sam looked up from his bed, where he'd sat pouting since he got home. "Nothin,' Momma." He sighed when she cocked an eyebrow disbelieving and leaned against his doorway, waiting for the truth with a smirk. "Maybe everything," he amended.

Sam's mother sat beside him, put an arm around him, and kissed him on the side of his head. "Wanna talk about it?"

Everything that had been troubling him raced through his brain all at once: the mystery of Valen's identity and his great-grandmother's strange accusation, the way Bradley didn't seem to know what to do with himself, and most painfully, Mary Rhodes dumping him. "No."

She cleared her throat expectantly.

Again, Sam sighed. "Well, I'm just real sad over Mary. I really liked her. I really *like* her."

"Mm-hm. I know, baby. But there's other girls. You gonna find one."

"But Mary was perfect. At least for me. She was so strong. Guess that's why she dumped me. She thinks I'm an Uncle Tom. She says…" he stopped and glared at his mother. "You *all* say I'm Valen's slave boy. And it really pisses me off!"

Suddenly and without warning, Sam's mother slapped him right on the mouth. "You watch your mouth in your granny's house, boy!" She held up a finger. "Now listen to your momma and listen good. You the only one who knows what's right for *you.* That man pays you. I know. The only reason everybody all bent outa shape's because his ancestors owned our ancestors. I know you think it's silly to hold a grudge. And I'm sure Mr. Alexas is a fine man. But it's not a grudge so much as a principle. The world don't give you much to work with, and self respect is hard to come by. It's an irresistible feature when you got it, and most folks don't got it at all. If you can work for that man, knowing our history, and still respect yourself for doing it, then that's what you should do. If you can run around with all white friends and still hold your head high, then there ain't no reason not to. Just as long as you never come to feel they better than you, or let them think it. You just hold your head high, whatever you do, and the girls'll come a runnin'. Being true to yourself is what makes you a man, and Mary, of all people, gonna see that eventually."

His mother kissed him again on the temple and stood to leave. "You're right," he offered quietly.

"Of course I'm right. I'm your momma." She laughed and left the room.

The clap of thunder caused Mary Jean Donavan to start. Vincent the cat leapt into her lap, as the thunder rumbled on, sounding almost like someone banging on her door. After a moment, she realized, someone *was* banging on her door. *The Vampire.*

Mary Jean set the cat down and went to the door, opening it as quickly as she could, sensing the urgency in Valen's presence. She gasped at the sight before her. "What happened?" She reached towards his face and stopped herself, deciding it might hurt him.

"It's Raksha. She's in the car…dying."

Again, Mary Jean gasped. "Who did this?"

Darkly, Valen answered, "It was Clarenda. Plain as the moonlight. She burned me. I would have died, if not for Raksha knocking me through the window into the rain. Raksha fell with me, unfortunately, and she's not an immortal. At least she's not intended to be."

Mary Jean noticed then that not all of the wetness of the vampire's face was from the rain. She reached out and touched his arm. "Valen…your face."

He looked away. "I'll heal quickly enough. It's Raksha I'm concerned with now. And Clarenda. She absolutely means to destroy me, and I have nowhere to go for safety."

"We'll get Raksha to the vet. It's late, but we can wake him for this."

"Yes. I did the same thing last year, when the serial killer stabbed her."

"What a creature you have." Mary Jean smiled. "And as for Clarenda, you must drop me off at your house. I told you I wanted to be alone with them, and tonight's the night. Otherwise you might get worse tomorrow night. Or even as you sleep in the daylight hours. A determined ghost is difficult to stop *or* reason with. I will try my hand at both. Of course, I'll need all of the truth on my side. Is there anything else you need me to know, before I confront her?"

Valen's eyes filled with tears, and they looked very pale, surrounded by his freshly burned skin. "I…we haven't time for telling stories. We have to get help to Raksha."

Mary Jean's eyes narrowed. "Very well, Valentinus. And afterwards you must take me to your home."

***

After Doris had shown herself out, Ray went to Brendan's room and found Bradley sitting on the bed, staring out the window. "Hey, can we…"

Bradley stood up suddenly and looked Ray directly in the eyes. "Fuck you. Don't even try." He pushed past Ray and ran downstairs.

Ray rolled his eyes and followed him. He found him pouting on the couch. "Look, I thought it was cool! You said you weren't into her! You have Helen now!"

Keeping his arms crossed, Bradley huffed, "Whatever, Ray."

"What do mean, 'whatever?'" Stop acting like a chick! What the hell is the problem? I didn't do anything wrong. You said it was okay."

"I said it was okay to *go out* with her. I didn't think you'd interpret that as calling her up two seconds later for a fuck." He glared at Ray. "In *my* bed!"

Ray took a labored breath. "Look, I'm sorry. I didn't know you still had feelings for her."

Bradley huffed and puffed like an old man before turning his wide eyes away from Ray and insisting, "I do *not* have any *feelings* for that cheap slut."

"Watch your mouth!"

"You *knew* she was a cheap slut, Ray. You said so yourself before you nailed her. And don't let her convince you that it was anything special, because it wasn't."

"Don't worry. I'm not that naïve."

"What the fuck's *that* supposed to mean?"

Ray closed his eyes, trying to get control of his anger and frustration. "Nothing." He looked at Bradley again. "Well, if you don't have feelings for her, then what are we arguing about?"

Bradley looked away again and shrugged. "You did it in my bed. I don't give a fuck that it was Doris. I just care that you got your glue all over my sheets. It's just disrespectful."

Ray ran a hand through his hair in frustration and utter confusion. "This is retarded. How do I fix this?"

Bradley stood up and shouted, "*Wash* my sheets!" He then stormed back upstairs.

"Fine. That's easy," Ray shouted after him. He went to the laundry room to start the water and found they were out of detergent. "Great."

Ray went up the stairs and shouted from the top, not knowing which room Bradley was in, "We're out of fucking detergent!"

"Then go *fucking* buy some." The answer had come from Brendan's room.

Without saying another word, Ray grabbed Bradley's keys and marched out of the house, into the rain, slamming the door behind him.

After waking the local vet who'd treated Raksha the previous year, Valen had dropped Mary Jean off at his mansion to be alone with the spirits, as she'd requested. So far, Mary had not made contact, though she felt *many* presences; far more than there'd been the time before. She found herself wondering if these others had actually been *hiding* from Valen.

Run! A voice in the darkness urged her. It had been a female voice, nonthreatening, concerned.

"Who's there?" Mary Jean asked. "I mean no harm. Please, speak to me. What is your name?"

Alexandria…but Momma calls me Dumplin.' Please get out of here. This place ain't right with the Lord…Run!

"I'm here to help."

Help yourself, my dear. It was a man's voice. *Dumplin' knows. Get out while you can.*

Mary Jean sensed only concern for her safety in these words. "Who is speaking to me now?"

Sedrick. I'm just a guest, but I'm trapped here. I should have listened to her. Please…take me home. My body's in the tunnel! He sounded urgent, terrified. *They took me into the tunnel! In the name of science, you have to get me out of here!*

"Who took you into the tunnel?"

Them…the vampires!

Get out, Miss! He'll get you too! He's not a mortal man!

"I know, Dumplin'. Thank you, but I'm safe for now."

I's so scared, Miss. He caught me in the kitchen! He took me to the grave! You got to run now! This place ain't safe for nobody!

This was getting creepy, even for Mary Jean, who was accustomed to spirits. She could feel more presences closing in around her, curious at the dialogue. She saw a flicker of an image in the hallway…a young man.

"I need to speak with Clarenda. Is she here?"

Oh, no, Miss! No! Get out now! You don't wanna see her!

I agree, my dear. I wouldn't recommend it. You'd be better off not attempting a civil conversation with that one. She's…mad.

"Mad? As in…?"

At the same time as Sedrick answered *angry*, Dumplin' answered *crazy*.

"I see. But that's the problem. I'm hoping I can help her. Maybe I can lead her to the light. Get her to let go of her anger."

No answer came.

"What about her brother?"

Can you help her? Another new voice had entered the conversation.

"Who is this?"

Didn't you just see me? It's Augustin. Can you…stop her? The spirit sounded worried.

"Stop her from what?"

She wants to hurt Valentinus. His voice became strained, *She wants to murder him.*

"And you want to protect him?"

Yes. I love him. I will come to him. I am trying.

"What do you mean?"

The voice sounded amused, *We're…soul mates.*

No! The voice was shrill, female…angry.

Fear took hold of Mary Jean. There was power in the room, dangerous power. "Clarenda Richardson?"

Once.

Mary Jean felt a sudden emptiness, as every other presence vanished from the room, aside from Clarenda and Augustin.

I won't let you stop me.

"Clarenda, I mean you no harm. I only want to understand why you want to hurt Valentinus."

He murdered us. He lied and murdered. He is a hateful man. Hateful to me.

No! Augustin argued. *You never understood. He loved us.*

Rage entered Clarenda's voice, *He lied! You lie! He murdered you in cold blood! He murdered us both!*

No…you did it to yourself! I watched you!

An image came to Mary Jean then: Clarenda falling from the window…the exact same window Valen had fallen from this very night. Suddenly, she understood. "You…committed suicide!"

Liar! He forced my hand! He murdered us both! She wailed in furious agony. A chair flipped over…then another.

Mary Jean's heart threatened to beat right out of her chest. She had never been so frightened of a ghost. "Clarenda…"

Shut up!

A candlestick came out of its stand on the wall and slammed directly into Mary Jean's face. She screamed and put her hands up, feeling the warmth of her freshly spilled blood. Before she could shake the oncoming dizziness, she felt her feet being pulled up from under her, and she fell backwards. She heard Augustin's horrified protest at the same instant as she heard a loud crack, and a gentle buzzing suddenly surrounded her head. She realized, too late to do anything about it, that she was on the floor, that she had hit her head. She couldn't move or speak, as the darkness overtook her. All she could do was realize with despair, *She's killed me.*

Driving home from the store, a wet box of detergent in the seat beside him, Ray fumed. It seemed every move he made got him into more trouble. He couldn't relax for anything. Bradley was mad at him. Lee was with the Nephilim across the Atlantic. The Nephilim had an agent here, watching him. His treasure was still hidden, last he'd checked. It wasn't at the Stevens house. It *should* be safe. Surely the Nephilim had no suspicions about its location. Then again…

Ray looked in the rear view mirror. No other cars in sight. It was impossible for anyone to be following him at the present moment. He paused at an intersection, sighing as he tried to decide which way to go. "I've gotta be sure."

Ray turned in the direction of his hidden treasure. He headed for the mansion.

A knock at the door took Mrs. Turner's attention away from her magazine. "Hold on! I'm comin'." She sighed as she made her way to the door, wondering why her nephews always seemed to be out back playing basketball whenever the phone rang or someone knocked on the door. "Always my job to get up from what I'm doin'."

She opened the door and inhaled with horror at the sight of the man before her, raising a hand to her chest involuntarily.

"Is Sam at home?" The man asked desperately.

The rain had died down, but the lightning in the distance that framed the horrific apparition did nothing to calm her nerves. She shook her head. "N…No. He ain't here."

"Who's that, Momma?" Sam asked as he emerged from his bedroom.

She tried to close the door. "No one, honey."

The man reached out and held the door in place with one very strong hand. "Sam!"

"Valen?" Sam went to the door and opened it, in spite of his mother's warning shake of the head. "Oh, shit! What happened? You're...burnt!"

"I'll be fine," Valen said matter-of-factly. "It's Raksha. We had to leave her with the vet overnight. She fell from the upstairs window. I won't be available to pick her up in the morning, nor at all until well after the office is closed. I was hoping you could pick her up for me."

The image of that old drawing popped into Sam's mind once again—Valen with fangs bared. "Why...why won't you be able to pick her up...during the day?"

"You *know* I can't do that. I have business during the day that can't be put off. Sam, please!"

"Sure, Valen. But...what happened? What happened to your face?"

"There was a small fire. Raksha pushed me out into the rain."

"Wait a minute...was this before or after she fell out the window?"

"It was the same event."

"She pushed you out the *window*? And you over here knockin' on my door? You should be in the hospital, Valen!" He looked in the shadows to see Valen's car in the driveway. "Gimme your keys. I'll drive you."

"No, Sam, that won't be necessary. I'll be fine."

"I don't *think* so." He shook his head, amused and concerned all at once. "You should see yourself. And why did you drive all the way over here in the rain all injured when a phone call would have done just as good?"

A horrified wail froze Sam's heart, and he turned to see his great grandmother.

"Jesus God Almighty!" She clutched her chest and began to falter, reaching out for the hall doorway with her other arm, trying to brace herself."

Sam's cousins ran in from the back at the sound of their great grandmother's shriek.

"The devil, Sam! You done brung the devil here!" She collapsed altogether, and Sam's cousins ran to hold her up.

Horrified, Sam's mother commanded, "Bruce, Jarrad, get Mamaw to her bed right now." She turned to her son. "Get that man away from here." She turned and ran to the phone, calling an ambulance.

Bewildered, Valen offered, "Sam…I'm sorry."

Sam stepped out onto the porch with Valen, closing the door behind him. "Let's get you home."

Bradley Stevens finally ventured into his own room. He studied the sheets that lay in disarray because of what Dori had done with Ray. *It should have been me*, He thought. *It's my bed, and Dori should be* my *lover. I had her first.* Angrily, he studied the bed, walking around it. Dori's panties were there on the floor. He knelt down and touched them, excitement coursing through his veins. He picked them up and studied them intently. *It should have been me who pulled these off of her.*

Bradley carried the little undergarments back to Brendan's room and lay down on the bed, holding them against his chest. *This should have been* my *trophy.* He clutched them fiercely, as if it could cause their former owner pain. *I fucking hate them.*

Ray stopped the car at a safe distance from the Alexas mansion, turning out the lights. The rain had finally stopped, which would simplify things. But not much. "Damn it." He couldn't stand it. The only way to see if it was still there was to get up close, but there was a light on downstairs. "God damn it," he breathed out dramatically. "Shit."

Ray got out of the car and closed the door quietly, hoping upon hope that the wolf wouldn't catch his scent as he crept ever closer to the old house.

After quite a while of creeping, he found himself caught in a pair of headlights. "Oh…hell." He'd been spotted. The only thing to do now was to act as if it were the most normal thing in the world for him to be skulking around the mansion in the middle of the night uninvited.

The car stopped right beside him. It was Valen's car. The man got out, narrowing his eyes at Ray. "Can I help you, Mr. Don?"

Ray offered a lopsided smirk. "Hey, Valen! What's happenin'." He suddenly noticed the man's state of appearance. "Jesus! What's all that blood?" He looked into Valen's angry eyes. "What the *fuck* happened to your face?"

"The *blood* is my dear Raksha's. My face was burned in a small fire earlier tonight. She was hurt in my rescue. And what about yourself? *Strange* time for a visit."

Ray shrugged nervously, not meeting Valen's gaze. "I was in the area. Thought I'd just stop in and say hello."

Sam got out of the car then and stared at Ray in confusion.

Coldly, Valen said, "Not likely." He regarded Ray with a sneer. "Won't you come in?"

As Valen walked onto the porch, Sam approached Ray and whispered, "What's up?"

Again, Ray lamely explained, "I was just driving by and thought, why not pop in on my old buddy Valen?"

"Because you hate him, maybe? Somethin's up, Ray." He looked to Valen, then back to Ray. "You comin' in?"

"'Course," Ray laughed falsely. "That's why I stopped by." He followed Valen onto the porch.

"Sam shook his head as he followed Ray and muttered to himself, "This night just keeps gettin' weirder."

Valen opened the door and breathed out a devastated, "No!" He rushed in.

Ray and Sam followed and stopped cold at the sight. Mary Jean lay on the floor, a pool of blood beneath her head, an enormous bruise and a gash on her face.

Ray walked in boldly. "What the hell is Mary the Witch doing *dead* on your floor?"

Valen shook her, and Sam ran to the phone to call an ambulance. "Mary Jean," Valen pleaded. "Please, wake up!"

After a moment, her eyes fluttered open, then closed, as she mumbled, "That could have gone better." She opened her eyes. "It's not safe for you here."

"What the *fuck* is going on?" Ray demanded.

Sam ran into the room. "Ambulance is comin'."

"Valen…tinus. It's not safe." Mary closed her eyes again.

Valen brushed her hair back with his hand. "We can talk about it later." He looked to his young friend. "Sam, come here and sit with her a moment."

Unquestioning, Sam did as requested, and Valen got up and went to Ray. He glared at the young man furiously. "Come with me."

Not sure at all what else to do, Ray did as the man requested, following him into a small room near the front of the house.

Valen turned on an antique lamp by the window and asked, without turning, "What are you doing here?"

"Like I told you…I was just in the area and…"

Valen turned suddenly. "No!" He walked right up to Ray, close enough for the other man to feel his breath as he spoke. "You must end this charade. I know that you have buried something potentially troublesome beneath my house. There's already enough chaos and confusion here tonight. So, I want the truth. I want to know why you've come here tonight. I want to know just exactly what it is you've hidden on my property, just exactly *where* you buried it, and just exactly *why* a Nephilim named *Dominic Babylon* came here looking for it.

Chapter 6
The Journal of Valentinus Alexas

Ray was only startled for a moment, before he decided to put on his angry face. He sneered at the man whose house he'd trespassed. "I don't know what the *fuck* you're talking about." Without another word, he walked past Valen, out of the room, as the sounds of the ambulance sirens filled the night.

Valen took a deep breath, annoyed. He turned to follow quietly. In the room where Mary Jean lay, he heard Ray say, "Come on, Sam. Let's get you away from your *crazy* friend."

"What?" Sam asked, still squatting beside the wounded woman.

"I said, let's get out of here. I can't take anymore of this bug house."

"What about Mary the Witch?"

The sirens blared until they were right in front of the house. A knock on the door followed, and Valen rushed to let the paramedics in. They asked him what had happened.

"We think she fell and hit her head," he answered. "She was there on the floor when we arrived."

The men went to Mary Jean at once, checked her vitals, and loaded her onto a stretcher.

"Let's *go*, Sam," Ray urged.

Completely bewildered by all that had happened in the past twenty minutes, Sam looked to Valen dazedly, "I promise I'll pick Raksha up in the morning." As he followed Ray, he turned and added, "Are you gonna be okay?"

Valen nodded silently, then looked pleadingly into Sam's eyes. "Tell your friend not to come back here, unless he's willing to answer my questions."

Not at all knowing what Valen meant, Sam nodded and followed Ray to his car, as Mary Jean was loaded into the ambulance outside.

Sam woke up the following morning and got dressed in a rush, eager to pick up Raksha and see the state of her for himself. He opened his bedroom door to leave and found his mother standing there, glaring. "Your Mamaw's fine. Thanks for askin'."

"Momma, I was gonna…"

She smacked him upside the head before he could explain. "You were gonna what? So you was real sorry if she died while you were spendin' time with your creepy friend?"

"He was hurt!"

"I saw that, but that don't justify walkin' out on Mamaw when she's havin' a stroke! She don't like that man."

"Tell me about it."

She pointed a finger right at his nose. "Don't you sass your momma, Sam! I'll take you right back outa this world I brung you into!"

Defeated, Sam said, "I'm sorry, Momma."

"That ain't gonna do, Sam." She turned and walked into the living room, and Sam followed, making his way to the front door. "You gonna go pick up that man's creature?"

Sam shrugged. "Yeah. I said I would."

"Mm-hm."

Just then, Sam's cousin Bruce walked in and said, "Go on then, Samuel. Massa's waitin'."

Sam glared at the older boy and left, slamming the door behind him.

He could hear his mother chewing Bruce out through the walls as he mounted his bicycle and headed for the mansion. He hadn't asked about borrowing Valen's car, but he knew Valen *never* had it with him during the day, and he couldn't be expected to take a full grown wolf home on his bike.

When Bradley got home from picking up Brendan and Kate, Ray tried to tell him about the previous night's adventure. "Bradley! You won't *believe* what happened last night!"

"Sure I will. It happened in my room, remember?"

Ray shook it off with a blink. "No…I mean what *else* happened last night. I was at the Alexas mansion, and Sam was there…Mary the Witch…"

"Did you get the detergent?" Bradley asked coldly.

"Yeah, I…"

"Did you wash my sheets?"

"No, I…forgot."

Bradley turned to leave. "Have fun at work."

When Bradley had gone upstairs, Brendan asked, "Did you guys have a fight?"

"No," Ray answered. "It's just Bradley's time of the month."

Sam helped Raksha to hobble into the living room and get comfortable on the floor. He had to hold her broken leg off of the ground, so that she wouldn't put any pressure on it. The cast clearly irritated the beast, but she seemed to be tolerating it.

"There you go, Raksha." Sam shook his head with wonder. "Amazing old wolf." The night before, as the vet had explained to Sam, Raksha had been suffering from serious internal injuries. He had doubted she'd last through the day. This morning, however, she had almost completely recovered, with only a few bruises beneath her fur to attest that she'd been so near death's door. As for the leg, the doctor expected it to take some time to heal. At least on the record. Off the record, the doctor had confided in Sam, there was something very unusual about Raksha, and she may not take as long to heal as most other wolves would.

Having been through more than her fair share of excitement in the past several hours, Raksha fell asleep almost instantly. Sam crept out of the room as quietly as he could and made his way to the library. Valen wouldn't be home for hours yet, and it seemed the perfect time for Sam to catch up on his reading.

Sam found the journals where he'd hidden them, pulling the one from 1917 out of the box. "Might just as well start here as anywhere else."

Sam found a cozy corner in the great room and sat on the floor leaning against it, as he opened the age-worn volume and began to read.

January 1

It was terrible. An omen of the year to come? I hope not. Last night was such a splendid New Year's Eve, celebrating with all the townspeople that I love. This letter was not the thing I wanted to start my year. It was from D'artagnan. Prince Tristan had warned me that D'artagnan had been seen near the end of the year. It was in September. How I miss my Tristan now. I wish he were still in Nightfire. I wish he were even still in the country, instead of across the sea, in his own forgotten kingdom. If ever he belonged anywhere at all, it was here. Alas, he's always been a wanderer. It's the fundamental thing about his nature. It's what makes him Tristan. As, I suppose, I am Valentinus for my desire to stay put. To stay in Nightfire and watch over my flock.

This is why the letter from D'artagnan frightens me. Once in a great long while, it seems he has to remind me that he's out there. I remember the first time he found me in the New World. I was lost, living in that cave, where the people believed me to be their blood god. He'd laughed at me, said it was appropriate, then, of course, refused to assist me. That is what makes him D'artagnan: his cruelty.

He showed up most recently near the end of the last century, and there was that horrid experimentation he'd been doing. His sick idea of a joke. But the power should never have been given to animals. Not in full. Thank God we managed to destroy them all. Well, all but the one. And I pray to God that one met its end some other way, for we've not heard from it in nearly twenty years.

Tristan said he'd been asking around about me in Europe. Now the letter, only four months later. He knows I'm still here. He thinks it's absurd. "I'll have to stop in and liberate you some time, my dear Quetzalcoatl." Why must he do this? Every time enough years have gone by that I no longer even think of him, he comes back into my thoughts. Willfully. So I read his letter and stood trembling as I let it fall to the floor. He's so like our "father" in his cruelty. Yet he lacks all of Tobit's finesse. Tobit had a splendid way of unleashing his cruelty. He would make his victims fall utterly in love with him, for his elegance, his grace and charm, that endearing laughter. The way he made us both believe we were all the world to him. There was an artistry to his vindictiveness. D'artagnan, on the other hand, D'artagnan the damned, has no grace. He is the worst sort of bully. A monster leaving a trail of blood in the night for anyone to follow. A monster without con-

science. A "psychopath" as all-too-clever Sedrick would have labeled him.

This old house has gotten lonely again. What better time for my once beloved D'artagnan to remind me of the wounds he left me. The scars will never heal that mark my soul where he pierced it. How little the vastness of time has done to sever our eternal bond.

I pray the letter was a tease. I pray the tease was satisfaction for him for another twenty years. I cannot cope with the turmoil that comes with a visit from D'artagnan.

Clarissa Jordan entered the room where Mary Jean Donavan lay resting at the hospital. She knocked on the door as she passed it. "Mary Jean?"

The older woman turned her head tiredly. "Who…?" She breathed in sharply as her eyes widened and her heartbeat quickened. It was the face of Clarenda Richardson, just as she'd seen it in her vision of the woman's suicide.

Clarissa held up a hand apologetically, clumsily holding on to her notepad and purse with her other arm. "I'm sorry. I didn't mean to frighten you…"

"No," Mary Jean assured her, calming herself. "I thought you were someone else." She forced a smile. "How can I help you?"

"Well," Clarissa answered, "I'm writing a book on the urban mythology of Nightfire."

Suddenly Mary Jean began to laugh hysterically.

Clarissa just looked at her.

"You're Ted and Liz's daughter, aren't you?" She smiled and narrowed her eyes.

"Yes," Clarissa answered nervously, feeling stared through, feeling naked.

"Hmm." Mary Jean studied her without seeming to see her. She cackled. "I see it now." She thought of Valen. "Funny no one has yet mentioned it to me."

"Mentioned what?"

Mary shrugged and grinned toothily. "You have deep roots here. You're connected to the Richardsons by blood. Tell me about that."

Taken aback, Clarissa looked at the woman vapidly, then stammered, "I…actually I was hoping to interview *you*."

"Then be fair, girl, and answer my question."

"Okay, well…"

"Sit down," Mary Jean snapped.

Without a word, Clarissa obeyed, not wanting anything to upset the old witch.

"Well?" Mary Jean asked.

Clarissa took a deep breath. "Well, my great-grandma was Clarissa Richardson. I'm named for her."

"Any kin to *Clarenda*?"

"Yes." Clarissa lit up. "They were sisters. Twin sisters. It's so strange that the name keeps coming up."

"You've spoken to Mr. Alexas."

Suddenly, Clarissa felt strangely cold. There was something very odd about all this; eerie. "Well, yes. I told him about her, because he accidentally calls me Clarenda all the time."

"I'm sure he does."

"What are you saying? It's not like he could have *known* her or anything. What's that tone in your voice…and what does any of this have to do with you?"

The witch shrugged and giggled. "Not a thing, dear. What does your *book* have to do with *me*?"

"Oh, well, I figured no book about Nightfire's legends would be complete without an interview with a *living* one."

"You flatter me. *They* call me Mary the Witch."

"Well what do they know?" Clarissa smiled reassuringly.

Mary Jean looked stricken. "Plenty. I've earned the name."

"Oh. Sorry. I…well. So how did you earn it? Do you mind if I quote you?"

Mary Jean sat up and reached over to put a hand on the young woman's arm. "Stay away from Alexas Mansion. You're in danger there. Things are not as they seem."

"What?" Clarissa remembered then. "You were *there* when you got hurt! What happened? You're not suggesting that *Valen* had anything to do…"

"Not really, no. But it is his house. And I see danger for you there. Terrible danger."

Spine tingling, Clarissa stood up. "Well, maybe I'll come back another time…when you're feeling better."

Mary Jean just watched her, as she hurried out of the room. "Valen, you fool," she said to herself. "Why didn't you tell me about *her*?"

Sam continued to read the journal. It was the strangest and most fascinating thing he had ever laid eyes on. Nothing more had yet been said of D'artagnan or the mysterious Prince Tristan who ruled a forgotten kingdom, but the accounts of Valentinus Alexas were strange enough without them. Sam realized, as he read, that nothing ever seemed to happen during the day. Every entry described, "tonight," or, "last night," or, "several nights ago." It should have creeped him out, but he found it fascinating. He read on and on, hoping for more about the past, knowing he would eventually have to read the earlier journals. He wanted to know how this man of means in the early twentieth century had ended up living in a cave, mistaken for a blood god. The name D'artagnan had used made Sam think of Conquistadors. He had no idea why. Just word association, he supposed. And what "power" had been given to animals that shouldn't have been? This Valentinus was a very intriguing figure. But Sam had to admit, nothing he read did anything but support what his Mamaw had told him.

As Sam read on, he learned that Valentinus had kept an old wolf as a pet, much as Valen did, named Tonkowa. He read about Valentinus' treasured friends Clarenda and Augustin. How they never seemed to leave the mansion. How they seemed to be almost *too* close at times. At last his heart stopped, reading the name for the umpteenth time and only just remembering. "Clarenda?" he whispered to himself. "But that's what he's always calling Clarissa. That was her great aunt's name." Sam considered the possibility that Valen *was* Valentinus; that Valen was an immortal, who had *known* Clarissa's family in 1917; that Valen was, in fact, a vampire. He closed his eyes and made himself keep going. "It just…*can't* be."

Sam read on.

August 17

I can't stand it any longer. I must get it out somehow. I am going mad, and Augustin is the reason! No one has ever shown me such affection. No one has ever enjoyed me the way that he does. Even D'artagnan only enjoyed me for the thrill he got out of hurting me. And I admit it thrilled me too. But not like this.

He tempts me. It's vile, I know, to want to take him. To want to make him like me, sharing my affliction. And Clarenda as well. I want them both. But Augustin has a way about him. A swagger. A sureness. And when he plays the violin, I tremble.

It was the worst last night. The furthest we had gone after years of embraces, countless episodes of innocently sharing his bed. Clarenda had retired, and Augustin and I were in the den, conversing about town politics. He stood up. "You're so intelligent." He emphasized the word. "Why aren't you the mayor of Nightfire?"

A strange compulsion drew me to my feet, and I walked over to him, soaking in his beauty, losing myself in the depths of his shimmering, dark eyes. The smell of him overwhelmed me. I had to have him.

He sensed my need on some level, I think. He put his arms out to take hold of me, and I went to him. We held each other as we had so many times, but this time it was different. There was an urgency. A passionate need of something. I ran a hand through his hair as the desire took hold of me.

I put my lips to his throat, and I took a deep breath of him, as I parted them there. I had to have him. My mind was a useless thing in the heat of this passion.

"Yes," I heard him say through the fog of my yearning. He began kissing my neck, and I felt the fullness of his mortal excitement pressed against me as I held him there. "I want this."

Instantly, I broke the embrace. "No." I turned away, and he reached for my shoulder.

"Valentinus, please. I want you the same as you want me. There's no sin in love. We should be together. We're David and Jonathan, remember?"

It was our joke, based on his favorite Bible story of that deep and certainly erotic friendship between two great men. "You don't understand. I can't. You're too precious to me. And that story ended in tragedy, if you'll recall."

He wrapped his arms around me from behind and rested his head on my shoulder. "Then we'll both be David and live on. We'll both be kings. I promise you."

Of course, I had no doubt we would both live on. But how could he know the irony of what he'd said. I almost did it right then. I almost turned around and took him where he stood. We might have been twin Davids, as he'd suggested. No mortal tragedy would ever come between us.

Instead, I managed the strength to simply walk away and up the stairs. I felt his eyes on me, as I always do, and I said without turning, "I'll see you tomorrow, dear friend."

***

Bradley and Helen were sitting in Bradley's car by Lake Nightfire, watching the sunset. Helen had managed to sneak off to the end of the block, while no one was looking, to meet him. "You know," Bradley said, "your being forbidden to see me without a chaperone is kinda exciting." He grinned, as he leaned over and kissed her. "Means we'll probably have to let Mati *watch*."

Helen pushed him away, laughing. Then she sobered, thinking as she had been for days about what her sister had said. "Bradley?"

"Yeah?"

"What do you like about me?"

He shrugged. "You're a good kisser."

"No, I mean *really*."

"Okay, you're a *really* good kisser."

"Come on, Bradley! Other than that. I mean…what do we have in *common*?"

"We…uh…"

"We go to the same school," Helen said excitedly.

"We both have sisters?" Bradley added, wondering if it would appease her.

"Yeah! See? I knew Mati didn't know what she was talking about. We've got lots in common." She thought for a moment. "We're both friends with Ray."

Bradley nodded. "We're both friends with Dori."

"Ha! We didn't both *sleep* with Dori! But I guess we have both been pissed off at her over her being a dirty slut."

Bradley laughed. "Yeah. I guess Mati told you?"

"Yeah. She said Ray nailed her in your bed."

Bradley growled at this. "He did. I'm pretty pissed at him too."

Helen smiled knowingly. "Well, you've gotta give him a break. He's a man. He has needs." Her demeanor changed then. "Of course, he could do way better than *her*."

"If you're so worried about men's needs, then why won't you let me..."

"Oh my gosh! Don't you just *hate* her?"

"Who?"

"Dori!"

Bradley shrugged. "No. I guess....she's just lost. She should have kept me when she had the chance. I mean, she *needs* someone like me. Someone like Ray's just gonna screw her up worse."

"Funny you should say that, 'cause I was just thinking we should find Ray someone like *me* to get him straightened out. He needs someone who can put up with all his crap, you know? Someone who can help him stay out of trouble."

Bradley nodded. "Well, it's their loss."

"I know." She smiled at him.

"So, ya wanna?" Bradley asked with a grin.

"Jeez! You and Dori *should* be together! You're both sluts!"

"I'm not! But I *am* a man. I have needs. You said so yourself." He laughed. "I know! You should use your powers of seduction to lure Ray away from her. Then I can win her heart and have a slut for a girlfriend like I deserve."

Helen laughed. "Sounds like a plan."

They both laughed at their little joke, then they sat in silence, wondering what else to talk about. Finally Helen jumped on Bradley, and they went back to making out.

Sam read on, not sure what to do with the revelation that Valentinus had been a fruit. He wondered how he could have ever had descendants if he was always making out with Augustin. The more he read, the clearer it became that long before Augustin, Valentinus had been making out with D'artagnan. It was also clear how completely the letter from D'artagnan had disturbed Valentinus. He mentioned it more frequently and with great loathing.

As the journal went on, Sam learned that things had gone back to normal between Valentinus and Augustin after their close call. They seemed to go on as if it had never happened. As if their friendship was all innocence and boyishness. Though the affection Valentinus felt for the young man was never in doubt. Sam turned the page, nearing the end of a very eventful August.

August 27

Tonight was a terrible night. Augustin wandered into the Mines...

Sam was interrupted by the sounds of footsteps. He hurriedly put the journal back in its box, hid it, and grabbed another book off of the shelf.

"Sam!" Valen said in surprise. "You're still here! Or did you just come back?"

Sam closed the book and put it away, hoping his friend wouldn't ask him what he'd been reading. "I'm still here."

"Where is Raksha?"

"Restin' in the other room." Sam stood up and dusted off his clothes. He studied Valen warily. The man before him and the man in the journal both only ever seemed to appear by night. They both had wolves as pets. They both lived in this house, and they had absolutely identical features. "I'd better get goin'," Sam said, needing time to think. "My family's pro'ly wonderin' where I got off to."

There was a knock at the door.

Valen held up a hand as he headed for the front door. "Don't go just yet! I want to hear what the vet had to say."

Sam slowly followed Valen to the front of the mansion. Valen opened the door. "Oh…I…didn't expect to hear from you tonight."

A tall black man stepped in through the door and said with a wide grin, "I have news for you…" He stopped, noticing Sam.

"Oh, I'm sorry," Valen said as he made the introductions. "This is my friend Sam Turner. He's been helping me get things straight and looking after Raksha during the days." He gestured to the other man. "Sam, this is Dominic Babylon; an acquaintance of mine who's staying in town on business for a while."

"Pleased to meet you, Sam," Dominic said.

"Yeah, same to ya'."

Dominic turned his attention back to Valen. "Well, I can come back another time."

Valen whispered, but not quiet enough that Sam didn't hear him. "What news did you have? Was it related to…?"

"No," Dominic smiled again. He looked at Sam and considered his words carefully. At last he said, "We just received word. Your friend Tristan has *died*." He smiled again.

Tristan! Sam's heart skipped a beat. Another parallel. Valentinus had written of a friend named Tristan, the prince of some forgotten kingdom.

"Oh! Well that's…" Valen suppressed his glowing smile, remembering Sam. "Will there be a ceremony?" he asked more soberly.

"You know the prince," Dominic answered with a laugh. "He just wanted to be left alone in that ratty old castle. Never been one for ceremony."

"True. Very true." Valen smiled thoughtfully.

Sam's heart was racing. *The prince? That ratty old castle?* Could it possibly be the same Prince Tristan mentioned in the 1917 journal? Sam thought about it. Well, if he was really old…and he did just *die*. But why did they seem so *happy* about it? It was just too weird for Sam at the moment. "Well, I really have to go." He made his farewells as quickly as he could and was out the door, realizing only after he'd started down the road on his bike that he hadn't answered Valen's questions about Raksha. He threw the thought aside as he kept on peddling.

Another realization struck him then. The night before, Valen's face had been badly burned. Tonight, however, there hadn't been the slightest trace of any injury. He'd healed completely…overnight.

Sam peddled much faster all the way home.

***

Much later in the night, another unexpected visitor made his way to the Alexas mansion. Only this one didn't want to be seen.

Ray turned off his headlights at a safe distance and got out of the car, choosing to walk up to the old house as he'd done the night before. No lights were on that he could see, save for the porch light.

Things were just too close to out of hand. Valen knew too much. He knew about the Nephilim. He knew about what Ray had buried. Worst of all, he knew *where* it was buried. Ray had to move it, and he had to move it tonight.

Ray moved as stealthily as he could manage, moving right up to the side of the house. He got down on the ground and started digging with his hands, moving away the dirt he'd piled up at the side of the house, where the structure was slightly raised off the ground. When he'd gotten enough out of his way, he shimmied under the house and turned on his flashlight. In only a moment he was digging again, stopping only twice to pry the dirt from under his fingernails.

At last his fingers hit the metal box. "There you are," he whispered. He breathed a great sigh of relief as he continued to free his treasure from the ground. When he had it in hand, he shimmied backwards, out from under the house.

The moment he was completely back in the open, he sat up and turned around, instantly wishing he'd just stayed under the house.

"Hello there, Mr. Don," said one of the two men with guns aimed at him. "I believe what you have in that box is the rightful property of the Prieuré de Sion."

Chapter 7
The Many Burdens of Ray Don

Ray's eyes shifted from the guns pointed at his face to a shadowy figure approaching in the darkness.

"Can I help you?"

The more talkative man turned his head to acknowledge the new arrival. "I think we've got things pretty well under control here, Mr. Alexas."

Valen's eyes narrowed, and he glanced down at Ray. "What precisely is it that you have 'under control,' Nathan?"

The man grinned. "You know. Sion business."

Valen laughed out loud. "You fool! Your father should never have trusted you with such a task. You aren't referring to what he's got in the box, are you?"

Confused, Nathan looked to his companion, both of their guns beginning to lower with doubt. "Yeah. Why?"

"Because it's a decoy," Valen answered sharply. "I watched him dig up that very same box earlier tonight. The Nephilim are on to him. He knew that everyone had figured out where he hid it, so he moved it. Now he's bringing the box back empty to bury, so that none will be the wiser." He glanced in Ray's direction. "But I guess he underestimated at least *one* of us."

"Don't listen to him, Nathan," the other man pleaded. "He just wants to get his own hands on it. We can't really trust *his* kind…can we?"

"Jude's right," Nathan said. He pointed his gun back at Ray, who looked bewildered. "Stand up."

Warily, Ray complied, staring at Valen with a combination of wonder and horror. *Who* are *you, and what are you doing?* he thought.

"Hand it over," Nathan commanded.

Ray looked furiously at Valen, who simply nodded for Ray to go along with it. Sneering, Ray shoved it into the arms of the eager Sion.

Nathan opened the box, Jude leaning over to see its contents.

"Well?" Valen asked.

Slowly, Nathan looked at Ray. "It's empty." He threw the metal box to the ground furiously and raised his gun, poking Ray directly in the chest with the barrel. "Where is it?"

Valen urged Ray with a subtle smile. Ray at last realized that Valen was rescuing him. He snapped defiantly at the Sion, "Like I'd tell *you*!"

"Well then," Nathan readied to pull the trigger.

"Now, Nathan," Valen said. "Do you really think we should kill him before we *know* where he took it?"

Nathan looked at Valen in confusion. "You mean you don't know where he took it?"

Valen shrugged. "Your superiors never thought to involve me. Besides, I lost track of him."

"What about Raksha?"

"If you'd been as good a spy as your father trusted you to be, you'd have realized Raksha had been injured. She's recovering inside."

Nathan put away his gun, and Jude followed suit. "Fine. So what are we supposed to do to keep him quiet?"

Valen laughed. "He's *been* keeping quiet. Do you really think anyone would take him seriously if he weren't? Now leave us." He looked at Ray. "I'll do what I can to get him to talk to me."

"But…"

"Go on, Nathan. I have my ways. And you know better than to try and linger without me knowing." He smiled predatorily at the man.

Nervously, Nathan answered, "Yeah. See ya, Valen." The Sions left without another word.

Valen walked past Ray, speaking coldly, "Come inside, if you value your life."

Still completely baffled by all that had just happened, Ray picked up the empty box and followed Valen inside.

As soon as the door was shut behind them, Ray all but shouted, "Where is it?"

"You're welcome," Valen answered.

"Look, I don't know what your connection is in all of this *or* why you just saved me, but I'm reserving my thanks until you give it back to me."

"Ray, do you even understand what…"

"Where is it!?"

Valen let out a deep breath. "I dug it up earlier tonight, and I put it in a safe place."

Angrier still, Ray persisted, "I *demand* that you return it! It's my future."

Valen laughed at this. "That may not be a good thing, Ray. It will be safer with me, I assure you."

"You have no right to keep it from me."

"You had no right to bury it on my land," Valen countered.

"Yeah, well, no one lived here when I hid it. How was I supposed to know you'd move in right after I buried it?"

Valen considered that and nodded thoughtfully, then met Ray's desperate eyes. "Have you had it translated? Do you understand what you're sitting on here? People are trying to *kill* you, Ray!"

Ray sighed. "Look, I can deal you in if you want. It's just me and my friend Lee right now, but I'm sure he'd understand. Just give it back. I should be the one to hold on to it. I'm the one who found it in the first place. I know it's dangerous now, but when we find a way to cash in on it, it'll be well worth all the trouble."

"I don't want *in*, Ray. I'm only trying to protect you. This thing may be your future, but it isn't likely to be a very long one." After a moment, he shook his head sadly. "It's in here."

Ray followed Valen into the den and watched the man open a drawer on a little table and pull his treasure out.

"You just had it in a *drawer*?"

"No one is going to rob me, Ray." He handed the tattered, centuries old papyrus to his guest.

Ray took the scroll, carefully, and placed it back inside the metal box. "Thank you," he said at last.

"It's a wonder that it's held up so long. Some would say it was *miraculous*."

Ray scoffed. "I say it's just great luck. *My* luck, if I can manage to stay alive long enough to make a fortune off of it. I just have to wait till I get all these freaky cults off my back." He nodded. "Well…see ya."

"Stay a while," Valen said flatly.

"No thanks," Ray replied, as he walked towards the door.

"You may want to give them time to ransack your home *before* you walk in the door with that."

"Ransack my home?" Ray remembered what had happened to his hotel room the previous year. "What about Bradley and the kids?"

"*Most* Sions are sneaky enough to ransack *around* people who are sleeping."

"Great," Ray said sarcastically. "*That's* good to know. How the hell do you know so much about them anyway?"

Valen offered a coy smile. "I'll make you some coffee."

The two Sions parked their car at the end of the street and quickly made their way on foot to the Stevens house. They turned and strode up the walk and were stopped on the porch by the two Nephilim who'd been waiting in the shadows. "Not so fast boyos," Christian Rivers said with a raised hand.

"This house in under guard," Dominic Babylon added.

Nathan sneered contemptuously and spat on the ground in front of Dominic's feet. "Well, well. I guess we got here too late. But then, so did you. Ray's moved it. It's not at the mansion anymore. He's already hidden it somewhere else."

"I *thought* that's what you meant when you said he'd moved it," Christian said with a smirk.

"It won't be long before we have it," Jude said. "The vampire's gotten involved. Might as well let us in. You're only postponing the inevitable."

Dominic spoke serenely, "This is disturbing news. But it makes little difference to me. There are children in there. We will not permit you to enter…alive."

"Fine!" Nathan groaned, as he turned to walk away. "But something terrible may *have* to happen in order to get Ray to give in to one of us."

As the Sions made their way back to their car, Christian and Dominic exchanged a serious look.

Two weeks passed slowly for Ray, as he worried over the fate of his discovery. He bound himself to the house, unsure where to hide it next. He kept the little box in whatever room he was in. He slept so lightly that even the sound of the air conditioner would wake him with a start. To pass the time, he started tinkering with Audri Stevens' car, which hadn't started since the night she'd been killed.

At the moment, the weather was fantastic. There were white clouds in the sky, surrounded by the brightest blue. The temperature was warm, but comfortable, as a cool and gentle breeze had remained a constant throughout the day. Unable to resist, Ray had opened the garage door before he'd gone underneath the car. He didn't have to leave the house in order to enjoy the weather.

"Old Man Morris says you've called in sick for almost two weeks now."

Ray rolled out from under the car. "Dori? Let yourself in," he welcomed her sarcastically.

"Hey, you left the door open." She leaned against the car, and Ray sat up. "Are we okay, Ray?"

"Sure. Why wouldn't we be?"

"I don't know, maybe because you're *not* sick, and we haven't so much as *seen* each other since…you know." She shrugged. "I thought we had something. I mean *really* something."

"We…you know…I've just had personal things. I'm trying to work it all out." He shook his head. "Has it really been two weeks?"

"Yeah, time flies when you're off the clock."

"No, I mean it seems so much longer than that." He smiled up at her. "We're not through yet, Dori." He held up a finger, as if scolding her. "But we don't have to see each other every day. We're not a couple. We're just…dating."

"Yeah. Right." She rolled her eyes and smirked. "So, I'll see you around." She walked off, her steps sounding sorrowfully slow. "But don't be surprised if I'm *dating* someone else."

"Oh, I won't."

"Ass." Her steps quickened as she walked to her car and drove off.

Ray shook his head. "Why do I say these things?" He rolled himself back under the car.

"Hey, Ray?"

"What?" he asked Bradley.

"Got a minute?"

Ray rolled back out and sat up. "Why is everybody so sneaky today?" He leaned against the car.

"Made any progress?"

Ray made a face. "Some. It's hard to tell. Seems like everything is wrong with this car. I don't know how it ran as long as it did."

"What happened to locking it up in the garage and forgetting about it?"

"I guess I just got practical. It's not easy us sharing one car. I can't afford my own. So I guess I'm just gonna have to get over it and face the reality of who's not driving the car anymore. I got over it with Donny's car."

"Ray, I just want you to know…I'm sorry about the way I've been acting over you and Dori. I've been a real…"

"Girl."

"Yeah. Actually, I guess I have. It's just…been a rough year. I've been taking it out on you, because you're here. But you don't know how much I appreciate you. How much I really do count on you. Nothing should ever get in the way of our friendship. Especially not some girl."

"Yeah, well, that's okay. We're cool."

"No, I mean it. I am so sorry for the way I've been behaving."

"Bradley, you're being a girl again." He smiled. "I forgive you. And I'm sorry I rushed into things with Dori. It was…inconsiderate. Oh, fuck, I can't talk like this. You wanna make up? Hand me the half-inch ratchet."

Ray rolled back under the car, and Bradley started digging through the tool box, laughing with relief at Ray's discomfort.

Later that morning, Sam made his way to the Stevens house, determined to get a fresh opinion on things. It was evident something was going on when Bradley answered the door. "What is it," he asked.

"Am I that obvious?"

"Usually," Bradley said with a smile.

"I need to talk to you." Sam added with a whisper, "Alone."

"Okay." Bradley led Sam up to his room and closed the door. Bradley sprawled out on his bed, and Sam took a seat in a chair in front of him. "So, spill it. You look crazed."

"Maybe I am, Bradley. I feel like it anyway. So, here's the thing. You can't tell anyone *anything* about this."

Bradley nodded seriously.

That was all Sam needed to give himself permission to unload. He told Bradley everything. He told him about the drawing that his great-grandmother had shown him from before the Civil War. He told him about the journal of Valentinus Alexas, the similarities in the hours they kept. He told him about how Valen and Raksha both seemed to have unnatural healing abilities. It was only two weeks since the fire that had burned Valen's face and led to Raksha's broken leg, and Valen didn't have the hint of a scar, while Raksha was walking around without a hitch. He told him about Valen's repeatedly calling Clarissa Jordan by the name of Clarinda, the fact that some guy he'd never seen had come to tell Valen that his old friend Prince Tristan had died, and that they'd been *happy* about it. He told him about his family, how they'd been treating him.

"What if it's all true, Bradley? What if Valen *himself*, not just his ancestors, owned my family. What if Valen isn't human at all?" A distance fell into his voice, as he nearly dared to say it, "What if Valen's a…"

"Holy shit!" Bradley said excitedly. "Holy *shit*! That is crazy! How have you held this all in for so long?"

"Please. I don't really believe it all *myself*. How was I gonna convince somebody else?"

"Well, you have to read the rest of the journal! We should tell Ray."

"Hell, no!" Sam shook his head. "Ray's got about as much tact as a tornado. Whatever the truth is, I still see Valen as my friend. I just don't know what to do with all this new information."

"You have to learn more and put it all together. That's all there is to do, Sam. You need to get some answers. I mean…" He shook his head. "I don't think Valen is a vampire. That's just…impossible. But there must be *some* explanation for all of it. Some reason he's *pretending* not to have any knowledge of Clarissa's ancestors."

Sam considered. "Yeah." He smiled at Bradley. "Thanks for letting me get that off my chest. I feel better."

"Good." Bradley laughed. "But now I'm all worked up. I want to know the rest of the story already."

"You should come with me tonight. I'm going by," Sam suggested eagerly.

"Sure," Braldey said. "I got nothin' better to do. Haven't seen Valen in a while. Why not?" He considered, "'Course he might try to suck my blood." He laughed again.

Sam shook his head. "He ain't sucked mine yet."

"Right, but you were never on to him before. I don't believe in vampires, I guess, but it never hurts to be careful."

With that, Sam had to agree.

Dori, Helen, and Mati were sitting around at Dan Parker's talking about boys. "So have you and Bradley done the nasty yet, or what?" Dori asked.

"No, bitch! I'm not that easy," Helen answered.

Dori shrugged. "Your loss. I've had him. Not bad."

"You fucking…"

"Helen, cool it!" Mati urged. "Dori's just playing around."

"As always," Helen said. "So how are things with you and Ray?" she asked spitefully.

"You'll love it, actually. Not so good. We haven't done much since we did it all. In fact, he's always at home. Something's going on with him, and I don't know what. Maybe he just can't handle me. Like, maybe he's a psycho who can't have sex without getting all weird."

"Maybe you gave him an STD," Helen suggested.

"Helen!" Mati shook her head. "You just say anything! At least y'all *have* boyfriends. No one has so much as looked at me in forever. Am I that ugly?"

"No," came a deep voice from behind her.

Mati turned to see Dirk standing there, smiling down at her.

"In fact," he went on, "I was just noticing how beautiful you were from across the room." Met with silence, Dirk held up his mug. "I was just stoppin' in for a cup of coffee. Needed to get out of the station for a while." He walked off.

As soon as he'd gone, Dori slapped Mati on the arm. "I taught you better than that! Why didn't you say something?"

"I just…froze! I wasn't expecting *Dirk* to say all that. Do you think he likes me?"

At this, both of the other girls slapped her. "Duh!" Helen said. "Why else would he go to all the trouble of saying something that *cheese ball?*"

"All these years, and he's never noticed me before."

Dori laughed. "That's how men work, honey. One minute you're blending in with the wallpaper, the next they can't wait to show you their bedroom ceiling."

All the girls laughed at this, then spent the next half hour talking about how hot Dirk was.

By 12:30, Ray had decided he had to tell someone what was going on. The only someone he could think of was Old Tom. He'd gathered his backpack and met Tom for lunch at a little sandwich shop called Darla's Lunch Box. While Ray had to spend his time staring at Darla Ann Jacobson's outlandish lunch box collection, which surrounded him on all sides, it was an out of the way place, where he was more likely to have the privacy he needed to tell Tom everything.

Unfortunately, after about fifteen minutes, Ray had accepted the fact that he couldn't tell Tom *anything*. He just couldn't bring himself to start.

"Ray, what's wrong?'

"Noth…"

"And don't say 'nothin' cause I'm on to you. Somethin's been buggin' you since you got back to town, and you haven't had the balls yet to tell me about it."

"Yeah? Well, since you put it like that…"

Tom held out his hands and shook his head. "I'm waiting."

After a long, thoughtful moment, Ray said, "Nothing. There's nothing going on. I'm just messed up a little. I'm having a hard time adjusting to being back here again, and all that's happened since I got here. Audri Stevens and all."

Tom crossed his arms and leaned back in his chair, while Ray took a bite out of his sandwich. "Uh-huh. Bull shit, Ray. I'm not workin' late tonight, so if you change your mind, just give me a call. You'll tell me all about it sooner or later." He smiled. "So how's life with the Stevenses treating you?"

Relieved that Tom had decided to drop it, Ray talked the rest of the hour about laundry, dishes, and the drama involved in getting Brendan and Kate to go to bed on time. Loving Ray the way he did, Tom pretended to believe that Ray cared about any of it for the remainder of their visit.

***

While Bradley was in the bathroom, Sam picked up the phone and called Mary Rhodes, not knowing what had driven him to do it. When she answered the phone, he was surprised. "Mary? It's Sam!"

She hesitated, then, "Hey, Sam. What's new?"

"Not much. Just missin' you."

She didn't say anything.

"Bradley and I are going over to Valen's tonight. Thought I'd see if you wanted to come along."

After a heavy silence, Mary answered, "Sam, do you remember that we broke up?"

"Yeah. I just miss you is all." He felt his voice quaver as he spoke.

"I miss you too, Sam, but we can't go back."

"Are you seeing someone else?"

"That's none of your business," she snapped.

"The hell it ain't!"

"Sam…I have to go now." She hung up abruptly.

Bradley walked into the room, noting the dazed look in his friend's eyes. "Take my word for it, Sam. Don't call her back. The more you call, the less they wanna talk to you."

Sam nodded his head in misery.

***

By sunset, Ray once again felt he needed to tell Tom everything. After about an hour of building up his courage, he picked up the phone and dialed the number. Abigail answered.

"Hi, Abi. It's Ray. Is Tom at home?"

"No, he's working late tonight. He just called to let me know."

"That's strange. He told me he *wasn't* working late tonight."

"Well, you know how fast things can change over at the paper."

"That's true. Thanks, Abi. I'll try and reach him there."

Ray called the office but got no answer. "Well," he said to himself, "I guess I could try and drive Audri's car over there and see if it makes the trip."

Sam and Bradley arrived at Valen's place to find him just finishing up an interview with Clarissa Jordan.

Valen greeted them and offered to let them sit in and listen.

Clarissa eyed the two teenagers, wondering if she should hold off on her last question. Ultimately, she decided to go for it. "Well, I would say that sums it up, Valen. But there is something that bothers me."

"What is it?" Valen asked with a smile.

"Why didn't you tell me that Clarenda Richardson and Augustin Richardson both died here in 1917?"

Sam and Bradley both started at this. They exchanged a look, trying not to let on that they had any knowledge about the people whose names had just been dropped.

Valen looked around to see all eyes fixed on him. "I…what makes you…?"

"Well, I'll tell you," Clarissa said. "I went to see Mary Jean Donavan in the hospital a couple of weeks ago. She seemed bothered by the fact no one had told her about *me*. She could see the resemblance I bore to Clarenda Richardson, which you keep calling me by mistake. So, how could she know that I resemble a woman who's been dead for fifty-eight years? And why would you have trouble keeping track of whether I'm Clarissa of Clarenda? Same problem. She died fifty-eight years ago. And yet, you clearly are both familiar with Clarenda Richardson. You both know her features very well.

"So I asked my mother about it. She looked in the family history she's kept and found her notes. All she had was that Clarenda Richardson died in Nightfire, on August 31, 1917…at Alexas Mansion. She'd been meaning to go to the library to dig up the specifics, but when doing anything in genealogy, Mom has always concerned herself first with direct ancestors. Clarenda was an aunt.

"So I went to the library and did the research myself in the archives. I pulled several articles from *The Nightfire Chronicle* up on micro-fiche, and then it all began to make sense." She paused and studied the faces of all in the room. Sam and Bradley were on the edge of their seats with anticipation. Valen looked horrified. She knew she'd hit upon the truth.

She went on, "Augustin, Clarenda's younger brother, was found murdered horribly in the foyer. It's a mystery that has to this day never been solved. All suspicion pointed to Valentinus Alexas, a prominent member of society, who was the grandson of the Valentinus Alexas who'd been among the founding fathers of the town. Seems strange such a scandal would wind up as it did. Perhaps money talked.

"Days after the death of Augustin, Clarenda Richardson seemingly committed suicide, leaping from the window of the room on the third floor that had been her brother's.

"Shortly after this, Valentinus skipped town and never returned. What's strange is there was never any attempt made at bringing him to justice. The precise cause of Augustin's death was never determined, since his body vanished from the coroner's. All that is known is that it was gruesome."

Oh, God, Valen thought. *She knows. She knows everything.*

"So it seems clear to me that the reason you kept this from me was because you thought you'd never have a chance with me, if I knew that your great-grandfather may have been responsible for two murders in my family."

"I...What?"

"It's obvious you're hot for me, Valen."

Sam and Bradley snickered at this. After a moment, so did Valen, so relieved by her mistake. Sam muttered to Bradley, "She always just blurts things out."

Clarissa went on, "And the reason you brought Mary the Witch into this was to make sure the ghost haunting this place *wasn't* Clarenda or Augustin Richardson, because you think maybe the rumors are true about this place. That there's a ghost. And you were trying to protect yourself from the inevitability of me finding out all the details."

Dumbfounded, Valen leaned back in his chair, holding up his hands. "I don't know what to say."

Clarissa smiled. "You don't have to say anything. And you don't have to prove anything. I'm not worried about the rumors, though it will add some grit to my book. The thing is, it's just a legend, about the haunting. It's just a story people made up to make it more fun to live in Nightfire. And it wasn't *you* who killed them, Valen. You aren't your great-grandfather, and I know that. So you don't have to worry about how it reflects on you." She ran her hand up his muscular arm. "You're too cute to be haunted. So let's see a smile on that face the next time I come by."

She stood and gathered her things. "Well, thanks for the time. I'll leave you to your guests. I've got lots of work to do. Thomas Johnson has expressed an interest in my work, and I've got a meeting with him tomorrow afternoon." With that, Clarissa abruptly left.

As soon as the door had closed behind her, Sam and Bradley broke into loud laughter. For Sam, the laughter hid his terror at learning the fates of Clarenda and Augustin.

For Bradley, it was pure amusement. "Oh, man, Valen. That is some fucked up shit. Is it true?"

Valen answered, "She's very clever. I'll give her that."

"She also totally wants you. You should go for it! How 'bout we all go out? You know, a *triple* date!"

"Triple?" Sam asked.

"Date?" Valen asked.

"Yeah! Why not? She was right. It is obvious you're hot for her, Valen." He turned to Sam. "And as for you, it's just time to move on. Besides, I know a girl who wants to go out with you."

"Who?" Sam asked.

"Shawna Smith."

"For real?"

"Yeah. So you take her, and Valen will take Clarissa, and we'll all go out and get to know each other."

"We all go out with you and Helen? That could be…annoying. All y'all do is make out."

"No, man, we talk all the time. It'll be fine, right, Valen?"

Valen shook his head. "I don't really have the time to date."

"Don't be retarded! You have time *and* money. Live a little. You're only…" Bradley stopped. "How old are you anyway?"

"Twenty…one."

Sam noticed the pause. Valen had needed to think before answering.

"I'll be twenty-two this October." He shook his head. "Anyway, when would we all be able to get together? And where? I'm hosting a party for the entire town on Friday, if you'll recall."

"What party?" Bradley asked.

Sam slapped him on the shoulder. "Don't you read the paper? It's the housewarming. He's showing off the restoration of Alexas mansion and inviting anyone who wants to come, since this house is such a part of the town's history."

"That's Friday? Okay. Then how 'bout tomorrow?" Bradley grinned. "Here. That way you don't even have to go anywhere."

"Well…I…"

"Great! Then it's settled," Bradley laughed.

Raksha peeked into the room then, and Valen could swear she was laughing at him with her eyes.

Ray entered the building where Tom worked and took the elevator to the third floor. There were a few people still around on the first floor, but the third floor was apparently deserted. He had seen a light on in Tom's office from the street though, so he pressed on. He had to tell him the trouble he was in. Someone had to know.

Ray stopped outside Tom's office door, hearing giggling. A woman giggling. He caught sight of something on the floor by Trish's desk. It was a bright red bra. "Oh, shit."

He turned to leave just as he heard Tom say, "I'll be right back."

Ray hurried, quietly, but when the door opened he caught sight of Tom in the mirror, and he saw Tom seeing him.

"Ray?" Tom asked guiltily.

Ray turned around slowly and miserably, trying not to notice that Tom wasn't wearing a shirt. "Hey, Tom. What's…up?"

Chapter 8
Ray's Decision

Tom Johnson tried to compose himself. "Ray, it's…" He gave up. There was no getting away from this. He'd been caught red handed cheating on his wife with the new secretary—caught by someone whose opinion of him meant the world to him.

"I'll see ya, Tom," Ray said icily, as he turned and walked away.

Tom just watched him leave, feeling sick inside, wondering what the hell to do next.

***

After Bradley and Sam had gone home, Valen made his way to Mary Jean's trailer, Raksha following at his side. He knocked on the door. "Come in," came the voice of his friend.

Valen opened the door carefully and peeked in shyly. It was not his custom to let himself into other people's homes. He found Mary Jean sitting at her table (her "work" table), pondering the weak flame of a single candle. He turned to Raksha. "Wait out here."

"I've been waiting for you." Mary Jean didn't even glance at him.

Valen allowed the door to fall closed behind him, his face barely outlined by the meager light. "I came to see how you were."

"And?" Mary Jean asked without looking up from her candle.

"And to discuss the situation…with the ghosts."

"Ah, yes." At last Mary Jean looked up with a smile. It was neither a friendly nor a cruel one. It was a habitual smile. "They are not in agreement with each other, the boy and girl."

"What do you mean?"

"They have different ideas about how they ended up as they did; different ideas about where to place the blame. They argue over *you*." She studied him, as his face visibly paled in the darkness. "Tell me what happened. Why should Clarenda be so upset with you?"

Nervously, Valen hesitated, then answered weakly, "Someone…killed the boy."

"Augustin."

Valen averted his eyes. "Yes."

"Tell me."

Valen met her stare, his eyes filled with tears. "It was…unforeseen. I…" He looked away. "I have to go."

Mary Jean watched the vampire make his escape. From what? Most likely from the past more than the present. It wasn't the question that had wounded him. It was the answer that he kept locked away in his heart, safe from all the world. But he wasn't safe from *it*. A black cat leapt up into Mary Jean's lap. "Vincent," she cooed. "There is a way to solve Mr. Alexas' problem. But he alone has the key. He alone has the information. The confession? The details to sort them all out. The only possible resolution is for Valen to tell them that story in his own words. The tale of young Augustin's death."

The next day, Ray was putting the finishing touches on installing the new alternator in what had formerly been Audri Stevens' car. It was the only thing he could do to take his mind off of things, and it wasn't working. The box containing his treasure was less than a foot away from him underneath the car. It was less than a foot away from him at all times and had been for the past two weeks. Now, as if his encounter with 'Count Dracula and the Freemasons from Hell' hadn't given him enough to worry about, he also had to wrestle with his feelings over finding Old Tom cheating on his wife. Then of course, there was Dori. Sometimes

Ray just wanted to disappear, or at least walk away from the world and watch how it all turned out without him from a giant window outside of the universe.

"Ray, is that you?"

Ray slid out from beneath the car and was startled to see Jenny. "Jeez, doesn't anyone knock anymore?"

"Oh, shut it. You haven't been to work in two weeks. Old Man Morris wanted me to come by and see how near death you were. Looks like he guessed it right. You're fakin' it."

Ray sat up. "Thanks for comin' by to spread your sunshine, Jenny, but I've got lots to…"

"What's going on, Ray? Can we just be serious for a minute? You *have* to show up for work. You're clearly not sick. What's the deal?"

Trapped, Ray sighed. "It's…complicated. I have personal things I'm trying to take care of." He looked at her pleadingly, which was an alien expression for him. "Don't tell Old Man Morris?"

She raised an eyebrow, clearly ready to make him beg. "I don't know. What's in it for me?"

"My eternal gratitude."

"How 'bout dinner?"

"Uh…" Why did women do this to him? Ray wasn't sure what to say. Jenny was a really fun girl and all, but he was dating Doris. Wasn't he? Actually, they were *just* dating…sort of. No one had made any commitments. Still, he wasn't in any position to go out with anyone at the moment. "I've got something with the kids tonight."

"Kids?" she asked skeptically.

"Bradley, my housemate, has two younger siblings. It's their house actually. Haven't I told you all this?"

She smirked. "Odd Couple meets Brady Bunch?"

"Sort of." He shrugged.

"You never stop surprising me, Ray. Dinner. Maybe not tonight, but some night. Your treat."

"Well, the kids…"

"Old Man Morris."

"Sounds great. I'll let you know when I'm free."

"You'd better." She smiled as she turned and walked out of the garage.

Ray watched her get in her car and drive away. "I've gotta start closing the door when I work out here."

Bradley and Sam walked into Dan Parker's with a mission. They found Clarissa Jordan sitting at a table interviewing Ned Tyler, the town's resident dirty old man. "It's a man made lake, you see. Used to be their territory. That's why the whole thing never did surprise me," Ned was saying.

"So did you know any of the men who were killed in the massacre?"

Ned laughed. "All of 'em. They all had it comin'. Messin' with Indian spirits ain't a smart thing to do."

Bradley motioned to Sam and made his way to the bar to order a Dr. Pepper. The bartender was not a very familiar face. He was a cousin, covering for Vicky while she was away on her cruise. Dan Parker's had remained a family business since the middle of the last century. "Hi." Bradley nodded. "Dr. Pepper?"

The man handed Bradley a bottle and took the money the teenager had put down on the counter. Sam caught the man's eyes then. "I'll have the same."

As if Sam should have known better, the man replied, "That was the last one. Sorry, boy."

Sam wasn't quite sure whether or not to be troubled by the way the man had said *boy*. He didn't want to jump at shadows the way that Mary and his family did. Racism wasn't inevitable. It wasn't in every word a white man spoke. He was young, he *was* a boy as far as this man was concerned, and they were out of Dr. Pepper. "That's okay." He considered. "I'll just have water."

The man shrugged. "Faucet's broke. This just ain't your day, boy." The man turned away.

Sam tried to put it out of his mind. Bradley handed him the bottle. "Here, have some of mine. Promise I don't have herpes."

"Naw, I don't need it. There's not enough in one bottle to really share. Thanks though."

"You know," Ned was saying to Clarissa, "I could tell you a lot more about this town's spooky history, Miss Jordan. I've been around." He winked. "In more ways than one. The lake massacre was nothin' compared to the werew…"

She sat up straight. "What…is that your foot?"

Ned cackled a bit. "Sorry 'bout that. I can't control him. He's just friendly."

She stood and extended her hand. "Thank you for your time, Mr. Tyler. You really are a tremendous resource. I've got to get to another interview."

Ned cackled some more. "An absolute pleasure, Miss Jordan."

Bradley and Sam stopped Clarissa on her way out. "What are you doing tonight?" they asked in unison.

Clarissa laughed. "No plans. Writing, I guess. Why?"

"We hoped you'd come see Valen with us," Bradley explained.

"What for?" She smiled at the thought of Valen.

"Well," Sam said, "we actually want to try and set y'all up. You seem to like each other. Valen just doesn't know what to do when it comes to this sort of thing."

Clarissa giggled. "Oh, and you two are the experts?"

They both offered wide grins and said, "Yes." They all laughed.

Clarissa nodded. "Sounds like a plan. I do like him. He's one hundred percent tasty."

Bradley and Sam giggled at this.

Clarissa turned to the bartender. "Can I get a Dr. Pepper for the road?"

The man put a bottle on the counter and took the money that Clarissa handed him.

"Wait a minute!" Sam was now sure that he wasn't imagining things. "I thought you said you were out!"

The man shrugged. "Try that little ol' place on Buxton Road, boy. I hear they got plenty to drink."

Sam's eyes went wide. "Oh, the *black* part of town? I get it. Wait till I tell Todd about this."

"Here, Sam," Clarissa said, handing him the bottle. "I don't really want it anymore."

Sam took the bottle, considering throwing it at the bartender's head. "I don't want it either." He handed it back and walked out.

Bradley and Clarissa exchanged a look. "Jackass," Bradley assessed the man as they left.

The man wiped down the counters, pretending as if no one had said a word.

Ray took a walk out to the mailbox, leaving his treasure behind for only a minute. A car pulled up, and one of the two men Ray had met the other night at Alexas Mansion got out. "Hi, Ray."

"Leave," Ray said.

The man held up his hands in surrender, as he slowly made his way to the mailbox. "I wanted to apologize for the other night. Nathan's a little bit overeager." He offered his hand.

Ray just looked at it, then met the man's gaze.

The man put his hand down at his side. "My name's Jude Sinclair. We didn't have the opportunity to make introductions."

"Right," Ray said. "There were guns involved. Makes it sort of hard to get all nice and cuddly."

"As I said, I *am* sorry about that. We just want to protect it…to protect *you*. From the Nephilim. They have an agenda of their own, you know."

"Actually, they tell me the exact same thing about you. And just who exactly are you trying to protect it from anyway? The people? Are you afraid it'll destroy the Church? I mean, considering the implications…"

Jude laughed out loud."No. Not that. We couldn't give less of a damn about whether or not this hurts the Church. In fact, *that's* who it needs to be kept away from. As well as some others. The Nephilim for one. The Nephilim would corrupt the scroll's message. The Church would destroy it. What are *you* going to do with it?"

"Right now, I couldn't say. Wasn't planning on using it to corrupt or destroy anyone. At least not today."

"Ray, give it to us! We can take care of it. We can take care of you. We've been at war with the Nephilim for ages. They read minds, consult demons. We can protect you."

Now it was Ray's turn to laugh. "All this shit about angels and demons is the real joke here. Do you have any idea what's actually on the scroll, or are you just guessing? Because nothing about it verifies either of your organizations' beliefs. There is nothing divine or damned in this world to speak of. We're all just what we can see with our own eyes. I *read* the scroll. I know! It's older than the oldest known copy of the gospels, and it blows them right out of the water."

"I'm comfortable with that," Jude said evenly. "Ray, the scrolls they found at Nag Hammadi, the Dead Sea Scrolls, all shed new light on the canonical scriptures. True light. But the one you have, it wasn't among those found. It's the most important secret the modern world could ever learn. Who knows you have it?"

Ray smiled smugly. "Leave." He turned to walk back to the house.

Jude sighed. "We'll stay in touch."

Ray turned back suddenly. "Wait a minute. I can't keep going on like this."

Jude's entire stance shifted with anticipation. "I'm listening."

"Meet me at Dan Parker's, tonight at 9:00. Bring that other jack ass too."

Jude smiled, exposing his perfect teeth. "You got yourself a date, Ray."

As Jude drove off, Ray found himself hoping that he knew what he was doing.

Bradley, Helen, and Sam stopped to pick up the girl they'd found for Sam. "I'm not sure about this, guys."

Helen slapped Sam playfully on the arm. "You'll like Shawna. She sits with me at lunch. She's fun."

"I'm just…I feel like I'm cheating on Mary."

Bradley turned to Sam. "Mary dumped you. It's over. Time to get back on the horse." He grinned. "So to speak."

Sam shook his head incredulously, as Helen got out and got Shawna. Sam gave Bradley a look of approval as Shawna approached the car. The girls got in, and Shawna slid right next to Sam and started petting his leg. "Mmm. You look good. We gonna have fun tonight."

"I hope so," Sam said.

"You hope so? I *know* so!" She called up to the front, "Bradley, you gonna let us use the car for a while, while you in the house?"

Bradley gave Helen a look of *did she just ask me that?* Helen shrugged, bewildered.

"Uh…no," he answered.

"It's okay, baby. We can find someplace else to get down."

"Wow," Sam offered uncomfortably. "You are one crazy person."

Bradley inwardly cringed at Shawna's behavior, hoping that Sam wouldn't kill him.

Ray walked into Dan Parker's at just after nine and smiled at the sight of the four men seated at the table in front of him.

"Ray," Christian Rivers said. "It looks like you've set us up for a party."

Jude Sinclair offered Ray a nod and a less-than-friendly glare.

"Sorry I'm late," Ray offered. "I had to drop the kids off at a friend's house for the night." He took a seat between Dominic and Nathan. "I've made a decision."

All eyes were eagerly upon him.

"We're listening," Dominic said.

"I've decided that there seems to be only one way out of this mess. I've decided to burn the scroll."

The Sions reacted in panic, while the Nephilim each just offered Ray a hard look. "You can't…" Jude spat. "You haven't…?"

"No, not yet," Ray said. "But it's the only way out. The world's been without this document for about as long as it's existed, and we all seem to be getting along just fine."

Nathan glared daggers at Ray. "I wouldn't make any rash decisions, if I were you."

Ray looked over at him. "I think that goes for all of us." He smiled. "There is an alternative."

"Give it to *us*," Jude pleaded. "It's the only way."

Dominic and Christian simply exchanged a look and waited for Ray to continue. He found himself almost wondering if it were true that they could read minds.

Ray went on carefully. "*If* I choose not to put the fire to this thing, there are certain conditions that *must* be met by all of you."

"Conditions?" Jude was outraged.

"Please continue," Christian said with a calm smile.

"You can't give it to *them*!" Jude insisted. "That's what you're planning, isn't it? That's why they're so calm. They're reading your thoughts!"

"Nonsense. That isn't his plan at all," Christian said, amused. "This is just our way. Accept what is. Remember what was."

"Prepare for what is yet to be," Dominic finished for him.

"Oh, we are *very* prepared," Nathan said dangerously.

"Actually, I was thinking I'd hold onto it a while," Ray interjected.

"Well, that gets us nowhere," Jude said.

"Oh, but you haven't heard me out, Jude. Let me lay out my terms, otherwise it burns tonight."

Jude forced himself to sit still, though his nervousness was evident. "We're *all* listening."

"I want you *all* to leave town. Tonight." He looked to Nathan and Jude. "Valen Alexas is clearly on your side in all of this. He can keep an eye on me on your behalf." He looked to Christian and Dominic. "For your part, the Nephilim will send Lee back home. You've apparently won him over. He can represent your interests." He looked around the table. "I keep the scroll for now. You all leave Nightfire. You each have someone here to keep tabs, someone that I don't anticipate killing any of the people that I live with before I make up my mind who I *am* going to give it to. Everybody's happy."

"Sounds fair," Dominic said.

"Very sound," Christian added.

"No!" Nathan said, standing, reaching for the gun inside his jacket.

"Nathan, wait!" Jude tried to calm his associate. "He means it. We don't need to read his thoughts to know them. He's never held back before. He really will burn it. We have to take him at his word. And, though I'm not happy about it, it *is* a sound plan. Valen has sided with *us*. Who better to have looking out for our interests? Your father will see the reason in it."

After a moment of angry contemplation, Nathan removed his hand from his jacket, empty, and sat down. "Agreed."

Valen scratched Raksha on the head nervously, as he visited with the four teenagers in the den. How did he get himself into these things? It provided him some comfort that Sam seemed just as unhappy as he was.

"I'm gonna go get another soda. Anyone want anything?" Sam asked as he quickly stood up from the couch and escaped the wanton clutches of Shawna Smith.

"I'll come with you." Shawna rose.

"No, no." He actually pushed her back down on the couch. "Let me bring you something."

"I'll come with you then," Valen offered. I want something too, and you've only got two hands."

Bradley and Helen added nothing to the exchange, because they were lost in each others kisses, just as Sam had predicted they would be.

Sam and Valen entered the kitchen and sighed simultaneously, then they started laughing. "Talk about your nightmare dates," Sam said. "She won't keep her hands off me."

"I know. Maybe we should just not go back in."

"But your date hasn't even arrived yet."

"Exactly."

They laughed some more.

The doorbell rang.

"I thought you liked Clarissa."

"I do," Valen said. "I just don't know what to do about it. I'm more *drawn* to her than anything else. But I'm not a good bet romantically. I don't want to get involved with anyone."

"Why not?" Sam asked suspiciously.

Valen looked at him, then answered quickly, "Because I'm rich."

They laughed again, and Valen finally went to answer the door.

He opened it to find Clarissa looking as radiant as he'd ever seen her. He inhaled sharply.

"Nice to see you too," she said.

As the night progressed, Valen found himself ever more drawn to Clarissa. She reminded him so much of his lost Clarenda and the happiness they'd known so very long ago. But the more he allowed himself to enjoy her company, the more things started happening around her.

Clarissa yelped and dropped her cards, as she avoided the liquid now racing across the table. "That's the third time tonight! And we're not even drinking alcohol. How do I keep doing that?"

Valen nervously handed her some paper towels. After the second spill, he had decided to keep them on hand.

"I didn't even see you touch it!" Bradley said. "And I was staring right at you. It's like your glass just fell over."

Sam exchanged a look with Bradley.

"What?" Helen asked. "I think she's just doing it so she doesn't have to show us her losing hand." She fanned herself with her cards and leaned up against Bradley.

"Stop cheating," he said, as he pushed her away.

"Oh my god!" Shawna stood up and pointed to the painting behind Clarissa, as it began rocking back and forth, just before it fell.

Clarissa turned and avoided the collision at the last moment, then stood up, "Oh, my…god."

Matilda Preston was loading the groceries in her car. Now that she was working, her parents had made it clear she was to help out with expenses as long as she stayed under their roof. Her mother was old fashioned and insisted it was already time for Mati to settle down and find a husband. Mati wondered if that's what Dirk had in mind when he had flirted with her the day before. Or did he have something else in mind entirely?

"Lookin' good these days, Mati."

She turned and saw one of the most gorgeous male bodies in Nightfire undressing her with his eyes. "Rubin? What's up?"

He shrugged, holding a bag in each of his muscular arms. "Just picking up a few things. Need any help?"

"Oh, no, I got it." She smiled at him.

He winked. "Well, give me a call if you change your mind." He walked on to his own car with a whistle.

Mati shook her head at the encounter. "My planets must just be all lined up this week, or somethin'."

"The house has…foundation problems," Valen offered. "It's very old." Nervously, he looked at his watch. "Look at the time! How did it get to be…?"

"Not this time, Valen," Clarissa said evenly. "There *is* something going on in this house, and you don't want us to know it. You don't want me to put it in my book."

Panicked, Valen tried to keep his cool, though he could feel the sweat on his brow. "What would you write, exactly? That you mysteriously kept spilling your drink?"

She simply pointed to the painting. "Foundation problems?" She let out a long breath. "Fine, I just won't drink. Lets play cards." Just then, she yelped and reached for her hair, having felt a sharp tug. She grabbed her shoulder. "Ouch! Something just bit me!" She rushed to the bathroom without another word.

Closing the door behind her, Clarissa let out a scream from the very depths of her heart. In the mirror behind her own reflection, the mad-eyed ghost of Clarinda Richardson stared back at her with unbridled hatred.

CHAPTER 9
THE JOURNAL OF VALENTINUS ALEXAS REVISITED

Helen and Shawna ran to the bathroom and were almost knocked over as Clarissa threw open the door and fled, completely terrified of what she'd seen. "What happened?" Helen asked.

Bradley, Sam, and Valen were standing, as the girls came back into the room. Clarissa grabbed her purse, then hesitated. "It was her," she said with a tremor. "She really is haunting this place, and she doesn't want me here. I'm scared to drive home by myself."

Bradley and Sam exchanged a knowing look. Valen simply stared, pale faced, as Raksha came to stand beside him.

"Who?" Shawna asked. "Clarissa, what are you talking about?"

"Ask Valen. He knows." She looked at her host, wondering just how to feel. "He'll tell you anything but the truth on the matter." She looked at the others. "You see, a long time ago, his great-grandfather murdered a relative of mine here. Another of my relatives committed suicide here just a little while later."

"I didn't do it!" Valen said.

Clarissa almost laughed. "I know *that.* But your great-grandfather *did.* And I saw Clarenda in the mirror…behind me. I think she's angry that I'd have anything to do with the descendant of the man who killed her brother."

"Oh…let's talk about something else," Helen offered.

"Clarissa, you don't really believe that, do you?" Shawna asked, concerned. "You just need some coffee. Ain't no ghosts in this house."

"No. I need to leave." She looked to Valen. "I'm sorry, Valen. Mary Jean warned me about coming here. She said I was in danger. She was right."

Helen grabbed her purse. "We can follow you, if you're scared."

"Thank you, Helen. I'd appreciate that."

"What…you wanna go? But we…" Bradley started.

"I don't like scary things, Bradley," Helen said simply.

"Okay." He looked to Sam and shrugged.

Sam noticed Valen, who just looked ill, noting that he wasn't arguing with Clarissa at all. "Well, I guess that's a night then. Thanks, Valen. Maybe we can do this again sometime."

Valen said nothing, as everyone began to file out through the front door.

"I'm sorry, Valen." Bradley shrugged. "Women are loony."

As the door closed, Valen wanted to scream out in rage, but he held it in, patting Raksha on the head, thinking sadly about all that was happening.

"Well, it's good of you to finally join us, Ray." Jenny crossed her arms in the locker room and smirked at him.

Ray looked around at her. "You just walk right in, don't you? I could have been naked in here."

With a smile, she confessed, "I had hoped…" She laughed.

"You're just trouble." Ray did his best to look offended.

"This from the man who almost burned this place down as a child?"

"That was a long time ago. It was an accident. But if I could travel back in time, I think I'd make sure it all burned down that day." He smiled mischievously.

"You're lucky the place is still here. Otherwise who knows where they would have put you when you came home."

"So what did you come in here for anyway, Jenny? Just to try and catch me without a towel on, or…"

"I wanted to ask you…"

"Ray," a new voice interrupted.

Surprised, Ray didn't really know how to respond. "Tom."

Tom Johnson looked to the young lady in the room. "Jenny, would you mind excusing us for a minute?"

"No, not at all, Tom." She smiled.

"No, you don't have to go, Jenny. Tom was just leaving."

Tom argued, "Ray, we need to talk. This hurt feelings bit just ain't gonna fly. We need to get this all out in the open, and I believe you owe me at least an opportunity to explain."

"I'll just…be outside," Jenny excused herself uncomfortably and left them to their business.

Ray stared at the floor. When Jenny had gone, he conceded, "Sounds fair. I guess."

"When do you get off for lunch?"

"Now."

"I'm buyin'. Let's go."

Tom and Ray got a table once again at Darla's Lunch Box. Ray had the scroll in its box safely in his back pack, now strapped to his chair. He knew he'd made a deal with his creepy occult stalkers, and he hadn't seen them since, but he still wasn't comfortable leaving it at home. Maybe when Lee got back, he would be. He wondered how long it would take for Lee to get home, now that the Nephilim would be sending him to take their place. He wondered how they'd managed to get to him in the first place. On top of all that, Ray really didn't want to be feeling angry at Old Tom.

"You seem to have a lot on your mind these days, Ray. I hate to feel like I've given you even more to worry over."

"It's okay, Tom…I…" He stopped himself, staring Tom down. "No, it's not okay. You're cheating on your wife. On *Abigail*! She's a little, old Sunday school teacher for Christ's sake! How can you do this to her?"

Tom shushed Ray with a hand gesture. "I know what you're thinking, Ray. I know how it looks. But I can't expect you to understand. Not now. You're young. You're free. I've been married for a long time, Ray.

"Now don't misunderstand. I *love* Abigail. And I'm not doing this *to* her. This has *nothing* to do with her. It's me, Ray. I love Abi, but I still need things she can't really give me anymore. When young men marry, they don't often know the difference between sex and love. They don't even know that there *is* a difference. For women, I don't think there is. But for us, well…"

"I'm not following."

"I know, Ray. I know, and I'm sorry. Look, what I mean to say is, I have no intention of leaving Abi. I would never do *anything* to hurt her. That's what marriage is. Marriage is all about love and devotion. It's about building a life with someone and caring for each other until death. Sex is nothing like that. Sex is about feeling good and not getting old. Sex doesn't require love the way that marriage does. It's a distraction. I have a very stressful job, Ray. I need to be distracted. Abi just isn't into distracting me the way she used to be.

"Again, hear me out. I don't hold that against her. She's paid her dues. She's a marvelous wife. She doesn't owe me a damn thing. That's why I would never hurt her with this, Ray.

"The truth is men weren't meant to be monogamous. Just look at nature. Look at *humans*. Why do you suppose men can father countless children in a year, while women can only pop 'em out about once a year? It's the way God designed us. I know it's not the popular opinion. I know it sounds terrible and shallow to say, but it's the damned truth. You'll see, Ray. When you're married, when you're as old as I am, you'll think back on this and say, 'Old Tom was right.' And I won't ever ask you any questions about what you do when your wife's not looking."

Ray considered it. It didn't seem like it should be right. It sounded like a cop-out. But how much of that was his own brainwashed Christian upbringing? He knew better than to let the Church's dogma of lies rule his life. And it was true: men were biologically designed to father children with multiple women at any time. He wasn't exactly comfortable with it, but it did make more sense to him to argue against dogma, rather than nature. *If there is no God, then all things are permitted.* He shook his head, confused. "It makes sense, I suppose. I just never pictured you being the type is all. And you're right; it really is what men are supposed to do, if you look at it from a *purely* biological perspective."

"Well, I don't mean to cut God and ethics out of the equation, Ray. 'Pure biology' doesn't care if your wife knows. 'Pure biology' doesn't even need a marriage. And as for God, He wired us. He gets it more than anybody down here does. I think as long as we're responsible and do our best not to hurt anybody's feelings, God's okay with it." Tom watched Ray taking it all in. "Are we okay, Ray?"

Ray smiled. The God thing was beyond him, but ethics were important. Maybe all things were permitted, but that didn't mean all things were right. *Just as long as one lover doesn't find out about the other...* Ray answered half-heartedly, "We're okay, Tom." Dismissing his reservations with a weary shake of his head, Ray expounded, "This is all kind of weird, and I'm ridiculously uncomfortable discussing it with you, but I think I understand what you're telling me. I can't say that I *like* it, but it's better than knowing you'd do anything to hurt Abi."

Tom smiled sadly. "I guess that's all I'd ever think to ask of you." He lifted a glass to his young friend, and Ray shook his head in bewilderment at the old man, still not sure just what to make of it all.

At the end of the work day, Ray was in the locker room, looking over his shoulder as he made his way from the showers to his locker, towel wrapped tightly around his waist. He opened the locker, then looked around one more time, then another just to be sure, before dropping his towel and pulling out his clothes. He heard a giggle, then turned his head just enough to see her standing at the edge of his peripheral vision. "Do you *teleport*?"

"Sorry."

"Yeah. Right." Even though she was only able to see his back side from her position, Ray lowered his wad of clothing to cover himself in front. "Can I help you with something? Or did you just stop by to enjoy the view?"

"Well, as long as I have you trapped, I was wondering, now that you're back and all, if you had thought anymore about maybe…you and me…?"

"Actually, I have." He turned around, still covering himself with his clothes. "The thing is, you're really, um, *hot*." He laughed. She laughed. He thought about Dori. "It's just that…um…" He thought about Tom and their lunchtime conversation—what Tom was doing behind Abi's back. "Well…"

"There's someone else?" Jenny looked disappointed, if not surprised.

"Actually, what I was about to say was…how 'bout tonight? *I'm* free." He looked down, then back up at her. "But if you don't mind, I'd rather not have you looking at me in this particular outfit until I've gotten to know you a little better."

Jenny laughed. "Sounds great! What time?"

Ray shrugged, feeling vulnerable. He'd never made a date naked before. "Um…eight o'clock?"

"Great. See you then." She sighed as she turned and left him to dress. "I sure do drive a hard bargain."

When he was more or less sure, aside from that apparent teleporting thing she could do, that Jenny had left the men's locker room, he got dressed quickly. "You better be right about this, Old Tom." He laughed. "Cheating *ethically*." He found it all too funny. Of course, he reasoned, it wasn't nearly the same as what Tom was doing. He and Dori were just dating after all. He had every right to date other people. They weren't even steady. And they sure as hell weren't married. No, he decided. There was nothing wrong at all with what he was doing here—especially if Dori never found out.

Sam had shown up at the Alexas mansion early that evening, determined after his conversation with Bradley and the strange events of the previous night to read the rest of that journal he'd picked out more than two weeks before. Valen had already been home from work, or whatever it was he did during the day, and they'd been visiting. All the while, Valen had seemed distracted.

"Have you eaten?" Sam asked, regretting the question instantly.

"Hm? Why? Do I look hungry?" He was starving.

"A little. You just look distracted, like Bradley when he hasn't had his tongue down Helen's throat in the last fifteen minutes."

Valen laughed at that. "No, nothing like that. I just have some business that I have to tend to tonight. I'm procrastinating."

"Well don't drag your feet on my account. Better to get it over with."

"I know. I just hate to kick you out. I won't be back for a couple of hours."

"I can just hang out here and read," Sam offered. "I can't get any peace at home these days. In case you didn't notice before, my family's sort of flipped out at the moment."

Valen seemed relieved. Then cautious. "Are you sure you want to stay here alone? I'm taking Raksha. If anything…"

"If there's really a ghost, it hasn't bothered me. I'm not a relative." Sam smiled.

"I…really don't know how to respond to that."

"Just go take care of your business, Valen. I'll be all right."

Valen smiled, deciding to feel confident. "Thanks, Sam. We'll hurry back."

Valen and Raksha left quickly after that. Sam wondered what sort of business required Raksha's attention. He wondered as well if he'd lost his mind. *Oh, please let me hang out alone in the haunted house where the vampire lives! I want to get into his secret stuff and risk having my throat ripped out.* Sam decided that he had.

He went into the library and found the journal, in the box behind the other remaining boxes of books, right where he'd hidden it. He picked it up and flipped through the pages until he came to where he'd left off. At long last, he was determined, he was going to get the answers he craved. He began to read. "Tonight was a terrible night. Augustin wandered into the Mines…"

Apparently he'd been wandering through the forest in the early morning, just before the sun rose. The story that was related to me was that he saw Bill Randal and didn't recognize him. Bill has always preferred not to be known by the townspeople. He always keeps to the shadows, feeds when he's hungry, then returns to the Mines. He hadn't noticed Augustin following him. He had probably been too panicked by how close to dawn it was. Augustin kept after him, until Bill apparently vanished. Augustin wasn't sure what to make of it, and he was tired from not sleeping the night before. He marked the spot with a red handkerchief wrapped around a tree branch, intending to return and investigate thoroughly.

Early this evening, Augustin rose and went to the spot he had marked. He searched the area like a bloodhound, determined to find how a man could vanish without a trace. Against all odds, he found the secret entrance. How it ever occurred to him to twist the angel around on the lone grave stone in the forest, I may never know. It's made to appear as part of the whole stone, unmovable. It's the same as the lion's head carved near the top of the grandfather clock in my own home; undetectable. But he detected it.

Of course, when he turned the angel, the secret entrance opened, and he heard the movement of the stone in the shrubs beside him. He discovered the opening, just large enough for a man to crawl into. He didn't know what it was. He had heard the tales of the Mines of Sangra Dios, just as any other man in the town had, but he didn't believe them. He thought it must have been a hideout for thieves, for vagabonds. He saw an opportunity to play the hero and run the bad element out of town. He of course crawled in to have a look, lantern in hand.

Once he got through the short tunnel and was able to stand, he noticed that this was no ordinary den of thieves. He no doubt saw the markings on the wall. The names beside the resting places of the Sleeping Ones. He found several bodies in a pit within the Mines and cried out. By then it was too late to make his escape. The sun had gone down, and the residents of the Mines were awake.

Bill, appropriately, is the one who found him first. "What's this? The meat has come looking for its plate?"

"Who are you?" Augustin asked. "What are you up to down here?"

Bill told him very bluntly, as others came to join him. "I'm a vampire, son. This is where we rest by day and where we hide the bodies of our victims before burning them to spare them our fate. A courtesy we'll shortly be extending to you."

Augustin laughed fearfully. "What? Vampires?" He noticed the others. "You're all madmen."

Word had reached me at this point that a human had invaded our sanctuary. This was alarming news indeed, so of course I rushed to the source of the panic.

Sam dropped the book. Valentinus had referred to the Mines of Sangra Dios as "*Our* sanctuary." According to this, then, he was one of them. It was all true. But what did that mean? Was this for real? Could it be a work of fiction? Sam toyed with the idea of running, of never coming back to Alexas Mansion. But it was too late for that, wasn't it? If Valen was the same as Valentinus, he would catch on. He would find Sam. Sam had to know *exactly* what had happened to Augustin. He read on.

I found them, Bill at the head. They had tied the human up. As I moved closer, I made out his features. "Augustin!"

"Valentinus!" The young man was in tears, terrified. "What are they doing to me? What are they? Get me out of here! Have you brought the police?"

Sadly, I slowed, as I approached Bill and accepted his accusing stare. I looked to Augustin, tears in my own eyes. "No, Augustin. I haven't."

"But they'll get you too!"

"No. They won't." I regarded him stonily, for I'd gone numb at the horror of the moment.

At first he looked confused, then realization dawned. "You're not...You're not! You can't be one of them!"

"What's this all about, Valentinus?" Bill asked. "He doesn't have your mark. He has no business being

here, and we have every right to kill him for it. Do you claim him?"

Many other voices protested the question. At this point, it wouldn't matter if I claimed him. I should have given him my mark, if I'd wanted to protect him. No human can enter our sanctuary and leave alive, unless the poor mortal "belongs" to one of us. Even then, these humans are not permitted in the Mines. "I dared not give him the mark. I love him too much for that."

Many voices moaned at this. Bill laughed. They often mock me for my love of humans. They find it riotous that I am so often fully involved in society. Some others are like me, but not many, and none on as grand a scale.

I assured them that I had never told him of the Mines, that I had never revealed my secret to him. I told them I hadn't the faintest idea how he'd found us.

"It was him!" Unable to move his arms, Augustin pointed with his wild eyes. He pointed at Bill. "I followed him!"

Now it was Bill who had the angry attention of the others. How could he be so careless? It was at this point that I heard from Augustin his full account of finding our lair.

When he'd finished his story, he pleaded. "Please! Be merciful! I'll forget I ever saw it! I'll tell no one! I'm endlessly loyal to Valentinus! I'll take his mark! I'll do whatever it takes! Please don't kill me! My sister would be devastated!"

At this they all laughed. How should Augustin have known how little mortal ties mean to the eternally damned?

I pleaded with them myself. "I give you my word. I trust this human with my very life. We have been inseparably close for years. He lives in my house. He is known in the town. Killing him would be too risky. It would be too suspicious. It would bring me under suspicion, and that would bring us all into danger."

Varney Jones, a creature I've never felt had any sort of soul, croaked out, "We can keep it far from your home. We can leave him in the woods to be found. The people will think it was murder, but they won't suspect you. We'll arrange your presence at that tavern of theirs when it happens."

"No. Listen to me, all of you. Leave the body to be found? Kill a prominent member of society? We'd need to break more rules in order to make up for this one mistake than would ever solve our problem. We would bring ourselves into more danger. And I'm telling you we are in no danger now. Augustin is trustworthy."

Several of the others discussed among themselves. As it appeared Bill had taken the lead for the evening, he was urged to speak on their behalf. "Valentinus, my friend, we are most displeased with this careless relationship of yours. However, I do hold partial blame myself. You were not careless enough to lead him to us, it is plain. So we give you a choice, and this will be the one exception. Kill him yourself, or give him the mark tonight."

"I am not in the habit of giving the mark to humans. I have never done it before. I would rather kill a human than burden them with such a curse."

"Valen! Please! Give me the mark! Don't kill me!"

I looked into Augustin's desperate, tear-reddened eyes, and I knew the chance that I would have to take. "I will take him home and explain the mark to him. I will let him calm down, get a good meal in him, before he makes the choice himself, whether to live...like that...or die."

Against all odds, as so much of the evening had been, my brethren agreed. I untied Augustin, and he threw himself into my embrace. I led him through the tunnels, all the way to my own entrance, and we entered the mansion through the clock together for the first time of perhaps many to come, as my mind was working then; for it was not only the mark that I thought to offer him, and if he wanted none of it, I was very willing to defy the others. After all, if he never went near them again, how would they know he didn't bear my mark?

Once Augustin was cleaned up and Clarenda was invested in some errand, I explained everything to him, all about the mark, and death, and the existence that I lead. As I spoke, I realized I had already decided to do nothing. No mark. No eternal partnership. No execution. Unfortunately I'd already filled his head with the possibilities of the mark. He begged me for it, eager to submit to the role and all that it implied. "I'm already yours, Valentinus! It would make me happy to let them see me as your property. I am. You've always had the freedom to do with me as you liked. You just never took advantage. And I love you for it. But now you have to. You have to. Take me, Valentinus. I beg of you." He kissed me deeply then, right there on the couch.

How tempted I was. How tempted I was to take him right there. To make him my equal, instead of my slave.

I wanted a partner in eternity. Augustin would be perfect. But I couldn't. I couldn't subject him to the sadness of living for centuries. His sister would die. All the people of Nightfire would die, and he would live on. And he would have to kill. To feed on the warm, living blood of other humans as it still pumps through their veins, pushed by their very hearts onto his lips. It is a horror. It might change his very soul. What if he became like Varney? Or what if he couldn't endure forever and became one of the Sleeping Ones? What if he became like D'artagnan? But I know that wouldn't be possible, even as I write this. D'artagnan was twisted to begin with.

I am so confused. I left him pleading with me, thinking I'd rejected him. But I haven't. I want him in a way that goes well beyond what he is asking for. He must not even realize that I could do it. That I could make him one of us.

Ray was just looking at himself in the mirror downstairs when the phone rang. Bradley called to him, "It's for you, Ray. It's Dori."

Ray went over and took the phone from Bradley. "You want me," he announced into the receiver.

Dori laughed on the other end. "You sound much better off tonight. Wanna make somethin' of it?"

"Oh, probably not tonight. I think I'm just gonna stay at home and relax. First day back at work really wiped me out. How 'bout I call you tomorrow?"

"Like you actually will. You'll probably be back to sobbing over your 'issues' by then."

"No, really. Hold me to it. Let's go out tomorrow. I want to. I'm really just not up for it tonight."

Dori's mood seemed to lift. "Well, in that case, I'll mark my calendar. 'Ray Don returned from the dead.'"

Ray laughed. "Do it. See you tomorrow."

When Ray hung up the phone, Bradley was standing there with his arms crossed, open mouthed, staring at him incredulously.

"What?"

Bradley shrugged. "Nothing. Your life. Your funeral."

As Bradley left the room, Ray shook his head and muttered, "Woman-man." He picked up the phone to get directions to Jenny's house.

August 28,

I have made a decision. Granted, I still have many decisions left to make, but I am on the move. I talked to Clarenda tonight about my desire to travel, and I asked her if she'd want to join me, and whether she thought Augustin would come. She was elated. I told her that I want to leave tomorrow, early in the evening. I believe she has already packed.

Augustin is another matter. He thinks that if we are going to run away, we should do it properly. Clarenda doesn't know "our secret." He is still bitter about last night, about my rejecting him. If only he had never learned the truth. He wouldn't be so desperate to have my mark if he'd never known it could be. He asked me tonight if I couldn't just make him like me. I had feared that question. I told him only that it wasn't an existence worth striving for.

What troubles me is my own mind on the matter. I have told none of the creatures in the Mines of my plans to leave Nightfire. It seems the only way. If I do not give Augustin my mark, I fear they will eventually find out and destroy him. We have to leave. The problem is, Augustin is wearing me down. I have never loved anyone as much as I love him and his sister. The more I think about losing either one of them, the more I want to cry out against nature itself. Then I realize that I don't have to lose either one of them.

I intend to prepare them slowly for immortality. As we travel the world together, visiting ancient cities and all the wonders of the globe, I intend to give them a glimpse of what forever could be for the three of us. I know I have said it's a curse, that death is better, but if they have years to think on what they would have to endure, if they are in their thirties perhaps when they make the decision fully educated, I might be able to bring them over without guilt. It simply pains me so much to see Augustin's yearning for me, and how he feels when I tell him that I don't want to mark him. He will wear me down. I know it. I might as well start planning for the future that he will demand of me. Eternity will be easier to bear, if I have this family to keep close all the while. To have a loving family at this point in my eternity is more than I ever dreamed possible.

I don't know how I shall tell Clarenda, but I suppose timing will be everything. I won't spring it on her all at once. I will work up to it over time. And if Augustin can be patient for just a few more years, we will have forever.

August 29,

I am dead. I can no longer endure living. If not for my beautiful Clarenda, I would give myself to the sunlight.

August 30,

This night has brought me no comfort. It's a chore to even breathe. I am writing now, only to have a record. Evidence against my vile 'brother' in the event of my self destruction. Someone must know the truth.

It was that damned letter. Months ago, D'artagnan wrote me. In my determination to leave Nightfire and begin anew, I'd forgotten it. In my love for Augustin. To even write his name now causes my heart to heave terribly, for he has been taken brutally from this world. All my dreams, all my plans, are now no more than dust and ash. It is only for Clarenda that I even bother to return to my "tomb" in the Mines before the sun comes up.

It was late. I had gone out to feed and buy flowers. Some idiotic whim had me convinced I should leave flowers in the living room as I bid my farewells to this place that has been my home for the past seventy years. I came home to a nightmare that will never leave me. Augustin was dead. Tonkowa was dead. I was torn in half with the pain in my heart. Augustin was laid out in the entryway, as if on display.

His neck was broken. His body was paler than it should have been. He'd been drained. A vampire had done this. I knew right then it was my fault. I should have given him the mark. They had ordered me to do it. I had promised to do it. He had himself begged me to do it. And I had not done it. I fell to the ground beside him in utter despair, wailing aloud.

Clarenda came home with some groceries. She found me holding him and reacted very much the same. We held each other. She asked who could have done this to him. It was then that it dawned on her that the killer might still be in the house.

I knew secretly that if this had been a message from the vampires of Nightfire, they had made their point. They had nothing against Clarenda and there was nothing more to be feared, aside from going on living without my lovely Augustin. She called the police out. I agreed that we should go into town and she should stay in the hotel. It was then that I noticed Tonkowa's absence. I found him in the shadows, lying in a pool of blood. His spine had been broken in half. His neck snapped. His eyes stared vacantly into the darkness. I knelt down and petted his glorious coat one last time. I knew the horrors that awaited me that night.

I told Clarenda about Tonkowa. She was horrified and fearful of the perpetrator. When the police arrived, I asked them to drive her into town and get her a hotel on my credit. I waited stoically as the police searched the house, as they loaded Augustin into an ambulance, though it seemed absurd to do so. He was beyond their ability. When they were at last ready to leave, I told them I would take care of Tonkowa's remains myself.

I carried Tonkowa to the clock, turned the lion's head, and carried him in. As I walked the corridors, carrying my beloved protector in my arms, haggard and unable to fight back tears, the other vampires appeared just as horrified as I was at Tonkowa's fate. I knew this was not their doing. Killing Tonkowa would have been a crime. Tonkowa did have my mark. This was the work of someone far more sinister. Someone able to kill a creature such as my noble wolf had been. Someone with no regard for our rules whatsoever. I knew in my heart that D'artagnan had returned.

My brethren followed me to the lowest levels, to the inferno. I laid Tonkowa out on the altar, drew the sword from the wall, and did what I had to do. The others lit the horrible pit below, and I lowered Tonkowa with the ancient chain elevator into the flames. I felt their hands on my shoulders as I did what responsibility demanded and watched until naught but ash remained of my dear friend.

Tonight was even worse, though I never would have dreamt such agony were possible. I couldn't bring myself to go for Augustin's remains myself, but I told the others that a vampire had killed him, and they knew we had to retrieve the body or risk discovery by the innocents of Nightfire. I waited at the inferno.

When they laid him out on the altar, I knew it would take all of my will and perhaps all of my sanity, but I had to do it all myself. I couldn't let them desecrate his body. I couldn't let them. I took the sword. I performed the ritual, and it had never been more horrible. I prayed aloud that his head wouldn't roll off of the altar. Bill was kind enough to hold him still.

When the deed was done, I nearly lost my sanity. I fell to my knees again. I couldn't take his body in that state. I couldn't lay him on the nightmarish iron hammock and lower him into the pit. I held my head and sobbed. The others were understanding. They stayed by me as Bill and Markus carried him to the device and began to lower him. The inferno was lit.

I stood and went to the crank. They moved aside, and I lowered him into the flames myself. I wanted to throw myself in with him. I made a break, and several strong hands grabbed me and held me back as I watched Augustin burn. I cried out his name. I struggled, but ultimately accepted my fate. I would go on. I would remain in the world for Clarenda.

When the ashes were brought up, they put them in an urn, as they had done for my Tonkowa and all of the guardians before him. This wasn't customary for a victim, but they knew I'd loved him. They didn't know I had never given him the mark. They saw it as a murder. I told them that D'artagnan had come back. I told them that I knew it with all my heart. D'artagnan the Damned. How could I have forgotten his letter?

August 31,

This is my final entry. Tonight, I wait for the sun to rise and take me from this world. In October I would have lived four hundred forty-three years. That is suffering enough for anyone.

September 1,

Julius has rescued me from myself once again. I didn't invite it. He simply knows me, and he heard of my loss. He sent Tristan in to force me into the Mines. I gave him a fight. I had nothing left to live for. Ultimately, I became too apathetic even to fight for my death. He pulled me into the Mines and "tucked me in" himself.

Tonight, Tristan escorted me out of town. I have left Nightfire behind forever. I don't know where my terrible existence will see me next. Surely Julius will find a way to magically make me smile again. I just don't see how. I was so in love. I was in love with both of them, and they were both in love with me. Now they are gone.

September 2,

We are on a train, Julius and I. He owns a car and has a special darkened room for me to sleep in when the sun comes up. I'm feeling a little more determined. I want revenge. I hate D'artagnan and would see him burn slowly.

Two nights ago, Clarenda and I were discussing what we would do. It was clear we would still leave Nightfire together, but at the moment she was far too horrified that someone had stolen her brother's body from the morgue. The police were investigating the disappearance even as we spoke. I knew they would find nothing. The body no longer existed. The night before, I had placed Augustin's urn in his room, and I'd laid the flowers from the night I'd found him at its base. How I longed to have my ashes in that urn with his.

What happened that night was so shocking that I was unable to even think clearly about it until now. Clarenda turned on me suddenly and completely. She went out early and came back quite late. She was in a rage. She attacked me. She hated me. She told me that it was my fault Augustin was dead, that I killed him. All I could manage to say before the tears overtook me was, "I know." She took a knife from the kitchen and came into the room, determined to murder me, I thought. I decided to let her, if she could. I had nothing to live for if she hated me. She stabbed me. I bled. I looked sadly into her eyes, wishing I could die so easily. She looked astonished with herself. She stabbed me again. And again. In the chest. In the side. In the stomach. Finally I told her, "You have to cut off my head if you want to do it properly." There was nothing but sorrow in my eyes as I met her stunned gaze.

She dropped the knife. "It's true. I know." She pointed to me with a trembling hand. "I know everything. He told me! I know what you are! You killed us!" She shouted hysterically, "You killed us both!" She ran for the stairs, and I rose in great pain and ran after her.

I caught up with her in Augustin's room. She knew. She was looking at the urn and the wilted flowers lying before it. Her eyes were mad, as I pleaded. "Clarenda, please..." I don't know what I would have said. I never will. She didn't give me the chance.

Clarenda said again, in a whisper, "You killed us both." She jumped through the window, screaming like a mad woman until she hit the ground, three stories below. She was dead. I had killed them both.

D'artagnan showed up almost immediately to gloat. I was lost in madness, just as he'd intended. "You did this," I said calmly.

"As I understand it, you did, Valentinus. Such a mess."

It was that word which set me off. He'd reduced all those years of love and friendship to nothing more than a "mess." I attacked him. "I hate you!" I threw him down the stairs. I looked for anything to plunge into his heart, to sever his head, to burn him.

He rose before I could find a suitable weapon and slammed me against the wall. "Don't act so surprised. I told you I was coming soon to liberate you, didn't I, my little Valentine?"

I lost my will. "Why are you doing this?"

"Because I love you." He looked at me as though he were addressing a child.

"Monster. The others know. They'll come after you."

"Like they always do." He seemed to enjoy that prospect. He smiled. I didn't have the will to go for his throat, as I'd wanted to only moments before. He had won. He had finally destroyed me.

"You have taken everything. I hope it hurts you what I'll do. I'll give myself to the dawn. This very morning."

He caressed my hair, and I felt the very devil was assessing the potential succulence of my eternal soul. "Then I shall return as soon as the sun has set and swallow your ashes. Then you can be inside of me forever. You are, after all, a part of me. You can penetrate me for a change. And I will keep you there, always."

D'artagnan saw that I was broken, that he could not get a rise out of me even by reminding me of what we'd been to each other when we were both still mortal men. I didn't care.

"Adios, my little Valentine." He left without another word, apparently satisfied with all he'd done in the past four hundred years.

When he had gone, I got a chair and sat before the broken window. The police came. I don't know how they knew what had happened. Maybe someone had heard the scream. I waited in the chair. They came in. I answered their questions. They didn't arrest me. I knew they wouldn't. I would have been out before sunrise if they had. When they were gone, and Clarenda's body with them, I went to my journal, wrote my farewell, and returned to my chair in Augustin's room, awaiting the sunrise.

It was soon after that Tristan arrived, just in time to save me. Very little has happened since. I fled Nightfire.

I am on my way to a place that Julius wants to show me. I know he will be stubborn enough to bring me out of this. I know him well enough to know he'll find a way. He has an unshakable faith. Perhaps I'll learn to live again. But I will always carry this pain. It stays with me, like a ghost.

Sam could read no more. He closed the book and trembled. He couldn't believe it. It simply could not be true. But it was. Valentinus Alexas was still alive today. He was back in this house. He had a new guardian. And he was a vampire, hundreds of years old, haunted by the ghost of a woman who'd committed suicide decades before, blaming him for her brother's death.

But it couldn't be true! Sam remembered in the book, it had specifically said how to open a secret passage to the Mines through the grandfather clock with a lion's head carved near the top of it. Sam knew the clock. It was on the first floor. If the story was true, then he could turn the lion's head. Otherwise, this was a novel, very craftily written. A book of absolute fiction, set against the backdrop of the mansion's history. Perhaps a fantasy that the mad, murdering ancestor of Valen Alexas had written to explain away all the terrible things that he had done. Sam wanted *that* to be the case. He couldn't cope with the other possibility. It was too ludicrous. He decided to prove it to himself.

He left the library and went to the grand old clock. He stared at the lion's head, gathering his courage. "I have to know." He reached up and took hold of the lion's head, twisting it, and was utterly bewildered when it moved. He turned it all the way to the left, and the clock moved aside like a door.

A dark passageway was visible where the clock had been. The air coming forth from within was cool. He tried to see inside, but it was too dark. The air smelled stale, like death. Suddenly Sam came to his senses. It was true! It was *all* true! He turned quickly to get away from the secret passageway and return the clock to its proper place. It was as he turned, however, that a powerful hand reached out of the darkness and held him where he stood.

Chapter 10
The Mines of Sangra Dios

Sam turned in horror to find an unfamiliar, corpse-like face glaring at him from the darkness. The creature bared its fangs and pulled him inside violently, throwing him to the ground. It then started dragging him down, into the depths of the secret caverns. Sam struggled. "Wait! Stop!" He pulled against his captor's grip to no avail.

The creature finally stopped and pushed Sam against a wall, now somewhere beneath the land that surrounded Alexas Mansion. Sam heard noises coming from the wall and screamed out loud, as emaciated hands began clawing their way through.

His captor laughed with a voice that croaked as though unused for years. "No mortal has invaded our sanctuary for quite some time. It seems you have awakened the Sleeping Ones. Now they must feed." The vampire pulled Sam away and pinned him to the wall on his left, as they watched the Sleeping Ones emerge from the walls that had been their graves for years.

Sam's voice was barely a whisper, though he was trying to scream, "I'm a friend of Valentinus! I'm his friend!"

Three living nightmares, covered in dirt, skeletally thin, shambled towards Sam now, looking like something out of a zombie movie. The Sleeping Ones.

"Too bad, little slave. We don't honor the human laws of ownership. Only our own. The Sleeping Ones have starved for decades. They *must* feed when awakened."

"Then they're going to have to feed on someone else!" Valen Alexas appeared in the corridor, having entered through the passageway in the mansion. His voice and face radiated anger. "You know the laws, Varney."

The other vampire sneered, as the Sleeping Ones came closer. "I *do* know our laws, *Valentinus*! This slave does *not* bear your mark—just like the *last* time! He has wandered into our sanctuary. He has awakened some of the Sleeping Ones. He is ours, no matter that you hold a receipt from some trader."

"You really should make *some* effort at keeping up with the world, Varney. The humans abolished the slave trade here more than a *century* ago. Sam is my equal."

Varney sneered even more devilishly. "Not your equal, Valentinus. You insult us all with such words. You are a *god*! *This* will never be your equal nor any of ours. *This* is our food."

One of the Sleeping Ones coughed up a great cloud of dust, then spoke hoarsely, "This argument is pointless. The human is in clear violation. We will feed now."

"What's going on?" another new voice, that of Bill Randal, entered the conversation.

Sam's eyes met Valentinus'. He found his own fear mirrored there, along with a deep sorrow. All he could manage to say with his now failing voice was, "You're a vampire."

Valen looked away from him, not making an answer. He spoke to Bill, "Sam Turner here seems to have gotten in the middle of something. But he's my friend. He is no threat to anyone."

Bill studied the twisted, hungry faces of the Sleeping Ones. He looked to Valentinus. "Does he bear your mark?"

Defeated, Valen answered, "No."

"How did he get here?"

"I don't know."

Varney provided the answer, "He opened the secret entrance in Alexas Mansion. I pulled him on in to protect our most precious secret."

"Valentinus," Bill went on, "this is more serious than the last time. This time none of us shares the blame. You have allowed a mortal, who does not have your mark, to find our resting place. The laws are clear. Aside from that, we know this is not the first time that one of your humans has entered our sanctuary uninvited. We must destroy him, and the Sleeping Ones must feed."

"Bill...please..." Valen was becoming desperate. "Once again, this *will* add suspicion to..."

"You returned to Nightfire for sanctuary," Varney said pointedly. "You can leave and hope the werewolves don't tear you limb from limb if all you're going to do is bring us trouble through your reckless relationships with mortals. That's why you're in this mess in the first place. If you hadn't helped them to kill Sebastian Barnes…"

Another of the Sleeping Ones coughed up a cloud of dust, his arm creaking as he lifted his pocket watch and found it unreadable. He struggled to clear his mind, to remember words. "When…is it? What…date?"

The vampire Markus had entered the corridor and answered, "June 25, 1975."

The Sleeping One groaned. "I have not fed in one hundred and twenty years! There is nothing to argue about here. The slave is destined to break our great fast."

"There is nothing you can say here, Valentinus." Bill shook his head. "*Learn* this time. Do not let these mortals so close that they discover our secrets."

"I…" tears filled Valen's helpless eyes. "Sam…"

Varney held Sam against the wall with one strong arm, and the Sleeping Ones approached.

A mist filled the corridor, and Varney's arm was pried away from Sam by some invisible force. The Sleeping Ones were pushed back, coughing out protests. The mist began to take a solid form, standing between Sam and certain death.

Valen cried out with relief, "Tristan!"

The other vampire smiled. "Yes, Valentinus. Seems I picked a good time for a visit. We'd hate to have to bring you back from the edge again so soon."

Sam recognized the name from the journal and from a very recent conversation between Valen and another man. "You're dead!"

Tristan laughed, as he regarded the young man. "Oh, that. That was only temporary." He let his gaze circle the room, locking eyes with everyone as he spoke, assuring himself that he had their full attention. "I'm feeling *much* better now."

Bill whispered in awe, "He's become an Ancient!"

"Yes, it seems I've hit vampire puberty. And so you children will do as I say." He looked to the Sleeping Ones. "Go and feed in the town. That's what it's there for. We need some time to clear this up. This is not a random human. A plan must be formed, one way or another, before we take his life."

"But he's…" Varney was cut off by a hungry glance from Tristan.

"Do you wish a full demonstration of my new power, Varney?"

Terrified, Varney backed away. "No. I only wish to see our laws enforced."

"They will be," Tristan promised. "Return here after you've fed. We will not leave the Mines until this is settled, and we will not be settling anything on empty stomachs. But rest assured, when you return, we will decide *just* what to do about young Sam Turner."

Without a word, and with many backwards glances, the other vampires left, save for Valentinus, Bill, and Markus.

"Thank you, Tristan," Valen sighed.

"Don't thank me yet, Valentinus. We still haven't gotten this lad out of the fire."

Valen looked to his young friend, so many questions forming in his mind. "Sam…"

Sam met Valen's eyes, letting the full impact of his situation sink in—then he promptly fainted.

"Lucky bastard," Markus said to the unconscious youth.

Tristan shrugged. "Can you blame him?"

Bill grumbled, "I guess not. We are a bit spooky, I suppose."

"A *bit spooky*?" Tristan laughed hysterically at that. He looked to Valentinus, who was staring unblinking at Sam with terrified eyes. "Don't worry, Valentinus. I have a plan."

Valen sighed, remembering his relief at Tristan's appearance, and looked up at last with a sad smile. "You always do."

"So, why don't I ever see you much around town?" Ray and Jenny had finished eating, and their date had gone exceptionally well.

"Oh, I have responsibilities that keep me home most of the time." Jenny smiled sadly.

"What? Like fluffing the pillows? I have responsibilities too. I still get out."

"Yeah, but you've got a roommate to help out. I don't."

"Well, yeah, but even if I didn't have a roommate I could still find time to fluff the pillows *and* hang out with friends."

"I live with my uncle. He's…not well."

"Oh." Ray was bothered by her tone. He decided not to ask for details.

She laughed. "Don't make that face. You didn't know." She shrugged. "My brother agreed to watch him tonight so that I could go out."

Curiosity got the better of Ray, as it always seemed to do. "So, what are you gonna do with him…I mean…if you were to live with someone *else*? I mean, is it like cancer, or crazy?" Ray cringed in his head as the question came out so bluntly.

"It's more like…crazy, I guess. He um…he has…spells."

"Well that's gonna suck if you ever get married. Can't you keep him in the attic, or in like a home?" *What the hell is wrong with me?* "I'm sorry. I'm no good at chit-chat. I don't mean to be such an ass."

Jenny laughed at Ray's helpless lack of tact. "It's okay, Ray. I like a man who doesn't waste time being careful. The truth is, we talked about putting him in a home about five years ago when it all hit the fan. What it comes down to is…" She struggled to find a way to explain without actually getting into it. This wasn't something she wanted to put on the table on a first date. "They wouldn't understand him. We have a pr…*nurse* who comes to sit with him during the day, while I'm at work. Then I take over when I get home."

Ray looked smug. "Wait a minute. Back up. You almost said something else. I know what that means. Anytime anyone *almost* says something around here, they seem to be covering up some weird secret. So let's not be careful. What were you going to say instead of *nurse*?"

Jenny laughed out loud. "Ray, you're so paranoid! I never would have guessed. You've obviously been through some trauma somewhere in your life." She took a sip of her drink.

"Well…?"

Patiently, she answered, "I was going to say 'private caretaker.' Nurse seemed more efficient."

"Oh." Ray was relieved and feeling a little bit silly. "Well, good. I'm just playin' around anyway." He smirked.

Jenny crossed her arms and leaned across the table. "So what got you so paranoid, Ray? Tell me some of these 'weird secrets' that people always have."

Ray sat back and laughed defiantly. "Well if I told you, then they wouldn't be secrets, would they? Besides, I'm much more interested in the two of us right now. To hell with crazy uncles and other people's weird secrets."

From there, much to Ray's surprise, the night passed smoothly. When Jenny's time to stay out was up, Ray paid the bill and drove her home. As he pulled up to her place, she leaned over and kissed him on the lips. "I had a nice time." She got out and closed the door.

Ray watched her leave; then he thought about Dori and laughed. "What the hell am I doing?"

"What the hell are you doing?" Bradley asked Ray incredulously.

"Huh?" Ray closed the door behind him and stared at Bradley as though the younger man were an alien.

"I'm pretty sure you don't wear lipstick."

Ray looked in the mirror by the stairway, wiped his lips, and laughed. "Oops."

"I'm also pretty sure that's not Dori's lipstick either."

"It's not," Ray answered. "So what?"

"So what? You're cheating on Dori! That's so what!"

Ray felt cold inside and was surprised by it. Hadn't he made the same disappointed argument to Tom at lunch? "Look, Bradley," he said gently. "It's not wrong. It's not cheating. I'm single. Dori and I aren't a set thing. I'm just dating around is all. I'm still into Dori. But single means single. I haven't picked one yet. What's wrong with shopping around?"

"Do they know that you're 'shopping around'?"

Ray shrugged. "No."

"Well *that's* what makes it wrong."

Bradley turned and walked up the stairs. Ray felt as if the wind had been knocked out of him. He looked in the mirror again, wiping the last traces of Jenny's lipstick from his mouth. He sighed. "What the hell am I doing?" He shook his head. "Oh, well. Que sera, sera." He snickered defiantly at his reflection.

The angry vampires returned to the Mines, no longer starved for anything but justice. "Well, *Prince* Tristan, we've returned," Varney announced. "So let's decide what to do with it." He regarded Sam, who was still lying on the ground unconscious.

Valentinus simply massaged his temples, as he silently died with worry.

Tristan knelt down and roused Sam.

"What happened?" the young man asked groggily.

"The others have fed. It's time to come to a decision." Tristan smiled down at Sam, trying his best to be reassuring given the circumstances.

"Fed?" Sam's eyes went wide, as he remembered and realized what the word implied. He fainted again.

Tristan laughed.

"I don't see anything funny about this, Tristan." Varney glared at the older vampire.

Tristan stood calmly. He seemed as out of place as he always had in the dusty Mines of Sangra Dios, especially in the company of the now former Sleeping Ones who were covered in utter filth. Tristan had always been considered a fop by the others. He came from a very privileged background and always dressed the part. Though his face was young, his long dark hair in mortal life had gone stark white before he'd reached the age of twenty-four. "You were born without laughter muscles, weren't you, Varney?"

"It's not funny! Our sanctuary has been invaded by a human *again*. It's Valentinus' fault *again*. He isn't getting away with it this time."

"Listen to me. We have an obligation to each other that goes beyond our secret tunnels." Tristan met the eyes of every vampire in the room. "The 'sanctuary' of the Mines is more than hidden doorways. We must care for each other as brothers and sisters. No one else in the world would give us the same respect as we can give each other." He nodded towards his dearest friend. "Valentinus is traumatized by all of this. We need to be sensitive to that. He's had more trauma than any of us during the two lifetimes since we founded this town."

"All because of his relations with the humans," Varney spat. "It's his own damn fault!"

"And where would you be, Varney, if Valentinus hadn't been up top during the first lifetime of this town seeing to our business with the government, covering all of our tracks, steering the humans away from our secrets far more often than he's accidentally enabled any of them to find us. This is really the *first* time it's happened. What happened with Augustin was ultimately Bill's fault, if you'll remember. Valen hadn't done a thing to lead him to us."

"I don't like the way your sort always uses their *names*. They're just cattle. They..."

"My point is," Tristan interrupted, "we have an obligation to help Valen through this. God knows he's done enough to help the rest of us in the past. This is his first offense. It's true, we may decide to destroy this unfortunate human, but Valentinus needs time to sort it all out. If we simply kill Sam now, Valen may go eternally mad. You know what it did to him the last time. We *owe* it to him. Give me a night to counsel our brother. We will keep the human under our power until tomorrow night, at which point Valentinus will be better able to handle the gravity of this situation."

Most of the vampires simply agreed. They had fed. Tristan had made a compelling argument for their responsibility to one another. What would it matter if they let it go one more night, knowing that the young man was under the watch of an Ancient? Varney Jones, on the other hand, was determined to have some extra security. "On one condition."

Tristan regarded Varney patiently. Valen regarded him with fear.

"We let *this* mortal go tonight, and only for tonight, on the condition that any mortal who wanders into the Mines before a decision has been made, and that means *anyone*, be it the Mayor, another one of Alexas' boyfriends or favorite pets, or Andrew *fucking* Jackson, is sentenced to die on sight. We kill them immediately. If there is any chance that…" he nodded towards Sam, "…*it* has leaked information about our resting place, we need this security, or there might not *be* a tomorrow night for any of us."

Tristan regarded the angry vampire stonily. After a brief silence, he made his judgment. "Agreed."

Varney cackled victoriously, seeming almost to *hope* for another mortal's intrusion.

There was a knock at the door, and Louise Turner put down her romance novel and went to answer it, worried sick. Sam had been out all night without a word, now there was a knock at the door, which meant it wasn't Sam, who would have just walked in. She feared it was someone come to tell her something had happened to her only son.

She opened the door and saw only a strange mist in the glow of the porch light where she'd expected to see someone standing. She looked down. "Sam!" Her son was on the porch, unconscious. "Sam!" She fell down and took hold of him.

He woke. "Huh? What?"

"Oh, Sam! You alright? Oh, my baby, what happened to you?"

"I'm fine, Momma. I just…" he considered what he thought he remembered happening. He couldn't tell her any of it. "I got sick. Someone must have brought me home."

"And just left you on the porch and run? This how those *white* friends of yours treat you, Samuel?"

"Ain't no regala friends brung him home." Sam's great-grandmother stood resignedly in the doorway, clutching her walker. She'd had time to accept it. She'd been waiting for the guillotine to drop ever since the night Valen Alexas had shown up at their door burned and pleading for Sam's help in the dead of night. "I knowed it. I tol' you. The boy has brought the Devil to this house. Now ain't no hope. No hope fo' any of us."

Sam and his mother both stared at the old woman fearfully. Louise feared that her beloved grandmother had become confused and addled. Sam only feared that she was right, and for all the attempts he made in that moment to dispel his fears with reason, he could not; and the thought burned into his mind. She was right.

Ray sat on a bench beside his locker after work the next day, waiting for the inevitable.

"You're moving slow today." Jenny giggled.

Smuggly, Ray answered, "No. I was just waiting for your appearance *before* I showered or changed clothes. I'm on to you."

She offered a glowing smile. "I had a really nice time last night."

"Yeah. Me too. We'll have to do it again."

"How 'bout tonight?"

Taken aback, Ray stammered, "Uh…" He had a date with Dori, but what good would it do him to tell Jenny? "I can't tonight. I have to make up last night to Bradley, help out with the kids."

"Got ya. I just thought since my brother was willing…He was glad I had a good time. He's been bugging me to get out there and get to know some people. Speaking of which, are you going to the party at the Alexas mansion tomorrow night?"

Ray cringed inwardly. "Uh…erg. I haven't decided." *No. Hell no. Fuck no. Why don't I just say so?*

"Well, I'm going. Uncle Joe has an appointment with a specialist. My brother and I are both off the hook. I think the whole town's going. Anyway, if you *do* go, maybe we can make a date of it."

"Uh…sure." He smiled up at her. "Sounds like a plan." He added, "*If* I go."

"You're so weird." She shook her head fondly. "I'll leave you to get naked. See you tomorrow, at work anyway." She winked and left the men's locker room. Ray breathed a sigh of relief, glad he'd decided not to go to Valen's froufrou housewarming party.

Matilda Preston was closing out her cash register at the downtown department store where she worked, when the sexiest voice she had ever heard asked her, "You come here often?"

She looked up to see Dirk Arnold staring at her from across the counter. "Oh, hi, Dirk. I…work here."

He laughed. "I know. I was joking. If you didn't work here and were going through the cash drawer like that, 'fraid I'd have to arrest you." He patted the gun at his side for emphasis.

Mati was so astounded at his hotness that she forgot to laugh, though inside she was laughing hysterically. Overdoing it in fact. Maybe it was a good thing she just stared at him dumbly.

"You're busy. I'll let you..."

"No!" She laughed at how loud she'd just spoken. "I mean, no problem. What's up? Need help finding anything?"

"Maybe. I mean...sort of. Ah, shit." *Why the hell is this so hard?* "I'm here for a reason."

She looked at him, waiting. "Most people that come here are." She giggled nervously, wondering what was the matter. She'd never seen Dirk come across so stupidly before. He was usually very articulate; probably one of the smartest men on Nightfire's police force.

"I mean...So, you heard about this thing at the old Alexas place tomorrow?" He leaned sideways on the counter, trying to be nonchalant.

"Yeah. Pretty much everybody has. I mean, it's been all over the paper."

"You goin'?"

She shrugged. "I haven't made up my mind yet. I don't know." *Yes, I'm going. Who isn't? So ask me out, damnit!*

"Ah, well...I'm not going if you're not. You know...I was thinking maybe we could...go together?"

"Pick me up at eight."

He laughed. "That was easy."

"Easy?"

"Well, no...I mean...I thought you'd turn me down."

She laughed. "And I thought you'd never ask."

He straightened, feeling taller than he had when he'd first come up to the counter. "Well, I'm making my rounds, so...tomorrow. Eight o'clock."

"Eight o'clock." She wanted to explode as she watched him leave, turning to glance back at her twice with a goofy little grin. The hottest cop in Nightfire had just asked her out on a date. Dori was gonna be *so* jealous.

Bradley and Helen were in his room on the bed. They'd been kissing and holding each other for the past half hour, having had the entire house to themselves while Ray wasn't back from work yet and Brendan and Kate were over at the Joneses'. She was catching her breath, giggling, straddling him as her hair hung down in his face.

He smiled up at her. "Come on, Helen. It's time. Have sex with me."

She laughed out loud and sat up, fixing her hair. "That sure was forward."

"Why beat around the bush? I want to. You want to. So let's do it."

He rolled her over onto her back, beneath him, and he kissed her tenderly, letting his hand slide up her thigh.

She moved like lightning, and was out from under him in a heartbeat, sitting beside him and rubbing his back.

Bradley was trying to figure out how she had moved so fast. "What the…"

She sighed. "Bradley, this isn't the way I want it to happen. I'm not there yet, okay?"

He turned over on his side, propping himself up on his elbow. "But, Helen, we've been going out for like a month."

"Two weeks. Six days. I know that seems like an eternity after the precedent set by your *previous* slut of a lover, but really, it's not. How long did you and the psychopath go out before…?"

"A month."

"Oh, well…see?" She decided the matter was settled. "So I think I'm gonna try to learn the guitar again."

Bradley rolled over on his back, groaning and laughing simultaneously, resulting in a very odd sounding grumble. "You were a *terrible* guitar player." He resigned himself to another sexless afternoon and sat up. "Wanna go eat?"

"Sure! I'm starving."

After letting about thirty inappropriate responses filter through his tortured adolescent mind, Bradley bounced off of the bed and suggested, "Dan Parker's then. Let's go."

Helen followed him down the stairs, glad to be on the way to a place where Bradley couldn't possibly try to have his way with her. Then again, she decided, she couldn't really put it past him.

Bradley and Helen arrived to find that Ray and Dori had already met up at Dan Parker's. They joined them at a table near the bar and ordered *lots* of food.

Dori regarded Helen as she chowed down on her burger and fries like there was no tomorrow. "Helen, it seems to me you're filling a void in your life with this particular meal. You guys still aren't doing the nasty, are you?"

Helen put her burger down and glared at Dori, trying to find just the right flavor of spite to throw back at her, but was interrupted when Sam walked in.

Bradley got up, relieved by the interruption. "Sam! Over here."

Sam was clearly dazed as he nodded at Bradley. He went over to the bar and didn't even register the fact that the man behind the counter was the very bigot who'd told him to take his business elsewhere the last time he'd been in. "Can I get a Dr. Pepper?"

James Parker regarded Sam condescendingly. "All out, boy."

Ray, who'd heard about the last time from Bradley, went immediately to the bar. "Hey, James. Dr. Pepper. It's for Dori."

James put a bottle down on the counter. Ray looked at it, then back up to James. "Thank you," he said, just an instant before punching James in the face from across the counter with all of his might.

Sam snapped out of his stupor, as James stumbled back. "Oh, shit!"

The others at Ray's table were all on their feet, rushing over to the scene. Bradley grabbed hold of Ray just as he was preparing to jump over the counter and go in for the kill, pulling him back. "Ray, shit! What are you doing?"

James raged, holding a hand to the place where he'd been punched as if he could keep the pain from spreading. "Get the hell out of here, you nigger-loving commie shit, before I exercise my right to…"

"Your right to what, you fucking bigot!" Ray was still being held back by Bradley, and he wasn't making it easy for him. "Your *right* to not give my friend a drink when he asks for it? His money's just as good as mine!"

"No it ain't!"

The two men exploded in a loud argument full of expletives and accusations. Bradley struggled to hold Ray back from jumping the counter and murdering James. Sam was between the two men shouting at the top of his lungs just trying to make them drop it and keep Ray from getting into more trouble than he was probably already in. Everyone else in the bar and grill was on their feet now, watching the exchange, hoping, as crowds often tended to do, that they were about to see a real fight break out.

Beau walked into the building, still on duty but thirsty and needing a break from the evening heat. He saw the shouting men, Sam standing between them. He saw the red mark on James' face where he'd obviously been hit. He marched over wordlessly to the group to diffuse the situation, ending Sam's shouts by grabbing the young man, pushing him over on the counter, and cuffing him.

"Get that nigger out of here, Beau! He's caused me too much god damned trouble."

"*What?!*" Ray was on the verge of loosing all self control. Bradley let him go, finally just hoping that he would.

Dirk walked in, wondering why Beau hadn't come back out yet, just in time to hear Ray shout, "He didn't do anything , you son of a bitch!"

Helen ran over to Dirk, followed by her boyfriend. "Dirk! Sam didn't do anything! He was just trying to calm Ray down when Beau came in and hand-cuffed him."

"James Parker's a racist sack of shit," Bradley added. "He never serves Sam drinks, and so Ray just went over and slugged him. The fight's between Ray and James."

"Please do something!" Helen pleaded. "Sam's not trouble. He's our friend."

Dirk regarded the younger sister of the girl he'd just asked out. No way was he going to let this particular damsel's request go unanswered. "I'll take care of it," he promised, and he made his way over to the bar. "Beau! What the hell's going on here?"

The other officer explained, "I walked in, and there was pandemonium. I put a stop to it."

"That why everyone's still yelling? What did you see *Sam* do?"

Beau considered. "Well…he seemed to be in the middle of it all."

"That nigger just comes in here to start trouble," James added smugly. "I never want to see him come around again."

Dirk was smoldering with anger, but he was a master of controlling his emotions. "I've seen him in here lots of times, James. Never seemed to be any trouble." He moved Beau out of the way and didn't even look at the other officer as he unlocked Sam's cuffs and handed them back to him. "It's not against the law to be black in the vicinity of a fight between two white guys." He looked between Ray and James, deciding out of pure hatred for the 'victim' that he wouldn't arrest Ray. "Go home and cool down, Ray." He looked to Sam, who was rubbing his wrists. "Sorry about all the confusion, Sam."

All the adrenaline of the past few minutes suddenly jolting him, Sam shouted out of every emotion, "*Fuck* this place!" He stormed out.

Ray pointed a finger in James' direction. "And fuck *you*!" He walked out without another word. Dori, Helen, and Bradley followed.

Sam was nowhere to be found when the rest of the group got outside. Dori ran up to Ray and hung herself on his shoulder. "I am *so* hot for you right now. Where's Sam?"

Sadly, Ray answered, "He ran off. I don't think he even saw me come out." He shook his head. "Mother fucking ass hole! I don't care if that *is* his cousin, Todd needs to fire that guy. I'm not comin' back until he does."

Eager to lighten the mood, Dori asked, "So are you going to Valen's tomorrow night?"

"No!"

"But you have to!" Bradley and Helen urged him in unison.

"Everyone else is," Helen assured him.

"Even Brendan and Kate," Bradley put in.

"See, Ray?" Dori cooed. "You'd be the only man in town *not* at Valen's party. And that's probably not far from the truth."

Suddenly Ray got a sinking feeling at the thought of being alone. He hadn't seen any of his stalkers since he'd made his deal with them, but that didn't mean they weren't still there, watching and waiting for an opportune moment to strike. He sighed loudly. "I'll be there."

"Good!" Dori bounced giddily. "Now I don't have to show up without a date."

Ray remembered Jenny, realizing at that moment just how deep into a lose-lose situation he really was. "...Right."

***

Much later that night, Sam was at Alexas Mansion, sitting on the couch across from Valen and Raksha, terrified beyond his worst nightmares. He would never have returned of his own free will, not after the night before.

He'd been hypnotized. After running off his rage and winding up at Hilltop in the dark of night, a mist had enveloped him, and Tristan had appeared, mesmerizing Sam with his voice and spiriting him off to the Alexas mansion. By the time Sam had come out of his stupor, he was already sitting where he was now.

Valen looked miserable. He and Tristan had talked the previous night until the sunrise was peeking over the hills and they'd had to race back into their sanctuary; back into the Mines that were the cause of the current problem. Tristan had calmed Valen down, made him understand. There was only one thing that he could do. Valen loved humans, but he wasn't one of them. He had been given no alternative to accepting that fact last night. The vampires had their laws, and he was a vampire. He had to put the safety of the Mines above all else. He wished that he could make Sam understand. He wished that he could travel through time, like in an H. G. Wells novel, and erase the mistakes that had led him to this moment.

"So, you really are a vampire."

"Yes."

"Are they gonna kill me?"

"I won't let them touch you."

"I read your journal. From 1917. I just had to know if it was true."

"So you went to the clock."

Sam nodded. "I'm real sorry, Valen."

The vampire shook his head. "It's not your fault, Sam. It's mine. I should never have revealed so much even in my private writings. That was a terrible year in my life. I wasn't thinking as I should have been."

"So how old *are* you?"

"I'll be five hundred and one this October."

Sam nodded, eyes glazed, just trying to absorb the information. He looked up. "So what happened to Tristan? I thought he died. Is he a ghost?"

Valen struggled to smile. "No. He's an Ancient. When a vampire has been a vampire for about five hundred years, give or take, they experience a metamorphosis. They die. Then they rise up again with near unlimited power. It will happen to me one day as well, in twenty years or so. The way it works when you first become a vampire is that you are bound by the confines of your mortal body. You are fatally allergic to sunlight, and you must feed on the blood of humans. So many of us used to get killed in the early years, because it was difficult to get away with our business, especially when we sleep as if dead throughout the day. When mortals find our resting places, they do not hesitate to use the daylight hours to destroy us. That's why there aren't many Ancients.

"After the metamorphosis, however, vampires can change form with only a thought."

"Like turning into bats?"

"If one so desires. Bats, wolves, mist, shrubs. No one can hide from or escape an Ancient. And they are notoriously difficult to track down and kill during the daylight hours, since they can hide themselves wherever they like."

Sam looked to the wolf at Valen's side. "So, Raksha has your 'mark,' like Tonkowa did? What's that mean exactly?"

"We give our guardians, human or animal, our mark. It's a bond we form that allows the creature in question to link with us psychically. I can call to Raksha from great distances, and she can send me images as well. For creatures such as wolves, the mark inevitably raises their intelligence. I've never put my mark on a human. I always felt it was too much like slavery, but worse, because there is no escape. Slaves at least were able to live their own lives. They weren't *really* my property. They didn't know what I was or what horrors I endured."

"What about Daisy Jacobs?"

Valen was startled out of his train of thought. "Why are you still so interested in that particular slave?"

"I can't…"

"Sam, she's your ancestress…isn't she?"

Sam fought back tears unsuccessfully as he spoke. "Don't hurt my family. Kill me, but not my family. All they have are stories. No proof."

"Sam, I'm not going to hurt your family. No one in the Mines needs to know about them. Daisy saw me that night. I would have liked to speak to her about it, but things changed so fast. The Yankees came in the very next day. All of my slaves were run off in the attack. Most of the men joined the army. I never saw Daisy Jacobs again. I always wondered what happened to her; the slave who knew. It's almost like being given another chance tonight. It's so astounding that *you* are her descendant, because I wanted to explain it all to her. I would have told her exactly what I'm telling you. I would have trusted her with my secret."

"You wouldn't have killed her?"

"No."

"You wouldn't have given her your mark?"

"No. She would have had nothing to fear from me. As long as she never went into the Mines. I wouldn't have told her about the Mines of Sangra Dios. The Mines of the 'Blood Gods.'"

Valen lost himself in thought for a moment, then went on. "And the man she saw me kill…we have laws. We don't kill townspeople, unless we have to. We kill vagabonds, travelers with no connections in the town, harmful elements such as the serial killer last year. I killed *him* myself, by the way."

Sam was repulsed. "You really…you chopped him to pieces."

"It had to be done. A message had to be sent. I came back to Nightfire, because I was in trouble with the werewolves. A particular pack has sentenced me to die. More than a century ago, I was involved in the death of their leader. He was a monster by every conceivable definition of the word. I did it for Nightfire. At any rate, they just found out last October that I'd been involved. A friend helped to get me and Raksha back into Nightfire, where we'd be safe."

"Safe?"

"Werewolves can't enter Nightfire. They can't cross the borders."

"Why not?"

"Long story. And it's another matter entirely. Just know that I am safe here from werewolves. The serial killer was an acolyte of theirs; a human servant sent to frame me and turn the town against me, which is why he made vampirism his gimmick. He wanted the town to figure me out."

A thought occurred to Valen, as he remembered Daisy Jacobs. Sam had her eyes. Eyes that reflected a deep thirst for knowledge, a cunning mind that deserved every enlightenment he had to offer. He could see it now so clearly, and he wondered how he'd ever missed it before. "Sam, I need you to know, I only ever owned slaves because that's the way it was in the world. Rich men had slaves. It wasn't really questioned until recent centuries. I admit that I *personally* never really questioned it. But I never treated a slave as subhuman. It was just their lot. I was used to it. I educated them, which was absolutely not done in those days. It was said that slaves who could read would learn what they were missing. They would rebel. I'll be honest; I had a few who *would* have rebelled. I set them free. It's my nature, Sam. I care about people. I want to see all of their needs met. If a slave asked me for freedom, I saw no reason not to grant it. To me, slavery was their job. It was no different to me than the man who ran a shop, or the man who tempered steel. If any of those had decided to change vocations, why should I question it? So it was with slavery.

"I know that atrocities were committed by some slave owners. I know now that slavery on the *whole* was an atrocity. I'm glad it's over and 'gone with the wind' so to speak. It's just as easy for me to *pay* people to work for me anyway. As I said, I was simply used to the way things were. Many of my slaves actually returned after the war and did work for me. I paid them very well. Daisy Jacobs, of course, was not among them. She was terrified of me. As I'm sure you are, now that you know."

"I'm terrified of the ones in the Mines. I trust you, Valen."

Valen stood up, and Raksha whined. He walked over and sat beside Sam on the couch. "I can't blame you for fearing them. After all, they've called for your death, just as the werewolves have called for mine. The thing about me is, I always look out for my own. I'm also a vampire. This whole situation…" He looked down, forlorn. "I'm so sorry…"

"Sorry for what? It's not your fault," Sam tried to assure him.

Valen looked up suddenly, and Sam noticed his fangs for the first time, wondering how he'd ever missed them before. "I'm sorry you trusted me, Sam."

Valen grabbed Sam so quickly that the youth could not cry out or even react, as the vampire sank his fangs deep into his throat and fed.

I'm so sorry.

Chapter 11
Immortal Heart

Valen walked miserably through the passageway to the Mines of Sangra Dios. "Varney!" There was no hiding the sheer hatred in his voice.

The heartless vampire emerged from the shadows with a twisted grin on his face. "Well?"

Several other vampires appeared behind him.

Valen looked down. "It is done."

"What's that?" Varney feigned that he had not heard, gloating.

Valen looked up, fangs glistening in the tunnel's dim illumination, the blood of his victim fresh around his lips. "I said it is *done*!" Tears began streaming down his cheeks freely, and he turned and hid his face against the wall.

Varney nodded, almost feeling sorry for him. "You did right, Valentinus. You sided with your kind. I imagine you'll have some explaining to do." His grin returned. "We'll leave you to your thoughts."

Varney and the others were gone just as silently as they'd arrived, and Valen *was* left with his thoughts. It was the worst sort of torture the others could have sentenced him to. He felt dirty. He hadn't felt this miserable with guilt since that unthinkable night so many centuries ago, when Tobit had manipulated him into killing his own mother.

A mist appeared in the tunnel beside him, then took form. "You did the right thing, Valentinus. You had no choice."

Valen turned to Tristan. "How were any of the choices before me *right*?"

Tristan looked almost as pained as Valen himself. "You spared him. Spared him from *them*." He nodded down the corridor.

More tears fell from Valen's bloodshot eyes. "Perhaps." It was only a whisper. It was all he could manage.

Tristan put an arm around his shoulders and led him from the Mines, back into the light and warmth of the old Alexas Mansion. "Now let's see what we can do to make this place a little more presentable. You've got a party to host here tomorrow."

***

Tristan and Valen worked late into the night, right up until the sun was about to rise, preparing the mansion for visitors. Tristan handled the books, knowing that finishing the tasks in the library by himself would have set Valen over the edge, considering what those tattered tomes had only just been the cause of. He knew that Valen was likely to overreact, to burn the books or something else he'd regret deeply in a century or so. He kept a close eye on his friend, making sure he had no opportunity to escape and wait for the sunrise as he'd attempted to do a number of times in the past.

Valentinus was still so human. He still formed connections and suffered on behalf of the people he loved. Suicide was his solution when it seemed the pain was too much to bear—the guilt, the shame of things he'd done or caused to happed to his loved ones. He was lucky to have friends such as Tristan, who would never let him do it. Tristan did worry though that someday Valentinus would suffer silently and meet the sunrise without any warning whatsoever. He hoped that evil morning would never come.

Tristan himself never really bonded with humans. He'd been conditioned by the one who'd turned him, as it was written in their laws should be done. He did bond with other immortals, however, and the thought of ever losing Valentinus could make eternity unbearable, even for one with such a zest for life as himself. He hoped that one night Tobit, the vampiric devil who'd seen to it that Valen was so vulnerable, who'd created the monster that was D'artagnan, would be apprehended and punished for his crimes.

As for the mansion, there wasn't really all that much left to do, since Valentinus and Sam had seen to just about every detail. Mostly they "polished" things. And they talked, which Tristan saw as a very good sign.

By sunrise, Valen seemed better. He made no attempt to run outside and embrace a fiery death. Perhaps he'd decided that his responsibility to stay alive was too great, after the night's events. Tristan wondered how Valen was going to cover up what had happened. They certainly didn't have the option of dropping Sam off at his mother's again. Questions would be asked, and Valen would have to answer them, protecting the monsters of the Mines from any suspicion. Tristan kept these thoughts to himself, pleased to see such a rapid improvement in Valen and fearing to bring the younger vampire back down with such realities.

The following night, they both rose early. Tristan went out to hunt. Valen greeted the caterers and gave them free reign to answer the door and welcome the guests on his behalf. The room where Sam still lay was declared off limits, as was the entire wing, until the matter could be resolved later that night. How Valen dreaded that moment, but he kept his thoughts within, retreating to an outside balcony at the back of the house, listening to the guests arrive, and watching the moon cross the sky.

A bat flew across the moonlight then and came right up to Valen. He laughed in spite of himself. "You're joking."

The bat changed form, and Tristan joined him on the porch. "But of course." He laughed as well. "Just thought I'd try it out." He shook his head. "Can't imagine why anyone would choose *that* form on a nightly basis. I'd much rather be…a deer." His eyes lit at the prospect. "I'm so enjoying this new phase of life. It's exciting. It's limitless." He put a hand on Valen's shoulder. "Just a few more years, and we can maybe turn into a pair of bloodsucking whales and feed on pirates throughout the Atlantic."

Valen laughed. "That would be the life." He shook his head at Tristan's strange imagination.

"Now why haven't they ever made a horror movie about *that*?" Tristan mused. "I should make movies. I think it would be grand. I would just shoot at night and call it an artistic eccentricity. I have the money. I really should."

"Oh, I'm sure the market for vampire whale movies would explode."

"Quiet." Tristan laughed. "You're just mad because you didn't think of it yourself."

"You found me out."

Tristan joined Valen in gazing at the moon. "I love the movies. I go to the theatres often. They are the paintings of the twentieth century. But more. They're the ultimate art form. I want to open a movie house, so I can watch whatever I want, whenever I want. Do theatres have to return the films?"

"How should I know?" Valen answered. "I'd thought about buying the theatre we have here. I think it would be nice to expand it. It has so few screens that people sometimes have to drive all the way into Dallas to see the latest films. It's unreasonable."

"Oh, let's do it together! I could be the manager. It would be fun."

Valen scoffed affectionately. "Until you got bored. You'd have to stay put to run a business you know."

"This is true. Speaking of which, I think I must move on."

"I figured as much, old friend. You've saved me once again from utter doom. Your work is done."

Tristan met Valen's eyes with concern. "Are you sure? Are you going to be all right? You're not going to…"

"I'm fine." Valen was amused at the worry in the older vampire's voice. "This isn't like the last time. I've not been left with nothing. I would never let the sunlight or anything else take me from this earth under these present conditions. Think of the consequences to others."

"I'm glad."

Valen hugged Tristan fiercely. "Visit often."

"Of course. Now get to your party. The guests will be wondering at the lack of a host." He morphed into the perfect visage of Count Orlok, the antagonist from a 1920s silent vampire film, and flew away on giant butterfly wings, just a short distance, before vanishing once more into the mist.

Valen shook his head and rubbed his eyes, too stunned by the odd vision to react otherwise. "Such a grand imagination." He turned and opened the door, meeting the light and sound of a full Alexas Mansion for the first time in decades.

In the instant before he was noticed, Valen surveyed the crowd. The caterers and hired hosts were doing their jobs magnificently. Everyone seemed to have food or drink in hand, and the rooms and other parts of the house not to be disturbed were subtly blocked off by the presence of the hirelings.

Valen studied the faces, recognizing a number of people that he'd encountered during his eight months back in Nightfire. He saw Angelina Cody admiring the curtains in the living room, while her husband, the sheriff, rolled his eyes behind her, shaking his head with tolerant affection. Alf Gardner and his wife Rebecca were there, though nowhere near their daughter Doris. They were in the company, however, of Wallace and Emmy Preston, the parents of Mati and Helen Preston. He spotted Mati not far from them, standing arm in arm with Dirk Arnold, who seemed to be subtly urging her to get some distance away from his own parents, Fred and Bette.

Other faces he picked out in the crowd were the police officers Bea Jurgens and Earl King, the high school math teacher Ted Krandall and his wife, historian and author of *The History of Nightfire, Texas* and *Founding Families of Nightfire and Their Descendants*, Elizabeth Krandall. He saw Beth Green gossiping with the editor-in-chief of *The Nightfire Chronicle*, Tom Johnson, and his wife Abigail. He noticed Barley and Lucy Paul, descendants of a Methodist preacher who'd lived in Nightfire during the nightmarish Wererwolf Plague of 1850; Barney and Wilma Hildebrandt—Barney a descendant of the town doctor from that same era; Darla Ann Jacobson, owner of a little diner called Darla's Lunch Box; James Parker, Mayor Delmar Strongbow, Jack Mason and his sons Robert and Jeffrey, along with the older son's new wife Barbara, and the immense Santana family seemed to be there in its entirety. Ned Tyler seemed to be ignoring Rufus ("Old Man") Morris as the other man spoke, instead giving his attention over to flirting with a couple of sixteen-year-old girls. Reverend Bob Michaels was there, as were the Joneses: Carl, Susan, and their daughter Eleanor. Gordon Kile and his very pregnant wife Melensy were giving a few people an impromptu tour of all the work Gordon's crew had done to make the mansion presentable. Still, all the people that Valen recognized were dwarfed in number by the people that he had never met.

"Big turn-out, wouldn't you say?"

Valen turned and smiled at the pungently filthy man before him. "Tips?"

One of the hired hosts rushed up to them. "I'm sorry, sir, we're going to have to ask you to leave." He put a hand, hesitantly, on the filthy man's ragged sleeve.

"Nonsense," Valen decreed. "This man is a local celebrity. Don't you read the paper?"

"Yes, sir. I just thought…well, he's an indigent."

"Not for the duration of our festivities." Valen winked.

The hired host nodded apologetically to both men and resumed his duties.

Valen addressed his old friend warmly. "It amazes me that you're still living like this, Tips. I'd have thought you'd have grown up by now. Two hundred years old and still a worthless bum." Valen laughed.

"They couldn't prove it y'know," Tips said. "That bit in the paper was just for fun. They treated me like I was crazy."

"You have this unexplained gift of *naturally* unending youth. You could have done anything or been anything you wanted by now, yet you live on the street, a non-participant, in a town that doesn't even make the maps. You *are* crazy."

The man shrugged. "I just like to watch."

Valen laughed. Tips looked rough and time-worn, but what people didn't know was that if he'd shaved and cleaned himself up, he would have looked about twenty-five. And he actually *was* two centuries old. He'd befriended Valen when the town was new, and the two of them had eventually caught on to each other's secrets. Tips was homeless by choice, but Valentinus had declared him off limits to the Vampires of Nightfire. The mystery of Tips was that he'd simply stayed young. There was no curse, no Fountain of Youth, behind it. He'd just stopped aging. Valen had always liked the man, though he never understood him. "It's good to see you're still the man I knew, Tips."

Tips winked. "Back at you, Mr. Alexas." He made his way back into the crowd, horrifying several guests at the punch bowl with his stench.

"You really have gone all out." Another timeless face approached.

"Harry!" Valen then noticed the other deceptively young-looking man approaching behind the first. "Jack! I'm glad you could make it. No one else from the 'family' would have dared."

Harry shrugged. "We like people."

"Always have." Jack added with a snicker. "Almost a shame we need to eat them and all."

At one hundred-sixty, Harry and Jack were the youngest of the vampires in the Mines and never failed to live up to their reputation as insolent, boisterous young pranksters. Valen had always liked them. "It's good to have you here. Just don't spike the punch." He looked out into the crowd again and sighed. "I'd better get out there and start mingling. I had no idea we'd have such a turnout."

"Yeah, it's a real party all right." Jack laughed.

Harry put a hand on Valen's shoulder. "Do let us know if you need any help." He nodded towards the hallway that was off limits—the hallway that held the room where Sam was. "We know it's not been easy for you."

Valen nodded sadly, appreciatively. "Thanks, Harry. I will if there is a need." He made his way into the crowd.

"What I'm saying, Mayor Strongbow, is that the roads are impossible to drive on. They tear our cars to pieces." Carmilla Franklin was on the job. Carmilla Franklin was *always* on the job.

"So move." Scott Beatty sneered at the woman from behind the mayor. "Your choice to stay there."

Carmilla turned on the young man wrathfully. "Listen, here, child! I *could* move. I could move right out of this racist little town, but then who would stand up for my neighbors! Most of the folks I represent couldn't afford to move even to another part of Nightfire. Why? Because all the good jobs go to whites. It's a crying shame that in a town this small there should be such an economic divide between the white part of town and the Black part of town, but it's there plain as day. The economic divide is the same as the racial divide. And I won't rest until it's made right. Starting with our pot holes! That's a city issue. The town council should finance the repairs, whether they need to be made on their own lily white doorsteps or somewhere else. We *all* pay our taxes."

"Ms. Franklin," the mayor spoke tensely. "Carmilla," he amended, emphasizing the informal air he wanted for the evening. "This is hardly the place for our debates to pick up. This is a party. We're here to enjoy ourselves." He gestured with an arm to the house itself. "We're here to enjoy the fact that one of our citizens has restored a part of town history for us." He noticed Elizabeth Krandall showing a scrap book to someone. "See? Look at Liz. She brought a scrap book with articles from the past hundred and twenty plus years relating to *this house.* This house is what we're here for."

"Don't you dismiss me, Mayor Strongbow!"

"I'm not dismissing you, Carmilla. I'm just pointing out that this is not a Town Council meeting."

"The Town Council is here, aren't they? We are all *meeting*, aren't we?"

The mayor sighed, "Carmilla…"

"Mayor Strongbow…"

"Call me Del. We're *not* in session."

"I'm always in session. Until I get justice for *all.* And *this house* is the *only* reason *I* came here tonight as well."

"You'd better watch yer damn mouth, Mammy."

Carmilla spun around towards the new voice so fast that it confounded the minds of all who saw it, especially considering her three hundred-fifty pounds of sheer determination. "Who the *hell* is speaking to *me* in that tone like they have the right to?"

James Parker continued, a look of utter contempt painting his face. "Just so you know. Ain't safe to be so uppity in this town no more."

"*Uppity*?" Carmilla shook her head and turned away, deciding that his comment had been so inappropriate and so grammatically offensive, that she'd cut the speaker deepest by not engaging him at all. "Mayor Strongbow…let's get back to our roads."

"Just sayin'," James went on behind her. "There's a certain organization in town has yer name on their list. Might give you a big ol' present some day *real* soon."

Carmilla spun back around and jabbed her finger at the man's face. "Are you threatening me? Because if you are, you've got another thing coming, sonny boy! I am *not* one to be trifled with!"

James looked away and smirked. "You're a fat bitch."

Two hands fell on James' shoulders. One of the two men now behind him said, "Mr. Alexas would like you to leave."

"Come with us," said the other man.

"Who the hell are you two?" James tried to break from their grip but found himself incapable.

"I'm Harry, answered one."

"I'm Jack," said the other.

Harry came around to face James, locking eyes with his, watching James' own eyes glaze over as he subdued him. "And you're not welcome here anymore."

"Besides," Jack added, as he came around and looked intensely into James' eyes, burning a command there with all of his will, "you've soiled yourself. You're a disgrace."

James looked down and found that he was wetting himself uncontrollably. "Oh, shit! How the hell…?"

"Come on," Harry commanded. The two "young" vampires each grabbed a shoulder and carried the man to the front door, throwing him unceremoniously from the porch to the yard. Everyone who'd seen the state of James Parker began whispering and giggling at once.

The two vampires returned to an astonished Carmilla Franklin. Harry spoke up with a grin. "We apologize on behalf of Mr…"

"Thank you, boys," Valen interrupted as he approached. "I can apologize on my own behalf." He winked at Jack. They nodded and melted back into the crowd. He caught Carmilla's eyes. "I am very sorry for that. I would have come to dispatch the man myself, but the Santanas had just put two babies in my arms." He laughed.

"Thank you, Mister Alexas." Carmilla, still amazed that she'd been rescued, offered her hand.

He took it. "Valen. It's a pleasure to meet you, Miss Franklin. I've heard so much about you."

"Carmilla." She smiled.

"Now what's all this talk about roads?" Valen asked, looking at the mayor.

Mayor Strongbow tried to blow it off, shaking his head. "It's a Town Council matter. Not something we need to discuss here. She's relentless, really."

"From what I've been told, it sounds like she has to be." He looked at Carmilla. "You'll be the first to hear this, Carmilla." He looked back to Mayor Strongbow. "I'm setting up a foundation first thing Monday morning. The Samuel Turner Foundation, to be used towards the betterment of buildings and roads in the more neglected parts of town." Turning his attention back towards Carmilla, he added, "I'd be very sad, if you weren't serving as the director of the board for this foundation, Miss Franklin. I need someone that I can trust to use it correctly. I wouldn't hand over several million dollars to just anyone."

"Several mi…" She put a hand to her chest. "I'm overwhelmed."

Valen smiled, satisfied.

"Who is Samuel Turner," Mayor Strongbow asked. His voice gushed with relief at having the issue settled at last without any commitment on one side or the other from his own office.

"A friend from Willow Bend Road." Valen looked directly at Carmilla. "A young man who continues to open my eyes. Let me know if there is anything else I can ever do for your cause, Carmilla."

She forced herself to say it. She had come to the housewarming for a single purpose, but she'd expected to be stating it in anger. Instead, it came out humbly. "The slave quarters."

Valen was taken off guard. He looked at her quizzically. "Yes?"

"Tear them down. That's all I came to ask you tonight. You fixed up this whole place and brought it into the 1970s." The passion began returning to her voice as she remembered her purpose. "This house is a symbol now. A symbol of something new. A brand new day for Nightfire. But the slave quarters out back; you left them untouched. Not restored, not torn down…just *there*. They too are a symbol. A symbol for a town that hasn't let go of the past. A symbol of a past where people were treated like animals because of the color of their skin. I'm asking you, as a gesture to the descendants of the slaves who lived in those buildings…tear them down."

Valen felt ashamed that he had never thought of it. Why had he left them untouched? Why did he feel reluctant to get rid of them? Was he holding on to the past as well? Did he, on some level, relish the days when buying human beings was a matter of course? He met Carmilla's humble, expectant stare. "Done."

As he said this, the people in the room who'd been close enough to listen in on the conversation began whispering and gasping; some with respect, others in horror.

For a woman who'd had to fight with all her strength for every victory, the ease of her success at Alexas Mansion simply knocked the ground from beneath Carmilla's feet. "Thank you," she breathed, as she managed to find a couch just behind her to fall into. She looked up at Valen. "Would you introduce me?"

"Introduce you?"

"To Samuel Turner. I'd like to meet him."

Valen looked away, then nodded once in her direction with a smile, not saying a word.

Carmilla smiled, taking it as a yes. When Valen had left them, she raised up her arms and said, "Hallelujah! Thank you, God! I'll be in church this Sunday!" The mayor laughed and sat in the chair beside her, congratulating her on her incredible victory, assuring her that he'd had her back behind the scenes all along.

Ray arrived at Alexas Mansion with Bradley, Helen, Brendan, and Kate. Brendan and Kate made a dash for the snack bar and the punch, and Ray slipped away into the crowd, letting Bradley and

Helen wander off without him. He searched frantically for Dori and Jenny, hoping to avoid them both.

"You're Ray Don!"

Ray turned, irritated by the man's loud voice, and saw an unfamiliar face. "And you are…?"

"Sorry," the man laughed apologetically and offered his hand. "Ben." When Ray looked puzzled, the man added, "Jenny's brother?"

"Oh! Hi." Ray took Ben's hand and shook it with forced enthusiasm, as he searched the space behind the man for Jenny.

Noticing, Ben guessed, "You must be wondering where Jenny is." He chuckled. "She's actually looking for *you.* She's told me all about you. Frankly, I'm grateful to you. She's really needed a distraction lately from all the stuff with our uncle."

"I understand that completely. I've got things of my own to get away from. She's a great girl." Ray was still looking *around* Ben, rather than at him.

"Ray! There you are!"

Ray turned in horror to find Doris Gardner smiling at him and rushing towards him. She jumped at him and wrapped her arms around his neck, but Ray pulled away quickly. He looked to Ben. "This is Doris Gardner…a friend of mine from way back."

Dori gave Ray a weird look but was cut off from asking him anything when Ben broke into her thoughts. "I'm Ben. Good to meet you."

Dori looked him up and down, impressed by his broad shoulders and muscular chest. She grinned in that oh-so-Doris Gardner way of hers. "I haven't seen you before. Where do you fit into the picture, muscles?"

Ben laughed. "I'm Jenny's brother."

"I'm sorry?"

"Jenny." He looked at Ray. "You know, she's…"

Ray saw no other way out. He fell into a sudden and completely contrived coughing fit, bending over double.

"Oh my god." Ben stepped back and looked to Dori. "Is he all right?"

Dori shrugged and put an arm around Ray's shoulders. "Ray, you okay?"

Ray affected a scratchy, coughy sounding voice. "Yeah. I think something just went down the wrong pipe. I'll be all right. Could you go get me some water?"

"Sure. Be right back." Dori rushed off into the crowd, searching for one of the caterers.

"I'd better go look myself," Ray wheezed. "Dori gets distracted pretty easily."

"I got distracted by *her*." Ben grinned. "Is she seeing anyone?"

A million territorial replies came into Ray's head, and he had to fight them all down against his truer nature. "Not that I'm aware of. I can probably get her number for you."

Ben nodded thoughtfully. "I…yeah. Could you? I mean…ask if she'd mind."

"Sure." Ray started up a cough. "I'll be back." He backed away apologetically.

As soon as he felt he was out of sight of Ben, he straightened up and tried to find the nearest door. Nephilim be damned, he decided, coming to this party was the worst idea he'd ever had.

"Ray! There you are!" Jenny was delighted to have finally found him in the crowd.

"Shit!"

"What?"

"Nothin'. Stubbed my toe. What's up, Jenny?" Now Ray looked all around for Dori, hoping she hadn't spotted him. A few people moved enough that he could see Ben again, and, to his horror, Dori holding a cup of water and speaking with him.

"What's wrong, tiger? You look pale."

Inspiration! "I'm…not feeling well. I think I got a bad cracker."

"A bad *cracker*?" She laughed and leaned over, kissing him on the lips.

Ray shot backwards and found Dori again. She hadn't turned to see him. Just then, Ben saw him and pointed at him with a friendly smile. Dori turned to see him as well. "Gotta go!"

"But…" Jenny was bewildered.

"Bathroom." Ray bolted. He was across the room in an instant, asking one of the hired hosts, "Bathroom?" The man pointed, and Ray saw an open door. He ran for it and got there just as Juan and Rubin Santana's grandmother stepped inside and locked the door behind her, likely for a much longer visit than would work for Ray. Panicked, he turned around and searched for something, anything, to get him out of the mess he had created for himself. He saw Valen and rushed up to him. "Dracula! How many bathrooms in this place?"

Valen saw the look of panic on Ray's face, then started to point, but saw the closed door and understood. "Upstairs."

Ray ran for it. As soon as he got to the top of the stairs, he decided the only open door must lead to the bathroom. Finding that he was right, he locked himself inside and said, "Shit," approximately thirty times. He tried the window and found it wouldn't budge. He sat down on the toilet lid and said, "Shit," again. As he sat there, wondering how he was going to survive this particular misadventure, he heard the faintest sound of violin music playing somewhere in the great, old house.

Helen held the guitar awkwardly, as she sat with Bradley on the fireplace. She began to strum.

"No." Bradley said flatly. "Why?"

"Why not? I used to play."

"No, you didn't. You used to try." He sighed and laughed in good humor. "Why don't you get Ray to help you?"

"I asked him, while you were getting ready. He said, 'Never again. Not since Donny.' I realized he hasn't so much as touched a guitar since he got back to Nightfire."

Bradley nodded. "Yeah. He and Donny used to play all the time. Remember their band?"

"The Wham-Bam Cockatoos!" Helen laughed, remembering. "Where did they ever come up with that name?"

Bradley shrugged. "I don't know. The surprising thing was always how good they sounded. But Ray says that he won't play the guitar or sing without Donny. Donny's dead. So…never again. He especially gets worked up over 'Let It Be.' Turns off the radio if it comes on. I think that was, like, their song."

"Oh, that's so cute. Ray's so cute." Helen sighed, dreamily.

Bradley saw Dori and stood up, waving her over. Helen barely noticed, as she *attempted* to tune her guitar and got lost in thoughts of Ray.

"Have either of you seen Ray?" Dori asked, an odd look on her face.

Bradley shrugged. "Not since we got here. I don't know where he got off to."

"Hm." Dori's eyes narrowed thoughtfully. "I'll go ask Valen."

Once she had gone, Bradley sat back beside Helen. "That's just retarded. If Ray really cared about her, he wouldn't let her out of his sight. A girl like Dori…I just don't see how he could." He stared after Dori, as she slowly vanished from sight in the mass of human traffic that surrounded them.

Helen perked up. "I know! And how could *she* lose track of *him*! I mean, really! Ray's just so hot! If I were Dori I'd be staring at him every minute."

Bradley laughed. "You already do."

"Yeah, well, you do the same with Dori."

Bradley laughed. "Yeah." He looked at Helen. "At least *we* don't have any problems like that. We've got each other pretty good."

"Yeah."

"So…" Bradley ventured. "I bet there're a lot of empty rooms in this place. You wanna…"

Helen didn't even look up from her guitar as she smacked him in the head with all her strength and went on tuning.

"Can't blame a guy for trying." Bradley cocked his head like a dog. "Is that violin music?"

Helen stopped tuning and listened. "I think so. Yeah. See? I told you it wasn't dumb to bring my guitar. If I can just get it in tune, maybe I can go and play backup."

Bradley shook his head. "No. You really, *really* couldn't." He smiled at her.

She smacked him in the head once more; then went on with her tuning.

"I don't mind it really. I take it as a compliment."

Rosemary Strongbow spoke in her most condescendingly polite tone, "Well, I can assure you that I would take it as an insult if anyone ever referred to me as 'Rosemary the Witch.'"

Mary Jean Donovan cackled quietly. "You're the mayor's wife. What makes you think that they *don't*?"

There she is. Valen approached his friend urgently. "Mary Jean, would you come with me for a moment?"

Rosemary Strongbow looked aghast that a man so socially prominent as Valen Alexas would actually be *familiar* with a common trailer house psychic. Mary Jean noticed this happily. "Certainly."

As soon as the two of them had found a relatively quiet corner, Valen whispered, "Can you hear it?"

Mary Jean paused, wondering which of the hundred million sounds she was supposed to be picking out of the party's ambiance. She recognized it suddenly. "The violin music?"

"Yes."

"It's not one of your hired people?"

"No. I didn't hire any violinists."

"Where is Raksha? Have you noticed anything in her behavior?"

Valen shook his head, verging on impatience. "No. She's with…Sam."

"Where is Sam?"

"Mary Jean…I can't. Why is he doing this to me? Why is he haunting me?"

"I think you must know, Valen. You have more answers than you let yourself realize."

"I have to find him."

"He's a ghost, Valen. Don't sacrifice your time with the living to spend time with the dead. His days are in the past. Enjoy the party. There will be a time to confront Augustin and his sister, so that they can move on and leave us behind. Don't forget that. This is not the time. It isn't *their* time."

"I wish I could see things as black and white as you present them. Unfortunately, that music is going to drive me mad."

"I don't like this, Valen. Let it go. Consider it a gift from a long gone friend, and just enjoy the music."

"But people keep asking me about it."

"Tell them something noncommittal. Tell them the identity of the violinist is a secret. They'll enjoy the mystery and speculate on who it was for years"

"It's no mystery to me. I have to find him." Valen left her abruptly to follow the music. Mary Jean simply sighed and shook her head helplessly.

***

Ray started at the urgent knock on the door. "Whoever's in there, hurry up!"

Recognizing the voice, Ray opened the door just a crack. "Sam?"

"Move it, Ray! I gotta go *bad*!" Sam pushed his way through, and Ray was forced to step aside.

"You sure get strong when you have to take a piss. Where have you…?" he shook his head. "Never mind. Just tell me where else I can hide in this place. You know it better than any of us."

"Three doors down on the right. Guest room. Nobody's there." *How do I know that? I can see it. It's all so big…Raksha's in there.* "I gotta go, Ray." *She's going down the hall now. This is too weird.*

"See ya." Ray hurried out of the bathroom and down the hall, closing the door to the guest room behind him. He noticed to his chagrin that there was no lock on the door. Suddenly it opened. "Doris!"

She laughed at his panicked state. "Saw you come in. Thought I'd take advantage. So what the hell's going on?"

"Just feeling kind of sick." He noticed the bed. "Sam said I could come in here and lay down." He eyed the door nervously. "'Course, now that you're here, I'm starting to feel a whole lot better. Why don't you shut the door?"

She grinned mischievously and did as he asked. She walked over to him, put her arms around him, and kissed him deeply. Ray found himself taking comfort in her presence now. They were alone. No one would think to look for him here. He was safe. He slowly led her closer to the bed, unzipping her dress and pulling it down below her shoulders.

The door opened. Ray and Dori both looked to the now occupied entryway. Ray's face was pure shock. Dori's was amusement, with a hint of utter disgust. Tears filled Jenny's eyes, as she slammed the door and left them behind her, perhaps forever for all Ray knew.

Dori smiled at Ray, pushing gently away from him as she shook her head. "I *knew* it."

"Dori…I…"

She slapped him across the face with unexpected ferocity, walked through the door, and slammed it behind her.

Ray exhaled dramatically, as he held a hand to his burning face. He sat on the bed and miserably groaned out the only word that could find form amidst the whirlpool of thoughts and emotions now bombarding his consciousness, "Shit."

The recently slammed door opened one more time. Sam walked in and shook his head at the miserable sight of Ray. He offered a sigh of exasperated, weary knowing and sat beside him on the bed, putting a hand on the other man's shoulder. "You're an ass hole of the highest magnitude, Ray." He shook his head. "But I'm still your friend."

For some reason not clear to Ray at that moment, the words of his friend brought tears to his eyes, and he simply let them fall.

Valen climbed the stairs, trembling, as the music grew louder. Would he finally see him again, after all these lonely decades? Would he finally be reunited with Augustin? He thought back to the previous times that he had followed the sound of his lost love's music only to find an empty room. This time felt different. There was an *electricity* in the air.

A door opened, and Clarissa Jordan walked through, approaching him with her hands behind her back.

Valen absently took notice of her. "Clarissa, I'd been looking for you…" Suddenly he felt as though he'd been punched, and an ice cold feeling of fear took hold of his gut. Clarissa had always looked like Clarenda. There shouldn't have been anything shocking about that. But there was. She looked somehow *more* like her late relative than ever before; but it wasn't just looks. It was the way she was walking. That bitter grin on her face.

"What's the matter, Valentinus?" She smiled.

"Clarenda…" Valen was horrified. This was no ghost. He felt his feet frozen in fear at the top of the stairs. It felt like hours, as his mind slowly realized what had happened, as his body struggled to react, to lift his feet and turn back down the stairs, to call out for help; but the horror of the vision before him was too great. He stood there, helpless, as she revealed the kitchen knife she'd been hiding behind her back and lunged at him.

Valen's voice quavered, as he managed to blurt out a single, whispered cry, "Clarenda…!" He was silenced harshly and unforgivingly, as the knife sliced through the flesh and bone of his chest and lodged in his heart.

The moment that followed seemed eternal.

In a single heartbeat, five hundred years passed before his eyes. He remembered his mother and father, the beautiful skies and shorelines of his childhood Spain, his bitter relationship with D'artagnan and Tobit, all the pain and loss…all the quiet moments of peace, the friendships that followed, his years with the Aztecs, travels with Julius, helping to found Nightfire, his relationship with Clarenda and Augustin, the pain and loss, the joy…the recovery that followed, Julius and Tristan never letting him go, adventures with Tex, earning a werewolf death mark, returning to Nightfire…Sam…

The whirlwind stopped, and it was over. He felt nothing, and he felt it profoundly. The world went dark. His ears heard sounds as though in a dream, and all they heard were screams. He struggled to make out voices and words, but his body failed him, and his immortal heart at long last ceased its beating.

CHAPTER 12
INTO THE LIGHT

The howl of an anguished wolf filled the night, and was followed halfway through by the terrified screams of nearly everyone present at Alexas Mansion, in that horrible moment when Valen Alexas was stabbed through the heart at the top of the stairs.

"Clarenda! No!" Sam staggered to his feet in one of the guest rooms as it happened, paling and trembling, clutching his chest. He caught Ray's eyes, as the other man sat nonplussed on the bed. "I'm…sorry…Clarenda…" Sam collapsed on the floor.

Ray jumped up. "Jesus! What the hell is happening?" He shook Sam, trying to get a response, but none came.

At the top of the stairs, Clarissa Jordan came to her senses and stared at the knife in one terrible, drawn out instant, as the blood fell from the blade and Valen toppled backwards, lifelessly, tumbling down the stairs and collapsing in a broken heap on the landing. She heard the wolf howl. She noticed the horror painted on the faces of all the guusts as they stared up at her. A man's voice right beside her rang out, "*Clarenda no! No!*" She turned her head right and left, but saw no one. She stared back at the masses below, as if in a nightmare. She screamed out in panic, "I didn't do it!" She dropped the knife and fell to her knees, sobbing, holding both trembling hands to her face.

Sheriff Cody and two of his men ran towards her. "Stay back. Everybody move back. Earl, call an ambulance. Dirk, cuff that crazy bitch and drag her the hell out of here right now." *I didn't do it?* Sheriff Cody shook his head in bewilderment. He'd heard some stupid justifications in his time as sheriff, but that one definitely took the cake. *Stab a man in the chest in front of hundreds of people, then tell them all that you didn't do it.* If Will Cody hadn't been so horrified by the scenario, he was sure that he'd have laughed.

As the sound of sirens grew closer to the mansion and the wild-eyed, screaming form of Clarissa Jordan was dragged in handcuffs from the house, Bradley Stevens came out of the upstairs bathroom, zipping his pants as he left in a hurry to find out what all the ruckus was about. The first thing he saw was Ray, pale as snow, emerging from one of the bedrooms. "Bradley! Help!" Ray was always uncomfortable with that word. He said it again, just to be sure he'd gotten it right. "Help! I don't know what to do!"

Frightened by Ray's uncharacteristic state, Bradley followed him into the room and found Sam lying on the floor. "Sam!" He knelt by his friend and tried to rouse him. He looked up at Ray. "What happened?"

"I don't know *what* the hell happened out *there*, but when everyone started screaming, Sam clutched his chest, said some weird shit, then collapsed. I can't get him to wake up."

Just then, Sam opened his eyes tiredly. "Bradley…it's real. It's all real."

"What the fuck?" Ray was certain that Sam had lost his mind, but he was powerless to explain how or why. The siren was right outside the mansion, then it was off. "What's happening out there?"

"Ambulance. For Valen," Sam croaked.

"What?" Ray looked helplessly to Bradley, but saw no help in the young man's frightened eyes.

Sam's head began to clear, and he realized he'd been talking. He looked to Ray. "Please, get me some water. I'm all right."

Thrilled to have something helpful to do in the situation, Ray moved like lightening from the room. "Right back."

When he was gone, Sam grabbed Bradley's arm. "Bradley, they can't take him to the hospital."

"Who? Valen? Sam, what's going on?"

"He's hurt. They're taking him to a hospital. He's being loaded onto the gurney right now. But they can't take him there."

"Why not?" Bradley was mostly humoring his friend, who appeared to be talking nonsense, but there was something about the way Sam was speaking that made him sound perfectly sane. It chilled Bradley to the bone, so he waited earnestly for Sam's reply.

Sam saw it all through hazy vision. *Raksha. She's waking up too.* He saw the mayor moving to stop them from loading Valen onto the gurney, but he was stopped by two men. *No, they're not men. They're like Valen. The mayor can't tell the medics. He can't reveal their secret.* He saw understanding on the mayor's face. Sadness on the faces of the vampires. *They can't help him.* At last he answered Bradley. "Valen's different. They can't take him to the hospital. They can't learn his secret."

"What secret?"

Sam knew he had to say something. He had to save Valen. He had to say something to Bradley before Ray got back. He trusted Bradley. Valen would have trusted Bradley too. Still, words failed him. How could he tell *anyone* such a truth as needed to be spoken? In lieu of words, he simply gave Bradley an urgent, desperate look, conveying his message through the sheer intensity of his eyes.

Realization struck Bradley like a punch to the gut. "You mean…?"

"It's all true. The journals…the picture my great-grandmother drew…" Sam could only whisper, "He's a vampire."

Bradley backed up, eyes wide with terror. "Then…Sam…what's happened to you? Did he…?"

"No. He's good. He saved me. Saved me from *them*…now we have to save *him*. He won't hurt us. Would never hurt his friends…"

"Sam…I…" Bradley though back to everything Sam had told him about the weirdness surrounding Valen Alexas. He remembered the kindness that Valen had shown him months before, when his mother had been murdered. Valen had never done anything to harm any of them. But a vampire? It couldn't be; but Sam was lying there, suddenly completely insane otherwise. Dismissing the possibility of madness would mean that Sam was seeing everything that was happening to Valen as it occurred, and Bradley saw only one way to learn the truth for himself. "I believe you," he said. "What do we do?"

Sam pushed himself up off of the floor. "We have to get to your car."

"Are you sure about this?" Bradley asked excitedly from behind the wheel. They had maneuvered through all of the other parked vehicles on the Alexas property to get the ambulance in their sights. The doors on the medical vehicle had just been closed, locking Valen inside for his journey to the hospital, where he would either be discovered right away or simply burn up in the sunlight when the relentless first light of dawn came in through his hospital window. Either way, according to Sam, the secret of Nightfire's vampires would be out. The mansion would be turned upside down. The others would be discovered in the Mines. And if that were to happen, no one could say what the outcome would be. Only that it wouldn't be good for *anyone*.

"Desperate times, Bradley."

"Right. You're right. We can't let him make it to the hospital." *You better not be crazy, Sam.*

The ambulance was moving, siren once again sounding out. "Go!"

Bradley hit the gas and took off after the ambulance, leaving a trail of dust between his car and Alexas Mansion.

"Go faster! We have to catch up!"

"I've got the gas pedal down to the floor, man! What else can I do?" Another siren joined in with that of the ambulance. "Great! I guess not every cop in Nightfire was at that party."

"Don't slow down," Sam urged.

"We're not gonna catch up with that ambulance, Sam!" Bradley didn't let off of the gas pedal as they continued racing down Nightfire's nearly empty streets, now pursued by the local police. "Wait! I know a shortcut."

"Huh?"

"We'll cut 'em off up ahead." Bradley turned suddenly down another street, tires squealing, a hubcap flying off of one of his tires and rolling right up to slam into someone's front door. The police car stayed on them.

"Right." Sam said. "Assuming we aren't too busy struggling to stay comfortable in our new handcuffs. And trust me, they *aren't* comfortable."

"I've got this. Hear that? We're ahead of them. If we can just make it before they pass at the next intersection…" Bradley couldn't push the gas pedal down any farther, but he added pressure anyway, as if willing the car to go faster would do the trick.

"We can't hit the drivers."

"Don't worry. I know what I'm doing."

"Do this often, do you?"

"Shut up. There…!"

The next instant was the loudest, most horrible instant of Bradley's life up to that point. Through sheer dumb luck, they hit the ambulance precisely where they'd hoped to, at the tail end, from the side. Both vehicles spun wildly out of control. Bradley watched, battling to take back control of the steering wheel, as the ambulance flipped over onto its side and continued to spin. Amazingly, Bradley's car stayed right-side-up and, once again through sheer dumb luck, didn't hit anything other than a lamp post, which they heard crumpling the rear end of the car like a soda can.

The two teenagers sat there in perfect silence, the ambulance facing them as it lay on its side up ahead. Bradley, feeling like more of an idiot with every passing second, prayed to God fiercely that no one had been hurt.

The police car had come to a screeching halt in the center of the intersection, miraculously not having been hit by either of the out of control vehicles as they'd spun away in opposite directions. Bradley finally spoke as he saw the doors open on either side of the police vehicle. "Oh, shit."

Bradley and Sam both got out of the car and started running to the ambulance.

"Freeze!" One of the policemen shouted in an unmistakable state of rage. "Stop *right* where you are."

Sam and Bradley noticed the guns and did as the men said. The police ran up to them. "What were you *thinking*!?"

Bradley stammered. "He's our friend. We had to get to the hospital..."

"We wanted to beat them there..." Sam added.

"*Idiots!*" The policeman shouted. "You better hope to *God* that everyone on that ambulance is okay. Don't move!" The two officers ran over to the fallen ambulance and began helping people out. The quiet one ran back to the car and called for another ambulance.

Bradley felt faint. *I've killed people. I was driving. I did it. I'm going to jail for life.*

"We did it." Sam smiled.

Bradley looked at Sam as though the other young man had just escaped from the nut house.

The two policemen met right by the two young men. Three paramedics were now sitting on the curb near the ambulance. "I called it in, Larry. They're sending another ambulance to check everybody out. Wrecker's on its way for the cars."

"Ours is drivable," Bradley offered.

"Yours is *impounded*," the much angrier officer countered. "Who was driving?"

"I was," Bradley answered weakly.

"You almost *killed* three paramedics." He shook his head. "God only knows what happened to your friend."

The other cop looked puzzled, "What do you mean?"

"He's gone. There was no one but an unconscious paramedic in the back. I would say the body was thrown, but the doors were locked."

"Gone?" the other police officer asked in unison with Bradley and Sam.

"That's what I said, Dick. Gone."

Bradley was starting to feel better about his situation. "So…impounded?"

The officer looked at Sam. "You have a license?"

"No."

He looked back to Bradley. "Then, yeah, kid. We're impounding it. First you're going to the hospital to take care of that injury. Then, I'm taking you to jail."

Injury? Jail isn't such a surprise…but injury? Bradley put a hand to his forehead then, and when he took it down noticed that it was covered in blood. "I must've hit it while we were spinning around. I…" He started to feel more lightheaded than before.

"Well, you're walking. You'll be fine. Meanwhile, I'm placing you under arrest for…"

And that was the last Bradley heard of it, as the ground came up to meet him.

"She's out cold," Sheriff Cody explained to Ted and Elizabeth Krandall. "We gave her some sedatives to calm her down. There's no question whether or not she did it, but we'll still have to ask her some questions when she comes to. You might want to go ahead and arrange for an attorney. But like I said, it's not a matter of whether or not she stabbed Valen Alexas. It's a matter of whether or not it's *attempted* homicide or just plain homicide. I doubt the man's gonna pull through, frankly. I've seen stab wounds before. She got him right in the heart. To be honest, I was shocked when they didn't put a sheet over his head right there."

Ted held his wife as she sobbed onto his chest. "This just doesn't add up," he said. "They were friends. There was nothing suspicious in the way she talked about him. She had nothing but fond feelings for him. She just *wouldn't* try to kill him. It has to have been an accident."

Sheriff Cody shook his head sadly, but was stopped from responding by a startling sound.

"And so it was." Valen Alexas was propping himself up against the wall on his shoulder, very visibly catching his breath. His clothes were tattered and filthy as though he'd been on the street for a week. The blood from his wound was still strikingly red on his shirt, though it had been torn to the side by the paramedics as they'd treated him. "I won't be pressing charges."

Sheriff Cody sprang to his feet. "Why the *hell* aren't you at the hospital?"

Valen waved him off as he staggered forward. "I'm fine, I assure you. I had to get down here, before things got out of hand, and let you know what really happened. Before charges are brought up."

"Well, Valen, you can't really say anything about it. This is attempted homicide. It's out of your hands. We investigate either way. The charges aren't yours to bring up."

Valen sighed. "Do you find it odd, Sheriff Cody, that Nightfire seems to have certain legal 'anomalies' that other towns lack. I believe you encountered some of them when you were wrapping up your investigation of the 'Vampire Murders' last fall, if I'm not completely mistaken."

Sheriff Cody looked annoyed. "From the sound of it, I'm willing to bet you know Nightfire law pretty well. You know somethin' I don't?" Sheriff Cody hated the oddities that were a part of their local laws. There were even exceptions to *federal* laws, and for the life of him, the sheriff couldn't understand why a town like Nightfire could trump the feds when it suited them. All he knew was that his predecessor had wound up in the loony bin for going against such a mandate the previous year, and Sheriff Cody had no intention of winding up like him.

"A great deal," Valen answered. "I'm fairly certain we can talk through this and have it resolved well before sunrise."

The sheriff sighed, offered Valen a seat beside the Krandalls with a gesture, grabbed a cup of coffee, then sighed again. "Sometimes I really hate this job." He took a sip, as Valen sat down. "So talk. What *really* happened, as *you* see it?"

"We were at the top of the stairs."

"I think we all got that much," the sheriff scoffed.

Elizabeth had stopped crying and was sitting up, listening attentively. "Go on, Mister Alexas. I believe you no matter what your story is. My daughter is not a murderer, and she had only the kindest feelings toward you."

"I know, Liz. She was bringing me a knife I'd left in an upstairs room. I was worried that someone would find it. A child especially. I didn't want anyone to get hurt. She tripped. Fortunately," he continued to lie, "the knife missed any vital organs. Clarissa is one of my closest friends. She really would *never* have attempted to murder me. It's preposterous."

"Why thc hell would you have a giant kitchen knife upstairs?" the Sheriff asked.

"I was showing it to Sam earlier that day."

"What the hell for?"

"It's an antique. Part of a set hand fashioned in Paris as a gift for one of my ancestors in the late 1780s. The maker of the knives had fought at his side during the last days of the American

Revolution. Sam had an interest in the history of the mansion, and he'd been helping me set up for the party. I thought the knife would impress him. So, I took it upstairs where he was working."

"Listen, Mister Alexas, we have procedures. Maybe you're not full of shit, but..."

"I can verify his story, Sheriff Cody."

The sheriff looked up. "Larry? You look like hell."

"Yeah. Me an' Dick were just at the scene of a wreck. Sam was in the passenger seat of Bradley Stevens' car. He actually told me that exact same story, about the old knife and Clarissa tripping. He saw her catch her foot on the carpet from upstairs, but he fainted when he saw all the blood. Says Bradley and Ray were trying to get him back to consciousness, and then he had Bradley drive him to the hospital to see Valen. They ran into the ambulance on the way. Literally." He noticed Valen. "So what the hell happened? You just get up out of the wreck and walk to the police station? Leave everyone else behind?"

"Pretty much. I guess I wasn't thinking clearly."

"You need to get to the hospital. Come on. I'll drive you. Your two friends are there right now." He turned his attention back to the sheriff. "I've got Dick waiting to take Bradley Stevens into custody just as soon as they patch him up."

Sheriff Cody nodded sadly. He really did hate days like this, and Bradley had been through so much in the past year. He hated to see it come to that. "What charges?"

"Let it go, Larry. The sheriff and I will handle it from here," a new voice broke in.

"Del? What the hell...?" Sheriff Cody studied the mayor incredulously.

"Let's talk in your office, Will." He turned to Valen. "Get home, will you, Valen? The party's cleared out." To the Krandalls, he said, "It's gonna be all right. We'll have this whole misunderstanding cleared up by morning. You have my word. Now get home and get some rest." He looked to Valen. "All of you."

"Now wait just a dang minute, Del! Just to *start* with, this man needs medical attention right now!"

The mayor shook his head. "Looks fine to me. How do you feel, Valen?"

The vampire stretched his arms and smiled. "Like a newborn baby being rocked to sleep in his mother's arms."

"Good. Somewhat melodramatic, but very Valen Alexas. That's good. Now get home and take it easy for a while. Larry'll drive you."

"What the…" Sheriff Cody stood up to protest.

"Will. Office." The mayor led the way.

"Excuse me a moment," Will Cody said to all present, as he rose from his chair and followed the mayor.

When they were alone in his office, the sheriff held nothing back. "God damn it, Del, what the hell do you think you're doing? We have to look into this! The man *needs* to be in the hospital! We *all* saw where that knife went. Wounded vital organs or no, he needs to be in the hospital. He's moving now on pure adrenaline, and I won't have it on my head if he dies in his sleep tonight back in his own bed!"

"No, you won't. And you *will* leave this alone. I told you when he came to town; leave Mister Alexas alone."

"But this is for his own goddamned good!"

"There are things you aren't aware of, Will. Federal government slash Nightfire government understandings that go *way* back. The way this plays out is simple. It's been proven that Clarissa tripped and stabbed Valen Alexas by accident. Bradley Stevens gets a ticket for speeding, but we all know he didn't *deliberately* hit that ambulance, and Larry and Dick didn't turn on their sirens to pull him over until the instant before the accident, no matter what they may have said. In fact, it was probably the fault of the ambulance drivers for running a red light without *their* siren turned on. By morning, this all goes away."

Sheriff Cody fumed silently for only a moment, considering the words of the mayor. "No. God damn it! No! I wasn't elected to sit here and let people drive into ambulances and stab each other in the chest and walk away like nothin' happened! I was elected to protect and serve the people of Nightfire! This is my town, and I will be God damned if I don't face its troubles head on."

The mayor nodded, understanding. "I hear you, Will. Sheriff Gilespe felt the same way. I respected his tenacity." Pointedly he added, "Right up to the end."

Sheriff Cody slumped in his chair and spoke defeatedly, "You're asking me to lie."

"No. I'm *telling* you…not to tell the truth. Whether or not you lie is entirely up to you. But this all goes away by morning. Make this happen for us, Will, and I'm sure your career as town sheriff will be long and prosperous." Mayor Strongbow stood to leave, offering his hand.

Sheriff Cody quietly considered the alternative. *And if I don't, my career ends with a room at 'Happydale' next to my old boss.* He turned away from the proffered hand. "I'll do my job, Mayor Strongbow. You have my word on that."

"Have a good night, Will."

When the mayor had left the sheriff to his thoughts, Will Cody picked up the phone. "Lana, get on the phone and sift through all the crap at Nightfire General. When you get Dick on the line, put him through to my office." He hung up abruptly, then hit the desk with his fist. "God damn it! I *hate* this shit!" Suddenly he wondered how much worse it was for Mayor Strongbow. Who was putting the pressure on *him*, and why? With a weary shake of his head, he decided he'd really like nothing better than to *never* have those particular questions answered.

Later that night, at Nightfire General Hospital, Sam and Bradley were ushered into the waiting room together, having been checked out and patched up. Sam's mother practically flew out of her chair and took Sam into her arms. "Oh, my baby! Oh, baby! I was so scared."

"I was fine, Momma. They just checked me out to be sure."

"I know, but you could have been hurt so bad. And after you didn't come home last night…"

Bradley was just wondering where the not-so-nice police officers had gone, when he felt a Herculean slap right across his face. "And you! You could have killed my baby drivin' all crazy! I wish they'd lock you up for life! But I guess I can't have everything. Long as I have my baby back, I'll be grateful."

"Mom…he has a head injury."

"Good! I don't care! I'll slap him again!"

Sam grabbed her hand and disguised it with a hug. "Thanks for waiting on me, Momma."

"Oh, Sam." She kissed his cheek tenderly. "You ain't never gettin' in the car with that damn fool idiot child again."

Ray walked up to Bradley, the muscles along his jaw line working, but accomplishing nothing. Sam was standing beside Bradley now. "Ray, thanks."

"For what?" he asked Sam sharply.

"For comin' down here and waiting with my Momma."

Ignoring Sam, Ray glared at Bradley, then shouted startlingly, "*You could have gotten yourselves killed!* What the *hell* were you trying to do?" His ire fading, he found his voice weakening. "God damn it. I could have lost you both." His arms moved, and Bradley was sure that another blow was coming his way. Instead, Ray grabbed him and Sam in a merciless bear hug and held them tight. "Fuck you," he said, and he let them go. "I could have lost you." Tears on his face, Ray walked out into the hall, leaving his friends in a state of speechless bewilderment.

In the hall, Ray leaned up against the wall, hoping they wouldn't come after him. He hated having his heart laid out for all to see. This night had been unrelenting. He hoped they'd leave him alone. He didn't want to think about them. He'd lost too much. He needed things to turn around already. He found himself beginning to suffocate under the weight of all his burdens. He didn't even have anyone to talk to about most of them. He was so tired of carrying on alone, and Bradley and Sam were the only things he felt he had to hold on to. *I could have lost them both.*

"They *told* me I'd find you here."

Ray looked up, unbelieving. "Lee?"

The dark-haired man smiled broadly. "Just checked in to the hotel. Asked about you. They told me they'd heard you were having a rough night."

Ray beamed. "You have no idea." The two friends hugged without another word, the silence finally giving way to merry laughter, as Ray welcomed Lee Paul home from his long global journey. At last, he had someone to talk to about the secret burdens he'd brought home with him. Someone he could trust. The Nephilim had kept their word. Granted, *they* still couldn't be trusted, but Lee was home. Sam and Bradley would be fine, and Lee was finally back. At that moment, nothing else even mattered.

After a night's sleep that was somehow both fitful and restful, Sam awoke to a gentle knock on his door. "Whazit?"

"Somebody here to see you, Sam. Thought you'd wanna get up and accommodate her," his mother answered.

Her? Sam sat up and rubbed his eyes. He noticed the sun coming in through his window, reddish gold as it made its way over the horizon. It was extremely early for unexpected visitors. He stared at the sunrise for a moment, letting all of the previous night's events sink back in. He was different. He had a vampire's mark. Bradley knew everything. *Everything* was different now. He found himself wondering if Valen could see the sunrise now through his eyes.

"Sam?"

He turned, startled. "Mary?"

She giggled. "Nice boobies."

"I wasn't expecting company so early."

"I couldn't wait. I didn't sleep last night."

"Why?"

"I just…" there was a pain in her voice struggling to take control, but she fought it down. "I went to the party last night. At the Alexas place. But I got there late. Things were pretty crazy. They wrote it up in the paper this morning. Mister Krandall's wife wrote about it."

"You were there? Sorry I missed you." He blinked and met her eyes. "What made you decide to go?"

"I thought you might be there. I guess…I don't know."

"I wish I'd known you were there." A harsh memory found him then. "Wait a minute. Why were you looking for *me*? I thought you never wanted to speak to me again."

Mary Rhodes sighed and sat down on the bed beside him. "Okay…please don't get angry, because why I went and why I'm here now are two different things. I went because I…missed you. And…I hoped I could make you leave and turn your way of thinking so that I could feel okay about the fact that…"

"What?"

"I hate being apart from you." She looked into his eyes and fought back her emotions. Sam could see them glistening in the water that layered her eyes.

He wanted to reach out and touch her arm, but he was wary. "But that's not the reason you came here at the crack of dawn to see me?"

"No. Please don't hate me for thinking it was my place to change your mind. I've been…stupid."

"No..."

"Let me finish, Sam." She paused and took in the sight of his disheveled hair with a strained giggle that had to fight through eager tears to get out first. "I was wrong. Not about what I stand for. Not about the fact that we have to fight for equality until the day that we die. I was wrong about you. I was wrong when I said you didn't care. That you just shrugged off our hardships and let your friends treat you like their side-kick. I didn't know what you were doing all along. And I feel so stupid, because I've wasted so much time trying to stay angry at you, and I didn't even need to be in the first place. I have my way of facing the fight. Carmilla Franklin has hers. But it's your way that got to them. Finally."

Sam was lost. "Mary...I'm really glad you've changed your mind about me, but...what are you talking about?"

Mary laughed, as the tears finally won out, falling down on either side of her broad smile. "The *Samuel Turner Foundation*? Sam...you did it! Valen told Carmilla all about it. How you've opened his eyes. You've been working on the richest man in town behind the scenes, and he's going to have our streets fixed, our parks restored. He's even going to have the slave quarters torn down on his property, just because she asked him to. Sam...how could I have called you an Uncle Tom? How could I have said all of those terrible things to you?"

She leaned over and hugged Sam. He held her, completely dumbfounded. He hadn't known anything about any Samuel Turner Foundation. He hadn't known anything about winning any great victories against racism. But he did know what he'd been through since Mary had broken up with him. He'd heard Valen's account of the casual acceptance of slavery in the Old

South. He'd been shunned for his skin color at Dan Parker's by a man who'd refused to serve him a drink. He'd been handcuffed at the scene of a fight between two white men that he was trying to break up. He'd seen what he had missed before the night that Mary had ended their relationship. He agreed with her that he'd been naïve. He felt deserving of every name that she'd called him at times. But there was more to it than that. Sam's world was anything but 'black and white.' The issues were there, and he owned them now, but that was only *one* of his problems. "No. You were right, Mary. You were right to feel that way. I'm the one who was stupid."

She pulled back and laughed, wiping the tears from her face. "Yeah. That's why *you* were the one to get us millions of dollars in funding to fix this neighborhood up, when our loudest politician has been trying unsuccessfully for years." She laughed." But, anyway, Sam…" The look of love in her eyes was unmistakable. "…I was hoping that, if you didn't still hate me…maybe we could…"

He kissed her, answering her question before she'd even had a chance to finish it.

That night, Bradley and Helen were at Hilltop, enjoying the cool summer night. Helen was strangling her guitar strings again, preventing Bradley from gathering his thoughts, as he'd been trying to do all day. He saw only one way to stop her. He leaned over and kissed her, pulling the guitar away from her as he did so and setting it aside.

Helen broke it off with a laugh. "You were just trying to get me to stop playing."

"You weren't 'playing' anything." He grinned. "Besides, I just wanted to kiss you."

"Then how come you always kiss me with your eyes closed?"

"You do the same. You told me so. You just open yours first when we stop."

Helen laughed it off. "It's more romantic that way. Last night was weird."

Bradley laughed loudly, still not sure what to make of his own experiences the night before; experiences he couldn't really talk about. "That's an understatement. Did you hear that Dori slapped Ray? He actually had the nerve to cheat on her! I don't get it! You just don't cheat on a woman that hot!"

Helen had to argue the point. "Dori just wasn't good enough for him. *She* set the precedent for cheating. She wrote the *book* on it! How could she hold it against *him*? It's *Ray*! He's definitely worth working things out with."

"They're supposed to talk tomorrow night. Ray told me." Bradley confided solemnly.

"Do you think they'll break up?"

"I kind of…" he looked at her and grinned.

Her eyes narrowed, but her smile remained. "Who do you think about when you're kissing me with your eyes closed?"

He shook his head. "Who do *you* think about?"

"Does it strike you that our main topic of conversation on our dates is always Ray and Dori?"

He laughed. "It is. I guess, yeah." He paused. "I think about Dori." *Did I actually just tell her that?*

"I figured. I think about Ray. Are you mad?"

He considered it, then shrugged. "No. Not even jealous. You?"

"No…" She snickered. "Actually, now that it's come out in the open, I don't think I've thought about you once the entire time we've been going out."

They both died laughing at that, and the fact that they were laughing at it made it even funnier to them. When they at long last caught their breath again, Bradley asked, "So, you wanna break up?"

Helen sighed with a smile. "Okay."

"Hm. *That* was easy." They sat in silence for a while after this exchange. It was the most ridiculous confrontation either of them had ever had, but it was so honest. So indisputably right. Neither one of them had any idea what to say now that their illusions had been so benignly shattered.

Helen broke the silence at last. "Yeah. So, do you think I have a chance with Ray?"

Bradley shrugged. "Do you think I have a chance with Dori?"

They looked at each other then laughed out loud and surprised each other by simultaneously answering, "Hell, yeah!" They laughed some more.

Bradley put an arm around her, and she leaned her head against his shoulder when they caught their breath yet again. "You know something, Helen?"

"This has been the most retarded break-up date of your life?"

"Well….that. But I was gonna say something serious."

"What's that?"

"We work well as friends."

"Totally." She hugged him fiercely, and both of them kept their eyes wide open, until they were once again consumed by uncontrollable laughter.

The following night, Abigail Johnson answered the phone at her home to the voice of Tom's new secretary Trish. She asked the young lady to hold on, and she let Tom know he had a call from Trish.

"Thanks, Abi. I'll get it in the other room." Tom got up from his chair and went into the kitchen.

Abi's suspicions got the better of her. This was not the first time Trish had called her husband on her day off. She covered the mouthpiece of the phone and listened in.

"I told you not to call me at home. It could cause trouble," Tom whispered urgently.

"I'm sorry. I just hate my days off. I couldn't help it. I just needed to hear your voice before I went to bed…alone."

Tom chuckled. "Well, now you've heard it. Maybe we can find a way to meet on the weekends. But really, Trish, this is serious. Don't call me at home. We have an arrangement. You know I'm married."

She sighed dejectedly. "I know. But I can still dream."

"Just make sure you dream about me."

"Every night, Tom. I love you."

Tom laughed. "Same to you. See you in the morning." In a much louder voice, he added. "I'm sure we'll have it all sorted out in time for the press. It was a terrific article either way." He hung up the phone.

Quietly, with a trembling hand, Abigail hung up her phone as well; tears of anger and betrayal glistening on her face as she made her way to the bathroom to think of a way to regain her now decimated sense of self worth.

At Dan parker's, Ray arrived to find Dori waiting for him at their usual table. He hadn't wanted to meet there, but she had assured him that James was no longer employed after his cousin Todd had learned what had happened to Sam. Ray couldn't wait to give Sam the good news. Dori was alone, which meant that she must have told the others she had business with him. He groaned and made his way to the table. "Listen, Dori…just let me say that I'm…"

She held up a hand to cut him off. "Stuff it, Ray. No B.S. We both knew what we were getting into when we started this whole debacle. It was an experiment from the beginning, and neither one of us had any real great expectations. It was fun. But it's history. The experiment was a dismal failure. Just like we thought it would be."

"Well, at least no one got hurt."

"No churches may have been burned down in the process, peaches, but I wouldn't say that no one was hurt."

"Right." He looked down miserably. "Jenny."

She looked away, subtly. "Yeah. So have fun at work on Monday, lover boy." She laughed it off and turned her eyes back to Ray, deliberately. "Now sit down and let's make peace."

"Can we do that?"

"Sure."

"How?"

She propped her elbow on the table and held out her hand. "Arm wrestling."

"Are you...*what*?"

"Chicken, Ray? Scared I'll beat you?"

"No."

"Well then." She moved her arm towards him.

"Ha! If that's all it'll take..." He sat down and clasped her hand.

They began, and Ray broke a sweat trying to move her. "What, do you bench press *cars* in the morning?"

Dori laughed. "Come on, Ray. Stop playing around. I'm serious."

His voice was strained. "So...am...I..."

She slammed his knuckles down on the table without much effort at all. "Pussy. Now we're cool, right?"

Massaging his arm, Ray looked at her as she stood. "Sure."

She winked. "So, do we go for one last absolutely meaningless tryst before we part, or do we just go back to being friends right now?"

"I vote friends. Right now."

"Me too." She smiled sincerely and walked over to the bar to get a Dr. Pepper, leaving Ray to his thoughts.

Ray sat, pensively contemplating the incredible strangeness of his entire weekend, until a horrible sound caught his ear. He looked over to see Helen sitting against the far wall *trying* to play

"Across the Universe" on her guitar. He got up and went to her, still rubbing his arm. "Helen! Can you even *tune* a guitar?"

She stopped, just as her heart seemed to stop beating in her chest. *You hate me.* She wanted to die. "I just tuned it."

"No." He reached for the guitar, and she handed it to him. He sat down beside her and started tuning it with a vengeance. When he was satisfied, he strummed it a couple of times, then smiled and began to sing, "Nothin's gonna change my world. Nothin's gonna change my world." It was the first time he'd picked up a guitar since Donny's death, and it felt surprisingly wonderful. He noticed some of the patrons beginning to look at him, as he sang. He stopped and handed the guitar back over to Helen. "There. All fixed up. Give it a try."

Helen took the guitar, zombie-like, while gawking at the man of her dreams. She got situated and began strumming.

"No!" Ray covered his ears. He met her terrified puppy dog blue eyes and laughed. "Look, you really stink at this."

"I'm sorry." *Oh, God, please strike me dead right here!*

Something about the look in her eyes pulled on him unexpectedly. This kid really needed his help. "You really want to be good, don't you?"

She nodded, as if God had asked her the question directly.

"Look…I can give you lessons if you want. I know I said no before, but…"

"You love me!" *Oh, shit! I'm a retard! I have to pee!*

Ray laughed out loud. "Actually, I just feel sorry for the guitar. You play just horribly enough to bring me out of a very determined retirement." He laughed one more time as he shook his head and reached for the instrument. "First, you need to learn the basic chords."

Helen hung on his every word as he taught her all that he could in an hour. It was the most attention Ray Don had paid to her as long as she'd been alive. By the end of the hour, her comfort level had improved, and they were both singing together. "Nothin's gonna change my world…nothin's gonna change my world." She burned every moment into her memory forever, determined to live in that hour for the rest of her life.

Valen Alexas sat down in a chair in his living room, stroking Raksha at his side, as he addressed his guests. Mary Jean Donavan sat off to the side, silently, just listening, knowing that this part was not for her benefit. Sam and Bradley sat side by side on the couch, staring at Valen expectantly. Bradley was far more nervous than Sam. Valen made a point to smile at him, to ease his mind. "Thank you. You cannot know how deeply in your debt I am. How deeply in your debt are all the vampires of Nightfire. All the *people* of Nightfire. We've kept our secret for a solid one hundred-twenty-eight years. To think that all it might have taken to undo that was a ghost…" No one said anything in response, but he knew what Sam was thinking, and Bradley's eyes were wide with bewilderment, telling volumes.

"Sam, I'm sorry that I had to do what I did to protect you. I'm sorry it had to be done so abruptly. But I had to strike fast, before I broke down and asked your permission. If you'd needed time to think, and I'd granted it, the others would have destroyed you that night, I'm certain. And I had to strike, before I lost my resolve."

"I understand," Sam assured him. "I can see it the way you do now."

"I know. That will take some getting used to. For both of us. I told you before that I've never given my mark to a human before. Not even the one human who begged me to." Pain briefly contorted Valen's face at the reference to Augustin. He was not looking forward to what lay ahead that night. "I promise you, I have no intention of holding you to me. I *have* a guardian." He nodded towards Raksha affectionately. "However, I am hopeful that we'll remain friends. We are bound for life now, one way or another. You will always be linked to my mind. I'll try to get acclimated to the new arrangement quickly, so that I can spare you all the tedium. I can dull the effect somewhat, but I can never break the connection completely." He tried to think of what else had to be said. "You'll be safe now. No vampire will ever harm you…not within our laws, anyway. I have only one enemy who may ever try."

"D'artagnan."

"Yes. But he's a pariah. The others in the Mines will help to protect you from him. As for me, I will do everything I can to make amends for the curse I've lain upon you. As I said, I won't hold you to me. You may remain in my employ if you choose as long as you're in high school. After that, I can send you away, to Harvard Law School. I have an old friend who's a tenured professor there. Only if it's your choice to go there, of course. But wherever you choose to go, your tuition is not an issue. I insist that you allow me to pay it as a show of my gratitude for all that you've been through on my behalf."

Sam didn't know what to say. He had not expected to have such a gift bestowed on him. College had been a non-issue for him up to this point. No one had offered him any hope. His grades were fair, but his financial situation was down right dismal. None of his cousins were planning to go. They would be jealous…but he'd always wanted to go to Harvard. "Thank you. You have no idea…"

"Ah, but I do." Valen winked at him, amused.

Valen looked now to Bradley. "I can see through Sam how necessary it was for him to tell you the truth about me. Thank you for being trustworthy. You put a great deal at risk in order to protect my secret. Including your own life when you rammed that ambulance. I don't know where the line between bravery and stupidity was that night, but I can only thank you for whichever it was that gave me the chance to get off of that ambulance. Things won't be as difficult for you as they will be for Sam, but still, you know the secret of the vampires of Nightfire. No further action will be needed, as long as you stay away from the Mines."

"I don't even know where they are," Bradley offered nervously.

"Count it as a blessing, my friend. You are a threat to no vampire save for myself at this point. And I count you among my confidants now. Tell no one what you know."

"Like they'd believe me if I tried." He laughed *very* nervously.

Noticing Bradley's nerves troubled Valen. He didn't want the young man to be afraid of him. "I've called Barley's Automotive about your car. They'll tow it in tomorrow and make all the necessary repairs, including body work, billed to me. And I've covered the impound fees as well."

"You didn't have to..." Bradley reconsidered. "Yeah you did." He chuckled. "Thank you." His nervousness was fading in light of his relief.

"It is absolutely my pleasure, Bradley." He looked to Mary Jean. "Mary Jean. I'm all yours."

She stood. "We should be alone."

Valen regarded the boys and nodded. "I agree. Please," he said to them, "it's important that this go right the first time. I need to do whatever Mary Jean asks of me in order to end this trouble with...my old friend." He was terrified to say Clarenda's name for the possibility she would come before he was ready. It had taken him a full two days rest and one full night to recover from the wound to his heart, a vampire's most sensitive organ. He didn't think he could endure another unexpected attack so soon. "If you could wait on the porch, away from the window." He shrugged. "You never know what might get thrown through it." He saw both disappointment and relief painting the faces of the two teenagers as they stood. "No problem," Sam offered.

"Yeah. Happy haunting." Bradley laughed. "We'll just be outside pretending to be oblivious."

Valen nodded to his faithful beast, and Raksha got up to go with them. He knew he needed to be completely alone with the ghosts of his past before they could be convinced to leave him.

When the boys and Raksha had left, Mary Jean asked pointedly. "Are you ready, Valentinus?"

The vampire nodded warily. "As ready as I can manage."

Mary Jean closed her eyes and felt the room psychicly. There were, as usual, a number of presences.

He killed me...a ten-year-old girl? There was something unnatural about her though. Something evil, but defeated. Not Clarenda...

Get out! Get out of here! She knew this one. Sedrick. Not who she was looking for.

Make me an offer...I want to borrow you for a few years. Let me live again...Let me live! Male. Angry. She put up her defenses and rebuffed his attempts to get inside of her. He left the room quickly. Feeling pathetic and depressed. So many spirits in this house that needed her help, but she was after only two.

She heard a whining. Like a dog. No...a wolf. Not Raksha. She opened her eyes to slits and saw the vague outline of the old beast watching from the shadows. Tonkowa. He wanted to see this resolved. He'd been waiting to move on until Calrenda was set right. Loyal even in death. No anger. Just concern. And hope. Hope that this would be the end of all the pain and confusion that Clarenda had been feeding on. "We're getting close."

Her eyes closed again. *She's coming.* A simple, sharp statement. A Woman. No time to identify. Everyone was gone now. No, not everyone. Tonkowa was there. And...

What are you doing? The question was both angry and despairing. It felt invaded. Indignant. It was Clarenda.

Save him. Augustin.

"We can begin." Mary Jean opened her eyes and looked to Valentinus, who was terrified. "Augustin. Are you strong enough to help us?"

Yes.

"No, Augustin. I need you to be stronger. Can you do it?"

"Yes."

Valen started at the voice. "Augustin..." A tear escaped from one of his eyes.

Valentinus... "Valen...tinus." The young man became slightly visible then, and Valen reached out to him. Augustin tried to take his hand, but it passed right through.

"Talk to me, Valentinus. Help me to be strong for you."

"I love you." Valen wept at the sight of him, as Augustin came into fuller view, still translucent, but much more visible.

"Valentinus." The ghost was beaming. "We have time...for a moment. Tonkowa's distracting her."

Valen laughed through his silent tears. "Tonkowa? He's here too? It's almost as though *I* were the one who'd been taken from the world."

"I don't blame you for my death, Valentinus. I know what happened that night. I remember. I've been watching you. I'm going to come to you."

"Come to me? But, you're already here."

"Get away! Get away, *murderer*!" A clock flew across the room and hit Valen on the forehead. He staggered back. The lamp stand came up off of the floor and flew at him."

"Clarenda! Stop it! You're wrong!" Augustin urged, as his sister took translucent form and walked eerily out from the shadows.

"He killed you! He was devious and perverse! You are too blind to see it. He's a monster." She began to wail. "He killed my baby brother! Left him on the floor...no blood! No heartbeat!" She screamed in agony.

Mary Jean spoke calmly. "Clarenda…let him speak. Listen to Valentinus…"

Clarenda turned her eyes on the psychic sharply. "Witch," she whispered. "Get out of this house, *you witch*!" Clarenda floated across the room with inhuman speed and struck Mary Jean across the face, sending her reeling. She lunged at her again and clawed at her, knocking her to the floor, grabbing her hair and banging her head against the ground ferociously.

"*No!*" Valen was aghast. "Clarenda! I'm the one you want. I'm the one you want to destroy."

The enraged specter looked to the man whom she believed to be her murderer and sneered. "I…will…kill you." She rose, slowly, menacingly. She glided over, very near to him now. Augustin was weeping.

"I loved you," Valen said simply. "I have always, *will* always, love you, my beautiful Clarenda."

She was taken off guard by that. "You loved Augustin more."

Valen shook his head. "Only differently. No more; no less." Augustin smiled warmly at that declaration.

Mary Jean didn't dare sit up, but she had to tell Valen what to do. She said simply, "Tell her. About that night. 'Confess.'" She cackled in spite of herself, then lay still, patiently.

Augstin was outraged. "There is nothing to confess!"

"Yes. There is." Valen knew what Mary Jean intended. "I want to tell you, Clarenda. I want to offer my confession. About the night that Augustin was killed."

The phantom's eyes narrowed. "I hate you!" She moved to attack him.

"*I hate myself!*"

The fierce declaration stopped her in her tracks. She looked at him, confused. "You should."

"Let me confess, I beg of you."

She simply looked at him, waiting, hovering a few feet above the ground, as if she were about to lunge at him again if this 'confession' didn't live up to her expectations from the start.

Valen took it as an invitation to go on, and so he did. "I hate myself for what happened. I hate myself, because I loved you both with such intensity. Augustin…was the love of my life. My heart was his, but I could never be with him, because of what I am. I *am* a monster, Clarenda. I was always a monster, but I loved you and never wanted that part of myself to touch either one of you…and it destroyed you. I was so happy in those years, when we were together all the time. I was so happy. Never in all the years that I've lived this cursed existence have I known such sheer joy. I do not expect to find that kind of bliss again. Augustin was…my soul mate. And you, you were the dearest platonic friend that I have *ever* had. You can't know how devastated I was when I lost both of you in the same year. It was nearly impossible for me to even put one foot in front of the other again for years.

"I blame myself."

"You haven't confessed. Tell me what you did. Tell me about killing Augustin and leaving him on the floor to rot!" Clarenda was losing her patience. "I know all about it. He told me."

Puzzled, Valen asked her, "Who? Who told you…and what? I don't understand."

"The man in town. He told me what you were. That you lived on the blood of mortals. That you had killed Augustin. He said was here to destroy you. I died in that moment of revelation. I died! Then I went to see for myself; to face you and know the truth. I saw the urn. I knew. It broke my heart. I trusted you...*and you lied!*"

"The man...in town..." Valen was lost, and then it clicked. "D'artagnan. Clarenda...I'm not through. I will tell you about the night Augustin died."

"Do," she said this single word with all the menace that could possibly fit into a solitary syllable.

"I received a letter from the monster who helped to turn me into what you now loath so much. He said he would come and 'liberate' me. I should have taken you both away right then. But I was blinded by my bliss. I can guess how convincing this man was, when he met you in town. He told you that I feed on human blood. I imagine he also told you that I slept in a tomb and could only go about by night."

"Yes. Vampyre. He said you were vampyre."

"He told the truth. And you realized we had, for years, only met at night. You had never once seen me take food or drink. No one had ever offered an explanation, but it clicked...especially considering the circumstances of Augustin's death."

"Yes," she spat the word with hatred.

"So here is what happened. I came home and found him there. Augustin. I knew it had been my fault. I hadn't taken him for myself. He had begged me to give him my mark, and I'd refused...but I should have done it. I wish I had done it. I wish I'd turned him fully into one of us, because then he could have defended himself against D'artagnan…the man you met, who told you about me. How did he know about me?"

"He…I don't know…"

"You met him at night."

"Yes."

"He was the one who killed Augustin…and Tonkowa. He did it to hurt me. He knew, because he was one of us. He hurt you even more, because you were grieving. You were lost in pain and needed a target. He gave you one, and he's been your master ever since, because you haven't moved on. Your dying thought was that I'd ruined your life, taken everything from you that you'd ever lived for. You threw yourself from the window, because your life had already ended…and I was the cause. But I wasn't the one who killed Augustin. D'artagnan came to see me just after you died. Did you see him? In the house?"

"I…yes…" Clarenda was thinking hard, considering what she was hearing. "I saw him. I didn't understand what had happened. I was supposed to be dead, but I wasn't. I was still there. I was still hurting. I saw him. He had come to destroy you, just as he'd promised. I was glad. I wanted you to burn in Hell for what you did to Augustin."

"He came to gloat," Valen went on. "To destroy me, yes. But not in the way you thought. Do you remember? Did you see?"

"I…did…I…forgot. I didn't understand."

"What didn't you understand?"

"I didn't know…" the ghost of Clarenda Richardson began to weep. "I didn't know what was happening to me. I was scared. I wanted to get back at you! You left though. The third man came and took you away. I waited for you to come back. Things changed. In the house. Things got old. Young people came into the house sometimes. I didn't know who they were. There were other people. Even Augustin. We sometimes scared the young ones away, but I didn't know who the other people were. I didn't understand. But sometimes I did. They were dead...like me. We were all in Hell together for having known you. And I wanted to hurt you."

"Clarenda," Augustin put a hand on her shoulder. "I've wanted to tell you all this time. It *was* this D'artagnan who murdered me. It is exactly as Valentinus says. I've been trying to help you."

"Help me? Augustin...what's going on? I'm so confused."

"I've been trying to guide you into the light."

"What light?"

"Over there."

Augustin pointed, and Valen could not see what he was pointing at, but he had no reason to doubt. "Clarenda, please, listen to Augustin. You can be at peace. If you wanted me to suffer...I will...always. I will never see you again as long as the universe endures, as long as I have something here to live for. I want to know that you are happy, that you are at peace. Think back. Could the Valentinus that you knew ever harm you or your brother? Did I not save you from that man who tried to ravage you? Could I not have fed on anyone else? If I'd meant to hurt you, why would I have allowed you to stay for so long, allowed myself to fall so in love with you? I could have killed Augustin at any time, but I taught him to fight, I made him my friend. Does it make sense to you that I would simply change my mind one night?"

Clarenda was confused, more so than she'd been in quite some time. "I always loved you…but you…I'm…hurting….so much…I don't know what happened to me. I knew if I hurt you, it would stop. I would stop hurting."

"Like when you jumped from the window, Clarenda? Did the hurting stop then?"

She looked stricken, as though the truth of those words had never taken root in her mind before Valen spoke them.

Augustin embraced her. "The hurting can stop now, Clarenda. Go into the light. People love you there. They're waiting for you to let go of your anguish and live with them in a place that is only happiness and sweet dreams forever."

"What can I do, Augustin?" She cried against his shoulder. "I don't know how to…" She looked over at something. "Is that…? It's…"

"Mom?" Augustin's voice faltered, as raw emotion overtook him.

"Father!" Clarenda let go and went towards people that Valen couldn't see. She began to fade, but turned to face Valen. "Thank you. I *will* see you again…my very dear friend." She turned away then and vanished from Valen's sight.

Augustin remained, smiling, tears on his ghostly cheeks. Mary Jean rose and made her way to them, holding her head as though it would fall off if she let it go.

"Augustin…" Valen began. "I wish I could go with you."

"Go? Where?" Augustin laughed.

"Into the light. With Clarenda."

"And Tonkowa." Augustin smiled. "He went in too." An amused look came over Augustin then. "But I'm not."

"Augustin…please…you deserve…"

"I deserve to be with my own soul…and I would only be half of that if I went into the light without you."

Valentinus didn't know what to say. It was a romantic notion, and he wished he could embrace it as zealously as Augustin, but he didn't find it very practical. "Augustin…I'm an immortal. I'm cursed to walk this earth forever. You *must* go into the light without me."

"Don't worry, Valentinus. I'm not going to go on like this forever. I'm going to be with you. Sooner than you think. I'm just as bold a ghost as I ever was a man." Augustin winked, then faded. "I love you, Valentinus."

As the beautiful vision of Augustin Richardson faded from view, Valen whispered, because all of his emotions had robbed him suddenly of his voice, "Augustin…I will *always*…be in love with you."

Mary Jean put a hand on Valen's arm. "It's done. You did it."

"No," Valen croaked. "Augustin wouldn't go."

"I know, but he's not in pain either. Augustin will go when he's ready. As long as he doesn't threaten you, we can leave him to his own devices. He's a very well adjusted ghost." She smiled, and Valen mirrored the gesture, feeling a sudden wave of relief wash over him like a cold wind. It was over. At long last, Clarenda Richardson was at peace.

"I don't suppose anything will ever be the same," Valen mused. "I don't feel all that guilty anymore, after carrying it with me for decades. And now...Sam and Bradley. No more haunted Alexas Mansion."

Mary Jean cackled. "Don't get carried away. This place is full of ghosts. Most places are. It's not a bad thing, as long as they keep to themselves, and we offer them the same courtesy. And, no, nothing will ever be the same. That's life. Today is distinctly different from yesterday, and tomorrow will be nothing like today. If it ever is, then you've already died."

Valen nodded. "Profound truth. That's what I like most about you, Mary Jean Donavan." Humbly, he added, "If there's ever anything I can do for you, don't hesitate to ask."

Still holding her head, she suggested, "A ride to the emergency room would be nice. I think I have a concussion."

Valen laughed, as he wrapped an arm around her and led her towards the front door in unquestioning compliance. "You'll be fine. I'm pretty sure we've both had worse."

She cackled her agreement as they went outside, light hearted, ready to embrace life once again, and all the friends who shared it with them.

In the hotel downtown, Lee Paul opened his Bible and read the passage that had captured his attention and not let go since it had first been introduced to him. "...The Nephilim..." He closed it and mused to himself. What a journey he'd been on over the past several years. Fleeing the country with Ray to avoid going to Vietnam, finding the Scroll, encountering the Prieuré de Sion and the Nephilim. Growing in his faith. It was incredible how the Scroll had removed *all* of his doubts about God, about the divinity of Christ, while at the same time it had dashed all the faith of poor Ray. They'd both heard the same translation, and they'd both taken completely different meanings from what they'd heard. The one thing they'd both agreed about was the seriousness of their find. And even when they'd learned what knowledge the Scroll contained, they hadn't expected anyone to try to kill them over it.

Indeed, nothing in Lee's young life could compare to the journey of these past several years. *Everything* had changed for him. Who knew that the Scroll and the struggle to determine who should be its custodian would ultimately lead him to unearthing all of those secrets about his grandfather after Ray had returned to the States. He had never really known his grandfather, and now he knew why. It was both humbling and awe-inspiring. He hated that he had to keep it all a secret, but who would understand? Not Ray "these people are crazy" Don. It was sad to him that Ray refused to trust the Nephilim. Ironic, that Ray had so much faith in Lee. Especially now that Lee knew the truth about his grandfather. About himself.

He looked at the photograph of his grandfather that he'd taken from the Nephilim hideaway in Lalibela. He recited the verse he'd learned again. "The Nephilim were on the earth in those days…and still today." He breathed out a sigh and fell back on his bed, wondering at how things were going to go, now that he was back. "Ray, Ray, Ray. I wonder if you'd still trust me, if you knew that I was *one* of them."

The Chronicles of Nightfire, Texas
will continue…

www.ingramcontent.com/pod-product-compliance
Lightning Source LLC
LaVergne TN
LVHW020534100826
845148LV00010B/1452

* 9 7 8 1 6 1 8 1 5 0 9 4 3 *